C0-GLI-504

RECENT HISTORY

Also by Annette Williams Jaffee

ADULT EDUCATION

RECENT HISTORY

Annette Williams Jaffee

G. P. Putnam's Sons
New York

DISCARD

Copyright © 1988 by Annette Williams Jaffee
All rights reserved. This book, or parts thereof,
may not be reproduced in any form without permission.
Published by G. P. Putnam's Sons,
200 Madison Avenue, New York, NY 10016.
Published simultaneously in Canada

The author would like to thank the New Jersey State Council
on the Arts for its generous support, 1987–1988.

She would also like to thank her son, Jon, for giving up a month
of his summer holiday to type a draft of this novel.

Part of Chapter Two, "Rosie," appears in a
slightly different form in *Ploughshares,* 14/1.

The text of this book is set in Sabon.

Library of Congress Cataloging-in-Publication Data

Jaffee, Annette Williams, date.
Recent history / Annette Williams Jaffee.

p. cm.
ISBN 0–399–13357–7 : price
I. Title.
PS3560.A317R4 1988 88-2442 CIP
813'.54—dc19

Printed in the United States of America
1 2 3 4 5 6 7 8 9 10

For Max—

who helped me out of the kitchen

and who continued to believe

The two children loved each other so dearly that they always walked about hand-in-hand whenever they went out together, and when Snow-white said: "We will never desert each other," Rose-red answered: "No, not as long as we live"; and the mother added: "Whatever one gets she shall share with the other."

—from "Snow-white and Rose-red"
by the Brothers Grimm

RECENT HISTORY

1

HEARTLAND

There is a heart in Chicago the size of a small house, a cottage in a fairy tale, with a door and six steps—one way in, no exit. The heart is pink, the pink of panties and tongues, and is made of plaster, and the inside is a relief map of veins and arteries, marked like the N roads on a French auto map. When you walk inside, it is as wide as your mother, as warm as your mother; the sounds primal as the ocean or an old washing machine.

This is Rosie's favorite room at the Museum of Science and Industry. There is a row of babies, nine of them, curled like peas in a pod, growing bigger and bigger. There is a fantastic invisible woman, hefty as a Maillol but cellophane clear, the arteries and veins running through her plastic body like a complicated web, the organs suspended like things to eat in aspic.

The older sister, Noonie, loves the street of Yesteryear, a faithful reproduction of the main street of a small American town at the turn of the century, with corset and shoe shops, a nickelodeon, and an ice-cream parlor with ceiling fans and ferns and curved chairs.

So, while Rosie climbs through the beating heart, tracing its mottled interior with her little hand, Noonie wanders through a past that does not belong to her, remembering.

What do we remember when we remember childhood? What flavors, what textures—an atmosphere sticky with something, not even your own. At some point it stops having to be your own childhood and just the mention of this word evokes those feelings and images.

Noonie remembers waking on a cold winter morning to the sound of her sister Rosie's heartbeat, her breathing, one cold hand flung across the covers, the pale worn silky covers of their grandmother's duvets, a legacy of the past, a mother's past. She remembers waking to cold, snowy skies streaked like herringbone tweed, and their mother Elsa is in the kitchen. She has already been downstairs to check proofs and things; Elsa is a studio photographer. The radio is playing, and the kitchen is so bright, it is like the spotlighted corner of a stage set.

There are snowpants to put on and mittens that Elsa knits by the dozen and are fed through the arms of your jacket on a long umbilical string of yarn, and the hot cereal to eat that lumps in your throat and remains in its original form to make its slow descent, as if to dispense comfort for hours. Your galoshes buckle and your shoes come off with them; caps buckle, too, with tiny teeth on a thick ribbon—too tight. The final stroke is the muffler wound flush across your face (the knot in the back, out of reach), tickling your nose, giving you a mouthful of wool with each breath, tricky as a *chador*. Noonie remembers cod-liver oil poorly disguised in orange juice, and sitting in underpants and goggles under a sunlamp; vitamins did not come in anything as handy as tablets then. All those clothes—and the annual stripping with spring, never a smooth course in cruel Chicago, but, like a bumpy marriage, an on-again, off-again proposition.

Noonie remembers the intense heat of summer. (Is it true that the summers and winters of our childhood were hotter and colder than now, or was it the newness of them, the rawness of our skins and souls? Never mind, those were hot summers, with no air-conditioning.) Some very hot nights they would get into the car, roll down all the windows and drive for hours, very late, all the way to the far South Side for a rainbow cone: seven slices of flavors balanced sideways on a waffle cone, like a ziggurat.

But the best thing, on the hottest nights, only two or three a season, she and Rosie are allowed to sleep nude, nothing but skin. What a treat, the feel of the sheets on your body, a single stiffly ironed linen sheet grazing your bare chest, nipples, shoulders, your limbs loose and free. Two fans are blowing and rotating, teasing as they make their way to you, then turning away, and late at night Noonie can hear Elsa tiptoeing into the room to turn them off because she worries about drafts, stiff necks, polio, but by then the small blessed breeze of cool air has entered the room, and in the morning, just as you are getting up again, the sun is hot and yellow on the sheets.

Morning as a child: you are always greeting it with pleasure, the search for shorts, sandals, a T-shirt, and Elsa is in the kitchen making a brown-bag lunch. If she is in a good mood she slices off the bitter hard crusts. Elsa feels strongly that bread crusts build character. (Noonie puzzled this for years before she understood that character building had to do not with sandwiches but with waste.)

The kitchen of her childhood summers: sunny, safe, Elsa's ample back, the neatly starched apron-bow just above the wide flow of her haunches as she moves from sink to counter to stove, producing things Noonie loves: fluffy omelets with mushrooms the soft brown of little minks, a mound of cottage cheese decorated with valentine-shaped strawberry slices, an orange sliced and arranged in concentric circles to look like the sun on a milky glass plate. Noonie's and Rosie's sandals are kicking the legs of the old wood-and-metal table with the checkered oilcloth cover held in place with white thumbtacks. The shelves are lined like this, too, with a row of red scallops along the edge, cups dangling from white hooks. Noonie can picture the day Elsa committed this artistic wonder, Elsa with a hammer in hand and tacks sticking out of her mouth, her brow furrowed in concentration.

Noonie remembers Elsa coming home late on Saturday night from taking pictures at a wedding; weddings are the best for Noonie and Rosie to hear about. She knocks off her shoes—high heels, suede—and sighs as she edges into the sofa. Oh, they can't imagine how exhausted she is, on her feet all night, those people . . . ugliest faces on God's green earth.

Sometimes she is given food and champagne, sometimes she is ogled and pinched and asked to dance the hora. (Sometimes she meets a man who takes her card and kisses her fingertips and promises to call soon.) Often she brings home tiny cakes and swans of sugar with ribbons tied around their lissome sweet necks and wrapped in square napkins with the happy couple's initials intertwined like frozen leaves.

She tells them stories: the bride who didn't show, the mother who passed out, the groom who couldn't swallow the wedding cake. He was marrying an English girl, she says. Fruitcake, that is the tradition, but he didn't know it and took one bite and just spat it right into her face.

Where is that picture? Rosie wants to know, hanging on Elsa's neck. That's the picture she wants to see.

"Dummy!" Elsa sighs, and eases her aching body up from the cushions. Why should she take and print a photograph like that; who would pay for a picture of the groom spitting at the bride? And why are they still up, don't they know what an hour it is?

They would want a picture of that, Noonie and Rosie decide later in bed, definitely. (They were that kind of naughty girls, Elsa said.)

Noonie's grandfather Otto had learned to become a photographer in *fin de siècle* Hungary. When he came to this country he bought a wagon and an old horse and went from town to town in the newly populated states of Minnesota and Wisconsin and took photographs of the farmers and their families. He would plop down in a field recently harvested or a barn hastily cleared with his spindly gilt chairs and potted palms and a large Oriental carpet and set up his painted backdrops. Would you like a ballroom in Vienna? A front parlor in Berlin? Perhaps the garden of the tsar's summer palace or the Tour Eiffel? The farmer and his wife had to hold very still for a long period of time. This gave their expressions a tension and tenacity that one was tempted to confuse with certain pioneer virtues.

By now, Otto had met Noonie's grandmother, a recently arrived blond beauty, while visiting mutual cousins in Council Bluffs, and settled down in a small farm town in Wisconsin near the border of Minnesota, although to Otto the Twin Cities would always be Buda and Pest. Soon there were Elsa and Tatiana and a brother named Byron, which Noonie was certain was a typo, but with the family's penchant for nicknames it didn't matter; he was called Baby. Much later there was another brother, Noah, but prophetically, Byron remained Baby: Noah died when he was two. Grandma and Poppa were a popular couple, but they were the only Jewish family for miles around. What this meant, being a Jewish family, was never clear to Noonie. She could not remember God ever mentioned except in anger or frustration. They embraced all possible occasions, Christian as well as Jewish (and would have done the Moslem as well, if someone had explained them properly); they celebrated all patriotic events enthusiastically. Otto hung the biggest flag on the street in the window of his studio on the Fourth. Once, at a church supper, they won the waltz contest; first prize was a sixty-pound sack of flour, Grandma told Noonie. Things were hard then, so she asked who had the biggest family, and gave the sack of flour to her. The woman had thirteen children, Grandma said, whistling through her teeth, but Noonie didn't believe her for a minute; she did some fast arithmetic and it didn't seem possible.

When Noonie was older, Elsa let it slip once that Otto had moved his family to Chicago and opened his studio on the North Side of the city after Elsa and Tatiana had started dating non-Jewish boys. So that was what they meant by being a Jewish family.

"Does that mean my father was Jewish?"

"Of course," said Elsa. She was busy flicking the television channels, looking for the news.

"So you met him in Chicago?"

"Nearby," she said. "Pa was taking pictures of the soldiers. He would go to the camps and posts and take the long official photograph—like a scroll, Noonie—of barracks and regiments. Group things."

"And you went along?"

"Yes. Move, Noonie, you're sitting on the TV listings."

"And you met him there?"

"Where? Shhh. My program's starting."

Elsa had always helped out in Otto's studio, and after his death she took over the business, although she would have never called herself a photographer any more than Mr. Wolfson, the jeweler next door, would have advertised himself as a gemologist. Elsa took pictures: weddings, bar mitzvahs, graduations, first communions.

Once, Noonie dragged her mother to a museum; there was an exhibit of famous photographs.

"A pepper!" Elsa shouted, looking at an Edward Weston. "A pepper sitting like a bride!" Noonie could barely get out of the gallery before Elsa exploded with laughter. "A portrait of a toilet! Oh, Noonie, ah la la!"

She didn't approve of his nudes, either. Elsa had a tricky old-world standard. She led a pretty spicy life, but, like photography, it took place in the dark behind a closed door. She didn't think Diane Arbus was courageous; she was not in the least surprised to hear what happened to her. And she felt sorry for everyone Avedon had recently photographed. Elsa tried to make her subjects look better, not worse. Be adorable, was always her advice to Noonie and Rosie.

It took Noonie a long time to understand that taking photographs (or making pictures, as it was referred to in her family) was Elsa's job, like teaching school or pumping gas. Art-schmart.

Noonie knows that when their grandmother was a little girl she lived in a tiny village in Galicia. Each year a man and his sons would come to clean the eiderdowns. They would slit them with strong curved knives and empty the feathers into barrels. Then they scrubbed the covers in a stream and hung them to dry from birch branches. The feathers would be stuffed back and the ends would be sewn up and the next winter could begin.

In later life, in America, Grandma traveled with her own comforter. It preceded her by parcel post when she spent six months of the year in Chicago with Elsa, or six months of the year with her younger daughter Tatiana in Palm Springs. It could get very cold in the desert, she informed skeptical Noonie.

Grandma was a mass of curves and hills, a mountain range of a woman. Once a year, when she arrived with Aunt Tatie on the Twentieth Century Limited, the first thing they did was order new corsets. (The second was eat pastries at Henrici's.) Noonie wondered why there were no corsets in California, but when she went along the first time she saw that her grandmother's shape was a miracle of structural engineering.

In those days, women visited the corsetiere more regularly than the gynecologist. You went upstairs in the elevator with the old birdlike man in the baggy uniform, who tried to pinch you, to a room with dusty blinds and peeling gilt letters on the opaque glass door: EVA's, it said. (Everything in Chicago took place behind these doors; you had your teeth drilled, you bought your toe shoes, you applied for a marriage license.) The corsetiere was a dark-haired lady with an accent like Grandma's (if Grandma had had a mouthful of pins). She had a small mustache, and she wore a tape measure around her neck and a fat pincushion on her wrist like a tomato corsage. She encircled you on her knees three times, as in a folk dance, and she placed the palms of her hands under your breasts like a friendly uncle.

It was nothing like nowadays, when ladies pop into Bloomie's on a lunch hour to snatch up a couple of flimsy purple or red things you can ball into a corner of your pocketbook. Grandma's corsets were alter egos; they stood by themselves like the dinosaur skeletons in the Field Museum.

Grandma could never understand Noonie's desire to be thin. It certainly did not run in the family. "Noonela," she would say, clucking her tongue while watching Noonie cut out the egg-and-tomato-juice diet from a magazine. "Why would you want there to be less of you?"

Sometimes Noonie wondered too, but then she remembered the sharp bones and elastics wide as a wrist, those straps and laces. So she Scotch-taped postcards of Rubens's beauties to the refrigerator door.

"Noonie," Grandma would implore, "what would you do if there was a famine?"

When Otto first moved to Chicago, his studio was on a street of shops connected to the Edgewater Beach Hotel, and when Noonie was very small, she and Rosie and Elsa lived in a small apartment in the hotel. Eventually, they all moved out, farther north and west, away from the lake to a three-flat building, where the studio was on the street and they lived above the grandparents, who lived above the studio. It was a more ordinary place, but even then their lives bore no resemblance to any Noonie knew about or read about: a working mother who wore trousers and took lovers, a father who simply disappeared in an unnamed war, two sassy little girls.

In Noonie's classroom readers, families lined up on a cobblestoned path: A girl for her, a boy for him; even the cat and dog declared gender allegiances, standing on corresponding sides of the path, as at a proper wedding.

Father wore house-slippers and a tie, Mother's pies cooled on a country windowsill, smoke circles rose symmetrically from the red-brick chimney.

Noonie is remembering this the day before her mother's next round of surgery is scheduled. She has just flown in and is perched precariously on one side of the bed, the other side balanced, as always, by her absent sister, Rosemarie.

"You don't look so good, Noonie," says the patient, propping herself up on one elbow. "Around the eyes, around the mouth." As a portrait photographer, she has made this her standard greeting.

Noonie ignores it, inspects the floral arrangements lined up around the bed. "Hey, what is this, a supermarket opening?" she jokes.

"Gus said that when Sarah was born," Elsa sighs, remembering. (Gus is Noonie's husband, Sarah is their twelve-year-old daughter.) "Sarah called me."

"That's nice," says Noonie.

"When I last saw her, Noonie, ah la la. You must get her a brassiere."

"She won't wear one," says Noonie. Sarah solves the problem these days by walking with her shoulders hunched, so they touch in the front, and wearing her father's shirts.

"She will stretch and sag," says Elsa, lifting herself onto the other elbow so she appears to be in a Yoga position: The Fish.

(In the mode of their family, Noonie and her mother will not discuss the main event, only allude to it, find topics related, like the most obscure definition in *Webster's Third International.*)

"Well, I've mentioned it to her," Noonie says, pleasantly.

"You must make her."

"Nobody makes anybody do anything anymore, Mother."

"I could never make anybody do anything then, either," sighs Elsa. "Only Rosie," she mouths.

Noonie rearranges the get-well cards on the windowsill. "Oh, you got one, too."

"Of course I got one, too. It's my sister."

They look at the invitation to Aunt Tatiana's sixtieth birthday party, a surprise, given in Palm Springs by Noonie's cousin Richie. He has even designed the card: a Playmate of the Month reclines on the front wearing Aunt Tatiana's face like a loose mask.

"Another example of the sensibilities of the men in my family," Noonie told Gus when it arrived.

He squinted appreciatively at the card. "Ummm. I had forgotten your aunt was so busty."

Noonie sighed. In the fruit bowl of breast metaphors—pears, peaches—the women in Noonie's family have melons.

"Cantaloupes," said Gus, kindly.

"I took that picture of Tatiana in seventy-three," Elsa is saying to Noonie. "Richie called me and asked for the negatives. How am I supposed to know what he's going to do with them?" Elsa looks out the window. "Richie never was a very nice boy."

Noonie remembers endless games of hide-and-go-seek with Rosie and him in the labyrinth of the hotel on wet afternoons. They would chase him down the long corridors, scour the butler's pantry and the banging dumbwaiter. They would brave dark closets, hearts pounding, waiting for him to pounce out at them. "He used to hide upstairs at the Weinbergs'. I could never find him."

"That was your problem, Noonie," says her mother, inspecting her fingernails (the nurse has removed the polish). "You played it week after week. You never learned." She taps the swinging bed tray. "None of you were very nice children."

"Except Rosie," Noonie finishes for her.

"Rosie has her own problems," says Elsa generously, "of which I do not wish to speak."

Noonie closes her mouth. The doctor knocks. "So this is the famous Natalie," he says, putting his handsome head into the doorway.

"Yes," says Elsa, grabbing his sleeve. "This is Natalie, the writer, the columnist, my Noonie."

"The famous Noonie." He smiles, taking Elsa's hand. "I was just going to give you a little sedative, Elsa. Why don't you take a nap and I'll buy Natalie a cup of coffee."

"Ho! ho! Watch out for my Noonie," says Elsa, rolling down her eyes just before the lids flutter down like thin purple veils. "She's on the prowl and she has a way with men."

"I'll be very careful," he promises, closing the door.

"What's wrong?" asks Noonie as soon as they turn the corner.

"I want a cup of coffee."

"You didn't ask me here for a cup of coffee," she says as they sit at the far end of the counter in the hospital cafeteria.

"Look, Natalie," the doctor says, and takes both of her hands.

(Touching is a bad sign. Noonie has been observing men for years and knows they are not meaningless touchers. Women go around all day wiping noses, patting bottoms, kissing foreheads, but for men touching is ritualistic, involving introductions, sports, sex.)

"What's wrong with my mother?"

"Natalie. Yesterday I ordered a biopsy of your mother's remaining breast. What we did was take a small wedge out. It doesn't look very good. It's spread."

Noonie watches as he takes an apple from a pile on a shiny white plate and makes a neat triangular cut in the fleshy top. She gasps, steps down from her stool.

"Sit, Natalie," he orders, chewing. "I've scheduled surgery tomorrow morning at eight. I'll go downstairs to tell Elsa when she wakes up."

Noonie stares at the bruised apple wobbling on the counter.

"I'm sorry about your sister. It would be a comfort to have her at a time like this," he says.

"What?"

"Your sister, Rosemarie. Elsa told me about her tragic death."

"Rosie isn't dead. My mother hasn't talked to her in over two years, but she isn't dead." (So Elsa has exercised the ancient Jewish prerogative of declaring a wayward child dead.)

"But . . . but she told me about her swimming and her medals and how she was lost at sea . . ."

Now Noonie takes his hands.

Noonie stands outside her mother's hospital room in time to hear the doctor's voice: informing, soothing, caressing, pleading at top volume.

"But, Elsa, you're sixty-two years old. I have young women . . . there's a young woman down the hall, twenty-nine. Twenty-nine and her husband's left her and she's been wonderful. Wonderful!"

Elsa stares at him, wraps her arms around herself. "I don't want to have more surgery," she cries, rocking back and forth on the bed. "I don't want to die."

Noonie rests her face against the cold tile wall, peeking into the tiny window, fighting her own tears. When she and Rosie were children, they had been taken frequently to the Shedd Aquarium by Mr. Horowitz, one of Elsa's admirers. Noonie remembers watching the squid tangle behind the yellowing glass walls near the tiled entrance. (They seldom made it past the main floor.)

"The squid has two hearts," Rosie had informed Noonie. "One's in here," she said, thumping her chest. "The other heart's in its head. No room for a brain, of course," Rosie would shout, poking Noonie in the ribs and running like hell.

Noonie wipes her eyes with her hand and knocks tentatively. The doctor shrugs on his way out.

"I don't want to talk about it!" Elsa shouts in warning before Noonie gets halfway in.

"You have to talk about it. You're having surgery tomorrow."

"My surgery, my surgery. When it's your surgery, you can talk about it."

"Mother." Noonie sighs.

Elsa looks at the ceiling, Noonie looks out the window.

"Why did you tell the doctor Rosie was dead?" Noonie finally asks.

"Oh, Noonie, the other version's so complicated. A man like that—problems, sick people on his mind, he prefers families intact. How could I? Hand me my pocketbook, I want you to check some things at the studio." Elsa shakes the large soft bag as if panning for gold. "Here are the keys, and here's a list of things you should get. Oh, and call Mrs. Wilson and tell her the portraits will take just a little longer." She hugs the bag to her like a favorite toy. "And don't call Rosie. I don't want her here, too. She's even more trouble than you are."

Noonie puts her coat on. "What shall I tell her, just in case?"

"Tell her I went on a trip . . . yes, yes, tell her I went to China. Just like that!" Elsa snaps her fingers happily; lying pleases her. "It's rather chic, I hear: the Great Wall, the People's Great Hall, the Hall of Complete Harmony." (Elsa has just seen slides at the public library.)

"And when shall I say you'll be back?" Noonie hopes to stump her on that.

"Just say I'm taking a long trip," says Elsa, closing her eyes, "and I'm not sure of the destination or when I'll return."

Noonie takes a cab to Elsa's studio. She tries to catch familiar landmarks, remember times she came home in taxis: Elsa hated driving (she came to it late), so they usually took buses and the El, taxis in times of triumph or tragedy.

Noonie unlocks the door of the upstairs apartment where she lived with her mother and sister. As the older daughter, she had possession of the key, wore it around her neck with the tense arrogance of a White Russian countess with her last piece of Fabergé. She was proud of the key, wasn't the least bit deterred by a photograph she had seen while flipping through a copy of *Life* in the drugstore: a small boy, dirty-faced and grim, thin and underfed, with a large rusty key on a string around his grimy neck. "Latchkey children," read the caption, "a serious problem for the future."

That was the fifties and that was all nonsense: the apartment upstairs was rarely locked, Elsa was usually downstairs working, and there was a plate of home-baked *spitzbuben* on the immaculate oilcloth covering the kitchen table. Noonie's friends' mothers, who lay around their houses with a nonchalance Noonie considered appropriate, barely managed to spread peanut butter on spongy cotton bread at lunchtime; Noonie and Rosie sat down to steaming goulash on beds of fresh *spätzle*.

Noonie looks around the kitchen. No cookies; there is still some coffee in the pot with the crack. Coffee was the women's drink in her family, pots of it, heavy and dark, its bitterness denied by mountains of *schlagsahne*, the whipped cream that accompanied every hot beverage, every pastry (no wonder they all weighed hundreds of pounds!). Noonie pours the dregs into a thin-lipped Meissen cup, puts her bag down, sips its coldness. Elsa must have made it before she left for the hospital (nothing to eat or drink after midnight). She must have been distracted or in a hurry: Elsa was a finisher—of pots, projects, punishments.

Noonie drops the keys into the cut-glass fruit bowl on the sideboard and sits, a solitary guest, at the family dining table.

When was the last time they had all been together at this table? Probably when it was at her grandparents', when they were still alive. There were parties then: dinners with fancy dress, gowns and tailcoats removed from crates that were like wooden caskets and shaken free of camphor. There were candied fruits in flat baskets with tiny forks and clear liqueurs poured into tumblers and tossed back in a swallow. There was dancing: Otto could still waltz in reverse.

Their grandfather Otto, alive but hidden behind the black curtain of his camera, like the master of a magic act. What was her childhood but a series of images, reflections? So many things were shadowy, like her father, missing in action but not thoroughly dismissed or properly accounted for years. Faces in the shadows cast by tall candles on this table, the way a figure grows and disappears: from the crack of her bedroom door Noonie caught the silhouettes of adults in the night, her mother's suitors growing and growing before fading into her mother's bedroom. Elsa insisted things were true beyond a shadow of a doubt; a sick person could be a shadow of her former self.

There was the shadow life of Elsa's negatives, merely the opposite, she said, but they were more, they were mysterious, you could not always discern the subject; they were like a map of the unconscious or a vaguely remembered dream.

At the end of the evening, there was the taking of the official family picture, the clapping hands to signal its assemblage. Linear, formal, posed; they were grouped so their hands draped each other's shoulders or waists, hands touching hands, as if the family were connected by an invisible string binding them together, tighter, like the laces of the grandmother's corsets.

But in Noonie's memories they do not stand at attention but circle wildly, like a painting by Chagall, where the ceiling is the floor and the inhabitants with green and purple faces are tethered not by gravity but by custom.

Was Rosie on roller skates? Possibly. The rug was just under the table as if it had been placed there to accommodate crumbs and spills. Elsa and Tatiana stood in the kitchen, probably reciting the old saw about its not being as fattening if you ate it standing up. Uncle Baby and his friend Roland sat to one side whispering, Baby's thin hand resting on Roland's tweedy shin.

Noonie loved Uncle Baby; he was her connection to culture. Thornton Wilder had been his teacher in college. He brought her novels to read, he bought her stockings and perfume. He and Roland took her to the Art Institute and fed her at Greek restaurants. They had been to Europe (Paris), a place others had come from and didn't miss much.

This was the baby brother who had played the silent tall piano with rose panels, his beautiful hands curved like the Chinese village scenes in the breakfront. This was the brother dressed in the sisters' hand-me-downs, their doll, their toy.

Noonie knows that Uncle Baby carved a life of the imagination while the others were rooted in the earth, in commerce. He dared to dream of distant places; his copy of *Lost Horizon* still sits on Noonie's shelf.

Noonie places her suitcase in the corner of Elsa's bedroom and lies down on the pink satin duvet. She opens the top drawer of the dresser and is attacked by Elsa's habitual *muguet* scent. She pulls out a quilted lingerie bag, slides her hand in: the contents are as smooth and icy as her mother's beautiful hands after she had fallen asleep.

Noonie had sat there for a long time, watching her sleep, wondering how the previous combative feelings could have turned to such concern, real panic, at the thought of Elsa's being afraid, or having pain. Or is she just afraid for herself, seeing her mother vulnerable, fragile, mortal? Elsa is a strong, large woman, the buffer between Noonie and the real world. Noonie always imagined herself riding upon her mother's back, like a tiny creature in a magic fairy tale.

Noonie in Elsa's bed: earaches, mumps, nightmares; the privilege of the unwell. Noonie has extended it to Sarah, although it made no sense in that big suburban manse. Gus would come home to crunched saltines, orange rinds, Magic Markers, bits of yarn between the sheets.

"What's the matter with her bed?" he'd sigh.

But Noonie clings to the healing powers of the mother.

Once, when Rosie and Noonie were sick at the same time (German measles), they were put to bed together. In her sleep, Rosie had taken Noonie's thumb and put it in her own mouth and sucked it.

2

ROSIE

Because of fate, history, birthdays, cut-off dates, Noonie, fifteen months older, went to school a full two years before Rosie.

For the entire two years Rosie had to wait to get to school, she went to school with Noonie in her mind, the route and routine etched into her soul as she sat in a corner in her coveralls, waiting.

The first month, Elsa and Rosie had walked Noonie to school and home again. One day, while Elsa was talking to the teacher, Rosie hid. She got down behind the puppet theater, that triptych that opened like an altarpiece of God, and wouldn't come out. If they forgot her, she thought, they'd have to let her go to school, they'd see she could go to school. But Noonie found her.

Then a big girl, Annelise McCarthy, the building superintendent's daughter, third grade, began to walk Noonie to school—there was a big street to cross right away, a crossing guard; there were stoplights.

Rosie knew the exact hours when Noonie was gone and when she would come home, although she couldn't tell time. She was just a smart little animal in the corner with her heart beating out the right number until Noonie came home: Noonie, her hero, her nemesis, her emblem, the big sister, the sister who went to school.

Noonie came home with pictures that had shiny stars, with maple leaves cut from colored paper, with scrapes on her knees and birthday-party invitations in tiny soiled envelopes. She came home with the stories of strangers: people Rosie didn't know, people even Elsa didn't know, Noonie's strangers.

Sometimes Noonie played school with Rosie. She put the dining-room chairs into a semicircle, then clapped her hands and said, "Now, children, we'll have a story." She put on Elsa's high heels and made Rosie call her Miss Taylor. She would sit in the middle and read a story (Noonie couldn't read, she just said words). Sometimes she'd say, "Now, children, it's nap time," and she'd make Rosie lie down on a rug in the corner and then she'd go off (to Annelise's, maybe) and forget her. Noonie didn't have a long span of attention when it came to Rosie.

There were no nursery schools, car pools. There was kindergarten and walking back and forth.

Until there was kindergarten, you stayed home. You played in Otto's studio while Elsa worked in the darkroom washing plates or in the front office with the plush fat sofas and appointment books and wedding albums.

There were no Creative Playthings. You played with what was there: painted backdrops, the crepe paper bouquets and dusty mortarboards or the rattling toys Poppa used to grab the attention of crying babies. There were ledger books to draw in and photographic-supply catalogues to read. Sometimes Grandma told stories about the lives in the Leatherette albums. There was a footed ashtray with sand in it, and you could draw with a lipsticked butt until Poppa caught you.

In the kindergarten room there was a sand table—big, very big, Noonie said—with a steel belly in the wide wooden frame. There was a doll corner with tiny chairs and a stove and pots and pans, all small. There was a rack with a tailcoat and hats and grown-up shoes.

The first day, Miss Taylor read *Peter Rabbit* aloud at story time. She held the book on her lap, upside down, and waved it in a graceful arc, like a beautiful lady with a fan, so all the children could see the pictures.

There was a big box with bright wooden beads and long colored laces to string them. You couldn't bring them home, but you could wear them there.

There was a big box with hundreds of fat square crayons, and stacks of manila paper and an easel with paints and a red smock hanging from the side and sleek-tailed brushes.

In the spring they hollowed out eggs and planted marigold seeds. You could not really see them, Noonie told Rosie, you could just feel them sharp on the tip of your finger.

At Thanksgiving Noonie cut out feathers and pasted them on the body of a turkey Miss Taylor had cut out for each child; Noonie's was green. Elsa put this on the refrigerator with a magnet shaped like a teapot. There was nothing by Rosie on the refrigerator.

At some point in the day, there were milk and cookies. Someone got to pass them out and someone got to take the money. Two cents. Milk came in short squat bottles with a pleated cap and under this was a cover with a hole for your straw to go through. The cookies had holes in them, too, and Noonie wore hers like a ring on her finger, taking tiny bites until it fell off. But she never brought one of these cookies home for Rosie. She just talked about them.

She talked and talked.

Then Noonie had a major triumph. She drew a picture of a stick woman, a woman in high-heeled shoes and a big hat and dangling earrings (this woman was Elsa—Rosie didn't need to be told that), and the teacher was dazzled: Noonie's woman had shoulders, and fingers on her hands (four on each), and her feet in the high-heeled shoes had arches. Noonie was sent to the principal with this picture and the principal wrote a note and attached it to the picture, and sent Noonie and her picture and this note to show every teacher in the entire school. There was talk of Noonie then, of Noonie and her talent, of Noonie having drawing lessons, of Noonie drawing.

By the time Rosie got to kindergarten, Noonie was in the second grade. She could read and write. She could add and subtract (sort of). Sure, there were milk and cookies, there was the sand table in the kindergarten room and the beads and Miss Taylor read *Peter Rabbit* aloud, but, in a way, Rosie had already done that, and how would she ever catch up?

Walking Rosie to school was dangerous, it was an adventure; it was Noonie's first job. She could never figure out how Rosie knew the way, knew the shortcuts through the Babbits' yard, through alleys, around a viaduct. She didn't know that Rosie had gone to school with her for two solid years in her imagination.

(Noonie never knew this, Rosie never told her, she probably forgot all about it. It just resided somewhere in her unconscious, near other things more terrible, and so it got pushed down like a forgotten single sock stuffed into the back of a crowded dresser drawer. Of course, Noonie remembered kindergarten: the famous drawing and the butter cookies and planting the marigold seeds, but it was all about Noonie. For Rosie there were always two experiences, two lives: her own and Noonie's.)

Once, early on, Noonie forgot Rosie at school. She was in the kitchen telling Elsa the story of her latest coup (a drawing or a spelling test or a composition) when Elsa asked, "Where's Rosie?"

"Rosie?" asked Noonie, as if it were a distant planet or something strange to eat.

"Rosemarie!" shouted Elsa. "Did you leave her at school? Oh, Noonie!" Elsa picked her up by her elbow and lifted her to the door. "You go right back there and get her—I hope to God she didn't try to come home by herself and cross that street!"

Noonie ran and ran, looking at every face for Rosie (she looked on the street, too, under cars); she had never run like this.

When she got to the school, Rosie was in the principal's office. The principal had given Rosie a cookie and was patting her little curly head, but she was crying pretty hard.

"Natalie!" said the principal, Miss Curtin, rising to her total height and sternness (she was tall and thin and they called her Curtain Rod). "Natalie, I am surprised at you! How could you do such a thoughtless thing? What a selfish, selfish girl. Leaving your little sister, a littler girl than you . . ."

(Being an artist didn't let you off the hook with Miss Curtin.)

Noonie's cheeks and ears were bright and she felt the

tears coming, but she didn't cry. She saved the tears because she knew that when she got home Elsa would be waiting for her and it would be worse.

Something happens in the water: first of all, you are weightless. This is the first thing Rosie noticed, remembers. She learns to swim the ordinary way many of us learn: a small rectangular pool in a day camp in the Indiana dunes, one hour's ride through smelly south Chicago, past the threatening smokestacks of Gary, in a yellow bus of dreamy little girls singing interminable camp songs: "Found a peanut, found a peanut."

First you hold on to the sides of the pool in the shallow end. You are a guppie and your bathing cap is pink and you put your face into the water and blow bubbles and turn it to the side and take a gulp of breath. Some of the little girls cannot do this, simply put their sweet faces in the water; they refuse with screaming and cries: no! no!

(Even the great ones begin like everyone else; even little Mozart sat down for his first lesson, his tiny fingers poised over the keyboard. So Rosie held on to the edge and learned to blow bubbles, then to kick, then to float solo: the dead man's float, the doggy paddle—what kinds of names are these to apply to an art form?)

But like a little prodigy, Rosie has pushed off and is swimming alone in the middle of the pool.

"Good God!" shouts one of the counselors, and dives in and grabs her, pushing her head under the water, so deep that she comes up sputtering. (It is amazing that she ever went near the water again.)

But what is missing is the fear; what is there is the sense of completeness, of this act completing you. There is no fear and there is no pain (or maybe she refuses to feel pain or maybe she doesn't feel it: "Hurt, pain, agony, and ecstasy," swimmers like to chant) and certainly Rosie is the child who holds her arm out to the doctor for a shot, who likes to watch, who puts her finger in the candle flame and holds it there longer than anyone. For Noonie, the thought is adequate, the suggestion; she begins to scream as the nurse's shoes squeak across the room and the hinge on the sterilizer is pushed up and out and it drops down—and all this time her head is buried in Elsa's lap.

Noonie, who was a pretty fair skater, always said skating was like flying, said this with bunny-fur pompons tumbling on her narrow toes as she did a figure eight. There was a small rink in this same park where she met her husband, Gus, some years later. Actually it was a fountain, and in the summer, neighborhood children could run through crisp needles of water and in the winter, it was frozen, with layers of water, and the little stand that sold Popsicles in the summer sold steaming hot chocolate with a marshmallow (life was that simple then). Rosie didn't like skating; she tried to blacken Noonie's old skates just to look different. Anyway, how could she compete with Noonie, all pink cheeks and flashing thighs.

If skating was like flying, then swimming was like dying, Rosie sometimes thought, the way the water would take your body, the soft weightlessness, the softness lapping into nooks and crevices. It could be your enemy, too, her coach tried to warn her, stressed that it could be like a dangerous lover (this coach will become the first woman to love Rosie, besides her mother, sister, grandmother). You mustn't let down your guard, ever, or not be afraid. It is this coach who, like a great teacher of dance can take the tiny feet and legs of a beginner and splay them in such a way that she can predict future success; so this coach at the Y took Rosie's body, touched her shoulders, waist, arms, watched her chest fill with air and blow it out.

"Butterfly," she said, then thought better of it. "This one can do anything. Go the distance."

"Feel this," Noonie says to Rosie the day she meets Gus.

"Feel what?" Rosie asks, warily. She is leaning back against the kitchen sink, eating a peach, and juice is running down her chin. Noonie hasn't paid much attention to her lately.

"Just put your hand here," Noonie says, "put your hand here and feel my heart beating." To make sure, she takes Rosie's sticky hand and presses it flat at the top of her breasts. "Feel it beating? That's what it's like to be in love."

What it is like to be in love, Rosie never forgot that; the stunning intimacy after the last few years of distance, the pounding heart (someone else's does not feel like your own), the notion of love. Once one of her lovers brought home a puppy from the animal shelter, a tiny thing with the thin tail of a rat, four, five weeks old, maybe, not old enough, and she put a large ticking alarm clock into the little basket with him so he would think he was sleeping next to his mother, hear his mother's heartbeat. (Does the fetus hear its mother's heart? Rosie doesn't know, but the image of this floating safe child/fish is something she thinks about often.)

This is the test that Rosie would put to lovers: the beating heart. Not only was Noonie's heart beating, she was flushed, the smooth triangle of skin rising from her breast to her neck and her long arched throat was mottled almost with a rash, as if she had run for miles.

Rosie would never have said that: this is what it is like to be in love. She wanted to feel safe, warm, comfortable—that's what she desired from love, not this beating heart, this fever. Hide me, she wanted to say to lovers, let me crawl under your skin, into your armpit or side or the crook of your arm, and hide me from the world, let me disappear, let me be gone. Noonie's love made her brighter, stronger, bolder, made her flash like the silver star on a Christmas tree; Rosie's made her smaller, let her fade, buried in the folds of something soft and warm.

The love of the other, separation anxiety, not of the child from the mother, but of sister from mirror-sister, whose reflection is frustratingly never your own.

(How we love stories of twins, of the moment the egg splits to become two persons, separate but identical. How we love stories of how, after years raised apart in families as different as Eskimo and Anglican, they choose husbands named Ed or drive blue Fords.)

The amazement of the baby in the mirror; Rosie remembers her tiny niece Sarah down on all fours, raising her hand to touch the hand in the mirror. "Baby!" she shouted in delight. "Hi, baby!"

Rosie's favorite trick of Houdini's, when at nine she discovered a biography of him in the school library, was something called Metamorphosis (later she would love the escapes, the water escapes—the filled water-torture cell, the milk-can escape—would fantasize them as she swam long distance, would imagine herself Houdini in the shark cage she had to use in the aborted Caribbean swim). In this trick, Metamorphosis, Houdini's assistant, his beloved wife, Bess, would be handcuffed and placed in a bag, and the bag would be placed in a trunk, which would then be bound with ropes and chains and padlocked in numerous places. Houdini would stand on top of the trunk, splendid in white tie and tails, would wrap a swath of heavy cloth around him and, within less than three seconds, trade places, so that he was in the trunk in the bag with handcuffs, and beautiful Bess in an evening gown was on the top!

In photographs of sisters they are always holding hands. Rosie's arm is wrenched straight out of the socket because she was always just that much smaller, and then the two hands are closed, into a tight bud of a fist, and Rosie, her head tilted slightly, is always looking up at Noonie.

From your hotel room in Dover, if it is clear and it is calm (and you pray it will be), you can see the shoreline of France on the other side, twenty-one miles. It is not the longest swim or the most dangerous. It is accessible (although only twenty percent of those who attempt it complete it), but the sea is a fickle lover and she can change her mind without warning: winds, the temperature of the water can plunge thirty degrees, even in the best-planned swim.

Rosie is seventeen when she swims the Channel for the first time. She has been taken there by Marie Marks, her first coach, mentor, not yet a lover; that will take another year of long glances, less and less subtle touches that linger, a kiss moving closer and closer to the mouth, lasting longer, tasting different. Rosie is so used to Marie's touching her (massaging, greasing her) she barely notices. How many times has Marie pulled her from the water, her hands touching Rosie's breasts?

But finally Rosie knows there is something different in the way Marie's hand wanders, flatters; it is slower, the quality of closeness.

(What did it feel like, the first time? Some of us remember—Gus—some of us don't; Rosie did not. It happened so quickly and she was frightened; she might have held her breath the whole time, if she hadn't cried out—it is such a mixture of pleasure and fear. It feels so good you are afraid it will stop. It isn't an entirely unfamiliar feeling, of course; you have touched yourself in these places, given yourself this pleasure for years, but this is the hand of someone else, that hand finding places not her own.)

Rosie is in the shower. Marie is toweling her off, when suddenly the towel is dropped and Marie has replaced it with her own dry urgent body. Then she drops to her knees, her strong, soft hands lifting, opening Rosie's thighs. ("Downstairs," Rosie called it as a child, her variation on "down there." Maybe she had some minor hearing problem, they never knew for sure.)

So Rosie is wet the first time she makes love, not unusual for her. The tiles are slippery, cold, Rosie grabs onto the faucets, her feet are splayed, the heels digging into the rubber edging of the stall, a slow trickle of hot dripping down her flat spine, wet hair in her eyes, the pattern of the nippled rubber mat on the bottoms of her feet for several hours afterward.

No, what Rosie remembers is standing on the Shakespeare cliff (that is the name of it) at three-thirty in the morning. (She was up at two-thirty to eat her pre-swim breakfast: six raw eggs mixed with yogurt, toast with honey, tea.) It is not quite black night at this time of year and trainers with rubber gloves have rolled down her thin nylon suit and are rubbing lanolin mixed with a base of Vaseline all over her body, pounds of it. She stands still, she feels so tall, still, like a statue, almost as if she is being modeled out of clay, almost as if she is being made.

Then they carefully roll up her suit and she puts on the multiple caps she wears for warmth and adjusts her goggles to her face. She is scared, she is terrified, it is not drowning, it is not dying, it is failing. (The Channel is approximately a thirty-hour swim; she isn't out to break any records, just finishing will give her a place in history, or her-story, as her later lover Alison will like to call it.)

There are two boats: an escort boat with supplies on the right (hot chocolate mixed with salt and glucose and minerals, jars of syrupy glazed imported fruits she likes sometimes, towels, blankets, extra goggles and caps, Vaseline) and Marie's boat on the left, so Rosie can swim a straight line.

Some of the tricks swimmers have, talk about, to make the time pass, make the unfathomable fathomable: counting in various languages, singing rounds of camp songs; Rosie sings drinking songs Otto taught them (in German), sings hymns Marie taught her ("Abide with Me"), begins to dream. Everyone can tell stories of hallucinations, imagined perils: huge swooping gulls about to lift you out of the sea and into the sky like a herring, the brick walls that appear suddenly and you are about to swim into.

Rosie settles deep, deep into consciousness, the level of profound memory, so she suddenly sniffs the little blue flowered nightie she got for an early birthday, sees the raggedy blue ribbon on the collar, remembers the taste of Noonie's thumb, Ivory soap and chocolate in the middle of the night, the almond crescents when Elsa pulled them out of the oven, so hot they have no taste, only burned nuts. And she sees herself as Houdini slipping her hands through the cuffs, bursting them with strength, untying herself, freeing herself, free, free.

3

MISSING IN ACTION (ELSA'S STORY)

Their father had not returned from the war. Whether this was sheer neglect or lack of good directions or hideous death was never fully explained. As a small child, whenever Noonie would ask Elsa, her mother would sigh dramatically and wave her arms as if warding off large threatening beasts.

"He did not return," Elsa would intone huskily and, peeking between two slick venetian blinds, intimate that he might be out there someplace. Or she would gather Noonie and Rosie onto her ample lap and conjure him wandering wounded and dazed onto a farm in Normandy.

Once, when a straggly-tailed dog followed Rosie home from the schoolyard and when they awoke to find her gone, Elsa told them that during the night Princess had been drafted, but they shouldn't worry—she was being shipped to their father, who would have a little uniform made for her and a tiny metal hat (that was the part Noonie liked best; she could see the thin leather strap dangling under Princess's scarred and chewed ear) and they were riding together in a huge tank, their heads popped out of the top.

At first it was easy to pretend; Noonie was young, other fathers had been to war, there were wars. Eventually most everyone returned or was accounted for and the stories became confused.

Noonie still remembers the thrill of recognition, the sweet shock when she read for the first time the Grimms' tale "Snow-white and Rose-red." (It was in a big green musty volume, with fine line drawings, not the kind of thing to appeal to children, but if not children, then whom?)

> Once upon a time, there lived in a lonely cottage, surrounded by a garden, a poor widow. In the garden grew two rose trees, one which bore white roses, the other red.

Noonie sat up straight: a lonely widow, with a cottage and a garden. It seemed to be just what she needed.

> Now this widow had two daughters, who so much resembled the rose-bushes that she gave to one the name of Snow-white and to the other Rose-red.

Didn't everyone comment on the peculiarity of one light sister, one so dark? Here was precedent to cite.

> These two children were the best, the most obedient and the most industrious children in the world . . . they always walked hand in hand whenever they went out together, and when Snow-white said: "We will never desert each other," Rose-red answered: "No, not as long as we live."

The part about being together seemed fine; maybe Rosie would live in California, as Aunt Tatie had done, but she didn't expect them to separate. The other stuff was harder to fit: Rosie was the obedient one, really. Noonie almost shook the book, turned it upside down, sideways, in order to make it fit—books were that real to her.

The story then lapsed into the usual fairy-tale stuff, which Noonie loved but didn't believe. There was a bear who came into the house on a snowy night and frightened the girls. But the mother invited him in (Elsa would certainly do that; she wasn't afraid of a thing) and told him to lie by the fire while Snow-white and Rose-red brushed him dry.

Then there were these curious words:

Snow-white and Rose-red,
Don't beat your lover dead.

There was more, of course: a pet lamb and a dove and a cruel demented dwarf and bags full of pearls and gold and stones. And the bear was really a prince when he was released from his spell and he had a brother for Rose and they lived happily ever after.

Noonie turned this into a play. There was an old bearskin rug where babies used to pose (in the twenties, Elsa said) that they propped up over a table for the bear and Rosie was Rose-red and Noonie played Snow-white and all the other parts. She was especially effective as the mother, slightly bent over, with a kerchief tied tightly around her head, and she was pretty good as the cruel evil dwarf, all hunched, with a shaking fist and spittle dripping from her mouth. (Rosie always admired this in Noonie, her ability to produce something from nothing, to carry on a conversation with no one at all in evidence.)

About this time a photograph of a handsome dark-haired man in uniform appeared on the mantel. But photographs were Elsa's business; how easy it would have been for her to buy a frame at Woolworth's and exchange the picture that came with the frame—the blurred features of Rory Calhoun—with one of the customers and claim this was Noonie's father. When Noonie read *Peyton Place* (finally!) in the seventh grade, she seized upon the similarity of her story to Allison MacKenzie's. Noonie was illegitimate, Noonie was a bastard child.

What saved her was Rosie; it was the only single time Noonie could remember being grateful for her sister's existence. There was a sign over the stage in the assembly hall of their school: FOOL ME ONCE, SHAME ON YOU. FOOL ME TWICE, SHAME ON ME. (This was attributed to Abraham Lincoln.) Noonie did not possess the fund of knowledge necessary to imagine two different fathers.

Elsa had taken up with a big blond ward heeler named Chick O'Connors. He was in the neighborhood passing out Election Day turkeys and had his picture taken.

What a change of pace from the others, Mr. Kleinert and Mr. Horowitz! Chick O'Connors sat in the front room looking calm and large, his buffed fingernails resting on blue-striped knees revealed by the parting of his camel's-hair coat. You could almost taste his ripeness.

Noonie tended to think of her mother's suitors as outfits. Mr. Kleinert: black mohair, pink shirt, diamond stickpin ("Diamonds are a girl's best friend!" he never hesitated to advise Noonie, giving her a wet kiss); Mr. Horowitz: gray sharkskin, nylon socks, polished brown tie-shoes.

Rosie, a simpler person, thought of them in terms of smells. Mr. Kleinert: Vitalis; Mr. Horowitz: wintergreen and mothballs. Rosie couldn't quite place Mr. O'Connors.

"Whiskey!" announced Noonie, a whole year older.

"Not just!" objected Rosie, a mere year younger.

Noonie would later be able to identify it as a cornucopia of male odors: tobacco, after-shave (lemony), whiskey, cold wool, sweet sweat.

Mr. Kleinert took them to the Chez Paree for Shirley Temples and the floor show; Mr. Horowitz took them to museums (he tried to snuggle Noonie in the coal mine at the Museum of Science and Industry!); but Chick took them skiing.

"Just wait'll I get you out on those slopes," said Chick to Elsa.

"I hate activity out-of-doors," said Elsa. "Skiing scares me half to death."

"Aw, nobody's taught you properly." He gave Elsa's shiny knee a little squeeze.

Noonie had noticed how men tended to blame what they viewed as her mother's inadequacies and failings on the man who had previously occupied that position in her life, as if Elsa's fears and quirks were mismanagement on the parts of Mr. Kleinert and Mr. Horowitz and Noonie's absent father. (Noonie also noticed how Elsa's behavior changed in the presence of these men: her voice was lowered in volume but raised in range; whereas she usually gestured with a whole arm, she tended to use just her fingers and wrists. Her whole frame softened, relaxed, folded, as if she were trying to make herself literally smaller.)

"I've tried, I've really tried," sighed Elsa. "Haven't I? Natalie? Rosemarie?"

In the back seat Noonie and Rosie smacked gum and turned the pages of their Katy Keene comics.

"Well, girls, I'm going to take care of that. You just wait and see. Tomorrow night, at this time, your mother will be whizzing down the highest mountain."

Ho hum, thought Noonie and Rosie, who had watched their mother try to mount camels at the Children's Zoo, ride ponies on Visiting Day at camp, stay afloat in Lake Michigan.

"My daughters are afraid of nothing," Elsa was fond of saying. "If they were to meet a lion on the street, Noonie would kick it in the rear and Rosie would stick her head in its mouth."

Elsa's daughters had pounded on her womb with their tiny feet, done perfect racer's flips, and entered this world as if shot from cannons. "It has been a real pleasure to watch," the doctor had told Elsa both times.

Sure enough, by the end of the first afternoon, Rosie and Noonie were schussing, Elsa was standing on the top of the mountain, frozen, paralyzed.

"I can't move my legs," cried Elsa. "This is real fear."

"Fear," snorted Chick.

"Fear is when things get worse and worse, not better," explained Elsa.

"Fear!" laughed Chick, who had been through the war (and returned).

"The most dangerous thing I did as a young woman was ride the down escalator at Marshall Field's."

(This was ridiculous. When it came to verbal abuse—snooty teachers, lapsed customers, sulky shopkeepers—Elsa was ferocious.)

Freed from skiing, Elsa waltzed around the cabin. Suddenly she was struck with a wonderful idea: she would cook a real Jewish dinner for Chick and his friends. How she wished to see chicken fat slip down those sharp jaws, horseradish bring tears to the corneas of those deep blue eyes, gastritis take up residence in stomachs flat as the Plains.

But she was stuck in a small town in northern Michigan; there was most likely not a box of matzo meal for miles around. Elsa stared at the Ritz cracker box, at the famous appleless apple-pie recipe. Of course, Ritzballs! No chicken fat, but there was a large jar of mayo in the icebox and dozens of envelopes of chicken bouillon. Elsa was about to embark on a new cuisine: a marriage of the worst of Jewish and American cookery.

But horseradish; French's yellow mustard was no substitute.

"Dear Chick," Elsa wrote, "take good care of my girls. I am going home for the horseradish!" She made a flag with the note and stuck it in the largest Ritzball.

(This was how Elsa liked to finish this story: "Then I wandered out in the snow to the main highway. A big truck ground to a halt. 'Where are you goin', little lady?' asked the driver, sticking his handsome head out of the window of his cab. He was a real gentleman. I didn't return for three days and nights. The driver was a country-western singer and wrote a song about me."

"You are the heartburn of my dreams," Elsa would sing in a heavy twang. "Do you remember that one?"

"Mother!" Noonie would shout; Rosie would just laugh.

"It really happened, you know," Elsa would say, getting up and leaving the room. "The part about the Ritzballs.")

"My father did not return from the war," Noonie wrote in her prize-winning essay for the annual Jewish War Veterans patriotism contest. "Sometimes I see him wandering wounded and dazed onto a farm in Normandy, where he was nursed back to health futilely by the farmer's buxom daughter, who presented him with two apple-cheeked children, posthumorously."

(This line was corrected, then deleted by Miss Tomlinson, Noonie's English teacher, for final publication in the Veterans' Day edition of the *North Town News.*)

"He died in France, a country he wrestled from the forces of evil and hatred. Not far from the beaches where his boat landed on June 6, 1944, Day of Infamy!"

One day, spreading mustard and sand on a hot dog at the Farwell beach, Noonie looked up and saw it cluttered with bodies. She felt sick.

"Oh, Noonie, your head," said Elsa, poking Noonie's skull with a finger. "They didn't leave them on the beach, like whales or something. They put them in cemeteries." Elsa turned her considerable profile out to sea (shallow Lake Michigan in this case) and began to recite, "In Flanders fields the poppies blow."

"Glad to see you using the books, kiddo," said Mr. Horowitz one night, sneaking up behind Noonie and pinching her bottom.

Mr. Horowitz had come to sell them *The Book of Knowledge* and had given Elsa the set instead. (She did a lot of business on the barter system. Mr. Kleinert was in ladies' foundations, useful with two developing daughters.)

"What's ya looking for?" he asked.

"My father's buried there," said Noonie, solemnly, pointing to the picture.

"Did your mama tell you that?" he asked cautiously.

"Not exactly," Noonie admitted.

"That was the First War."

"I want to know what really happened to my father," said Noonie. "Mr. Horowitz says that was the First War, 'Flanders Fields.' "

"Oh, he does?" said Elsa making a mental note. She was hanging up wet contact sheets.

"And my teacher says there's someone I can write or call. My congressman, she says."

Elsa sighed and signaled Noonie to sit. Noonie leaned against a stool in the corner.

"Ho ho! Noonie! Take a look at this!"

Noonie watched as a bride's anxious face surfaced from chemicals in the sink.

"Thirty-five, if she's a day!" said Elsa, rolling her eyes. "Wearing white, no less!"

"Don't change the subject!"

Elsa shrugged, drained the sink.

"Mama, pay attention, I'm fourteen years old. I have a right to know the truth about my father!"

"The truth? He never returned," Elsa sighed, shaking out the portraits. "He put on his uniform. He combed his thick hair. He went to war. You didn't know where people went."

"He didn't write?"

"Letters were secret stuff, letters were forwarded to someplace else. It was not like the stream of postcards that you and Rosie sent from Camp Juniper Knoll."

"People don't just disappear," Noonie objected.

"In a war they do. In a war, the rules change, things happen you don't count upon in ordinary everyday life, Noonie," explained Elsa, hanging up the proofs with clothespins.

"Didn't you get a telegram or something from the government or the Army? Miss Tomlinson says . . ."

" 'Miss Tomlinson,' " she mimicked. "She should stick to teaching English."

"She says she can find out for me. A few phone calls."

Elsa stripped off her rubber gloves, opened the door, walking through the studio to the stairs, up to the apartment. Noonie followed, out of breath. Elsa went directly to her bedroom. Noonie was silent, frightened. She watched as Elsa squatted heavily, down on her knees. Noonie was afraid she might faint, but she didn't stop her. Elsa reached under the bed and pulled out an old chocolates box: a red plush valentine with a satin ribbon across its width, withered silk gardenias pinned to a gilt arrow.

Noonie was terrified; what if his ashes were in the box, something terrible? (Her best friend Cheryl Ann's grandfather was in an urn on the closet shelf at her grandmother's; sand and small bones, like a construction site. Cheryl Ann had given her a handful to take home, but she threw it on the street as soon as she got out of there.) She watched Elsa untie the ribbon, unpin the arrow. She wished she could stop the whole thing; she hated Miss Tomlinson (and she would forever) and Mr. Horowitz for meddling.

Elsa passed Noonie several folded foolscap pages, soft and worn as old kid gloves. They were sent from Detroit and dated March 1946.

For years Noonie had imagined her father, his face planted firmly on every prince, every hero, movie star, rock-and-roll singer. Now she discovered that he was a welder, also a philanderer, a shirker of familial responsibilities.

"You like stories, Noonie," said Elsa faintly, her eyes narrowed as she watched Noonie read the letter. "I taught you to pretend, to make up things, to imagine it as it might have been."

"You lied," said Noonie. "You lied to Rosie and me. This isn't a book . . . you can't make things up! You lied!" she screamed. "He was alive all this time and living in Detroit and you didn't tell us!" She slammed the door to the bedroom.

"Sometimes," Elsa shouted, "the truth is not so interesting."

Noonie grabbed the photograph of the man in the uniform on the mantel and threw it against the wall.

"Wait, Noonie!" Elsa shouted, running over to her. "I didn't lie about the picture. The picture's him!" she sobbed, bending and picking up the pieces of glass. "The picture's really your father."

This is the true story of Elsa's life, at least the part that is relevant to the existence of her daughters, Natalie and Rosemarie.

At the beginning of the war, Elsa is twenty-five, a broad-hipped, big-bosomed girl with dark wavy hair worn in a long pageboy with a side-part, a deep wing of hair over one eye. Otto has been commissioned (what luck!) to take photographs of the soldiers at Fort Dearborn, outside of Chicago. So imagine Elsa in her high heels and stockings (you can still get nylons then with the dark long straight seams that Noonie always admired and once purchased, a bit early, frankly, in her marriage, to wear with some whorish underthings that sent the wrong signals!) climbing on a tall ladder, her fine legs showing under a short dress, one foot higher than the other, to hold some equipment for her tiny father, hidden (for a change) behind his black drape.

This is as beautiful as Elsa will get; it is the younger sister, Tatiana, who is the beauty: everything the same, but everything smaller, finer-tuned, her small head balanced on a slender neck, on shoulders so frail they seem the wings of a balsa glider, her nostrils quivering—a thoroughbred versus a brood mare, and indeed there is trouble for Tatie delivering her one brute son, Richard. (Noonie inherits this fineness, this bone structure like a Gothic cathedral, so that from the waist to the chin she is Tatiana all over again.) Have you noticed when there are two beautiful sisters, still one is described as the beauty? Elsa is the peppy one.

The photographs are taken with a special camera, equipped with a wide-angle lens that sweeps across a wide frame, allowing for hundreds and hundreds of faces to appear on a single plate. Tinting is done for preservation and also allows for a sharpness, so one can locate a loved one in this vast sea of strangers, and, ironically, the color is so close to that of the uniforms, it lends an air of authenticity, too.

(How many thousands of these photographs, rolled up, crackling, litter our basements and attics? So many of these men, the survivors, must be dead anyway, and everywhere there must be the bewildered bereaved searching the rows for a curly-haired, youthful father they can't possibly remember like that.)

Inevitably, one man steps out of the crowd, one soldier, who is assigned to them: who helps Elsa down the ladder, who sits next to the driver of the jeep that takes them out to the field, the boxy camera bouncing in the back seat between Elsa and Otto, a gloved hand restraining the tripod, and who jumps out on both feet in that instant before it comes to a stop, offers a hand, a tip of the cap, pulled from his head in one swift gesture, his dark curly hair slightly mussed, a gold tooth in the back of his wide white grin.

(Like horse traders, they are suckers for men with strong teeth—Elsa and her daughter Noonie.)

All Elsa can remember of the farmers' sons in Wisconsin, the sons whom they left town to escape, is teeth and their hair, hair so blond it is white in daylight, darker under electric light, and the pale sharp hairs in their wide nostrils and thick ears; big brown hands, rough, covering yours, and the sweet smell of hay and horse and their heavy laced shoes worn everywhere, even with their Sunday suits to the church dances, albeit polished to a shiny finish, but a dead giveaway of something raw and American, not like Poppa's fine kid buttoned shoes.

And the sons remember the Gluck daughters, their fancy airs, their tiny waists and small even teeth, the diamonds in their pretty ears, and elaborate hairstyles, no braids for them.

"The little Jewesses," their mothers call them, as if they were straight from the desert of the Old Testament, not the mittel-European cuties they are. "If you marry them," they would warn, "you will have to work in the house, as well as the fields."

So until now there have been the farmers' sons, and an occasional refugee-cousin hastily dressed up and brought to Sunday lunch, whose accents and exaggerated fine manners Elsa and Tatie mock behind their backs in the kitchen between the soup and nuts, and now this handsome soldier Victor Kamensky.

At first he comes occasionally, then once a month, every pass, taking crowded trains, hitching a ride: what a strangely friendly time. Victor and Elsa take the El downtown to stroll along the lake or to frequent movies, restaurants.

Elsa allows him to make love to her one afternoon when the whole family is out—surely they know this will happen, it is time for it to happen and she is ready for it to happen (there is a war on!). Why would she allow this, except that it is time for it?

They make love on her single bed in Tatie's and her room, although she doesn't let him smoke in there and she changes the sheets while he shaves in the bathroom (she thinks the room smells of sex—not an odor Tatiana or anyone could place if you did not know what it is or were not expecting it). After he showers and dresses, they lie back against the cushions, and Elsa strokes his black hair, strokes it over and over as he closes his eyes and pretends to sleep. Elsa is sitting against the wall, one leg straight along his prone body, next to his left cheek, her other leg raised slightly so that when he opens his eyes, partially, he is greeted by her white inner thigh, her lace slip, a garter, the darker edge of her stocking: a place he likes to press.

Although it would not have comforted Elsa and it would have enraged Noonie to know this, Victor carries these afternoons around with him for years, through the war and back to Detroit, all those years in a double bed with a less pretty woman, his wife. Over the years, Elsa's leg, a good one to begin with, becomes longer and paler, silkier, so that it is almost that of a marble Venus in a Roman museum instead of the hot flesh of a young woman on a green chenille bedspread in the back bedroom of an apartment in Chicago, circa 1942.

(We have, most of us, mere mortals, filled this role for someone out there, so somewhere your fresh breasts or legs, a broad chest or shoulders, the hollow of a young throat, lives in the memory of some aging person of your past, and because of the good luck that we never meet again, we remain like that for someone forever.)

This is not the self that Elsa displays to her daughters;

there are hints of it, of course, this sensual self who allows herself afternoon indiscretions. In her heart of hearts, Elsa is a secret dancer and there is a selection of sepia-toned shots of his daughters taken by Otto with the greatest pleasure: such *Mädchen,* such cream puffs, dumplings, beauties, costumed as Spanish queens with combs and castanets in polka-dot dresses with shoulder flounces or as swans, *en pointe,* wearing hats like tulle baskets, upside down. There is a dog-eared copy of Nijinsky's biography, written by his brave broken wife, Romola (and rumored to be ghostwritten by the evil Diaghilev himself!), and there are the crusty brown gardenias—Elsa's flower—whose petals crumble as they fall from the gilt-edged pages of a Leatherette edition of *The Rubáiyát.* (Then there is all the lingerie.)

All of this contrasts nicely with Elsa's pile of starched aprons, her stern looks, her admonitions about work ethics and feminine hygiene, but it opens a crack, a tiny space that Noonie in her way squeezes through, and creates an entire persona based on a mother's youthful fantasies.

But here is the chronology:

Meets Victor Kamensky at Fort Dearborn, becomes pregnant with Noonie, marries him at Thanksgiving in a cream-colored wool suit with a broad matching hat and a cascading bouquet of gardenias in a small ceremony in a suite at the Edgewater Beach Hotel, Noonie is born, Rosie is conceived, Victor is shipped overseas (later she will learn it is to the Normandy beaches), he doesn't return.

Missing in action, Elsa conjectures when it gets to be 1946 and the war is over and she has heard nothing official, or unofficial.

"Missing in action!" snorts Otto, a tiny granddaughter bouncing on each bony knee, redeemed in his first impression of this no-goodnik Russian Jew from Detroit with the shiny teeth who holds his fork like a shovel. "I can just imagine the kind of action he is missing in!"

Then there is the letter of goodbye, explanation, apology; there are real dates, succinct as if they are carved on a tombstone. So why the lies, the mystery, this hesitancy, this reluctance with fact; why wait until Noonie at fourteen pushes her to tell the truth?

Because it was like this to Elsa: fleeting, shadowy, over almost as if it hadn't happened or had happened to some other girl, a heroine in a novel, someone on the screen, a series of black-and-white images. This is how she remembered it and this is what she did not report to her daughters.

Can Noonie remember her father? This seems out of the question. We are absolutely certain that Rosie cannot because he disappeared over the horizon several months after dropping his sperm in Elsa's womb again. Some souvenir. Noonie was, after all, a baby when he lived with them: Noonie in a wobbly crib in Elsa's bedroom, Tatiana now on a divan in the dining room, Uncle Baby in the Murphy bed in the hall, Poppa and Grandma with the big carved headboard in the front bedroom.

But it is part of the edge that Noonie always had over Rosie: she knew their father, she could comment on him, imagine him with an authority.

"No," she would say to Rosie, "he was not like that." No, taller or darker or smarter. He didn't eat tomatoes. He liked peanut brittle. Peach ice cream. He said he'd never wear a brown suit when he got out of the army.

These things were true; Elsa, closemouthed about the matter, of course, allowed a certain amount of factual information to escape in an innocent way. "Oh," she'd say, "you couldn't put eggs in his potato salad, he was allergic, or seeds in his rye bread." That kind of thing, and Noonie, ever alert, like a court reporter, was there to gather anything and fit it into a sketchy framework she called "Father."

So we have a picture of a dark handsome man who is a picky eater and is dressed in navy blue.

What should she tell Rosie? All during dinner, Noonie watched Rosie slurping her spaghetti, her red nose dripping from chlorine. Once they had gone to the grocery store and were walking through the cereals aisle when Rosie took Noonie aside, pulled a box of Wheaties from the shelf, and, pointing to the picture of Bob Richards on the front, said solemnly, "That's our father."

"Guess what?" Noonie said casually as they were getting undressed for bed.

"What?"

"He's alive, our father. She lied to us."

Rosie narrowed her eyes. "You're lying now."

"No. There's proof, letters. I saw them. He left her. He left us. He lives in Detroit and makes cars."

"Yeah?" Rosie disappeared under her nightie for a minute.

Noonie took out the letters from where she had hidden them under her underwear and a box of Kotex. She opened them for Rosie, smoothing the creases as gently as Elsa would push the wrinkles near her eyes; the words smeared under her fingers. The letters were written in number-2 pencil in a large and formal handwriting, the Palmer method, the kind Noonie had been taught to write. (Noonie was old enough to appreciate the place awarded penmanship in a pre-Sputnik world. It pleased her that her father had such a lovely and accomplished hand.)

The letters were pretty straightforward: he was leaving

because he could not compete with her family, her father. It was crowded in Elsa's affections, what with her parents, sister, brother, daughters. The girls were his, he acknowledged this, he admitted this to the attorney, but he gave up any legal rights to them; Otto would raise them. He didn't know Elsa very well, it turned out, after these years away in the war. He was going home to his own people. If she would not try to contact him again he would make no trouble for her. Sincerely yours.

"Sincerely yours!" Rosie breathed.

Noonie stared at the stranger's words, stared at the stranger's face (she had taken the picture back). Why had Elsa lied to them? Was she ashamed? Was she still in love with him? Did he have another woman, children? Although she would not have guessed it, nothing was answered or made easier by the knowledge of his whereabouts.

"We have to call him," Rosie said.

"Where?"

"Call him on the telephone, tell him who we are, tell him the game's up, we know about him."

Noonie stared at Rosie. "You're nuts. He doesn't care, don't you understand?"

"Maybe he changed his mind. Call him."

"You call him."

"You're older," Rosie said. She yawned and turned off the light. "You know him, remember?"

Noonie waited a long time, and then one day when Elsa was downstairs working and Rosie was swimming, she picked up the telephone and, hands shaking, dialed 0.

"I want to call someone in Detroit," she whispered, having no idea how to do it.

"What number do you want, please?"

"I . . . I . . . don't know."

"What is the name, please?"

Noonie started to stutter; she had never said his name before. She had never even seen his name before she read his letter. Then she hung up.

4

DIRTY GAMES

Who started the dirty games? And how did they end? For they ended with an abruptness that can only be unspoken.

They began with whispers and giggles and foraging through Elsa's drawers. Elsa's lingerie, hidden in sateen envelopes with sachet members: filmy, lacy, red, and black. Then the amazing tray they saw at Aunt Tatiana's: Marilyn spread naked on a velvet sheet while highball glasses balanced on her private parts, leaving faint circles and wet patches. Or the book Cousin Richie showed them on the same visit to Palm Springs, a book you flipped through and saw not ducks dancing or tennis players serving but a long-legged woman undressing with grace and élan (you could control the speed with a flip of your thumb): Fifi La Rue, straight from Paris.

(The pieces are always there and we merely have to assemble them, like the props in a recurring dream.)

Two little girls perched on a wide sill in front of a

picture window, giggling behind the draw-drapes in their flowered cotton underpants, their feet blue with cold. Outside there was snow piled in the yard, and the neighborhood boys were hidden in storm coats with squirrel collars, hats with earflaps; they are waiting. The curtains were heavy faded cotton, tropical scenes of huge floppy flowers with bristling stamens and elephant-ear leaves. They whispered behind the curtain, their chests goose-fleshed. Rosie was so thin you could trace her breastbone, count her ribs; Noonie was fleshier, already showing promise.

How had all this been synchronized: the boys, the act? How did they know to be there in the yard; they were trespassing, cutting across people's backyards, the shortcut home from St. Jerome's. The dangers were many—not only trespassing, frostbite, but what if Elsa came upstairs unexplained, early? Noonie had checked their mother's appointment book: she was taking Mr. Mahoney's picture for the local paper. He was being cited for bravery beyond the call—fire; he rescued a widow and her three small brats (said Elsa).

(So they were down there this minute, Elsa probably with her bodice undone and his dutiful hand somewhere between her knee and crotch. Uncle Tootie said Elsa was a hot ticket, a hot dish. Noonie didn't know what this meant but she knew what it was about.)

Rosie took the platform first, dressed in an approximation of a man's outfit. There were some men's things around: a wide orange-and-gray striped tie of Mr. Horowitz's that she wore with a silk blouse of Elsa's, a pair of soft house-slippers, a loden hunting cap from the costume box in the studio, Poppa's tailcoat.

"And now, presenting Miss Natalie La Rue . . . straight from the streets of Paris!"

Noonie took the stage now. (Rosie hopped down; they always worried about the sill holding both of them.) She strutted in precariously high heels, wearing a long black chiffon robe of Elsa's with a pink ostrich boa. She carried a small paper fan from Chinatown: FEN WONG, CHINESE RESTAURANT, it said, CANTONESE-MANDARIN, CARRY OUT. The fan was Noonie's latest trick (they sometimes wore masks, they wore makeup, they never removed their panties); she had practiced in the bathroom for an hour last night. She moved her hips back and forth, then she began to lower the boa, slowly allowing it to shimmy past her shoulders and down her hips. Rosie was singing all this time: "Come On-a My House."

Noonie allowed the robe to slip down, revealing Elsa's amazing fur-trimmed bra; a masterpiece of the structural imagination, black satin trimmed with mink, the circular-stitched cups standing out like generous mountaintops: Mr. Kleinert's last Christmas gift.

The Carrigan boys went crazy now, stamping their feet, beating their thick leather mittened hands together over and over (maybe they were just cold). Noonie opened the robe and closed it, like a fireplace bellows, finally allowing it to slip off, when Rosie picked it up and, with an entirely original and unrehearsed gesture, buried her face in the filmy collar and gave it a kiss before tossing it into the corner.

Noonie could have stopped with that, but she continued. She removed the brassiere; the hooks, done up incorrectly by Rosie's shaking hands, took a while to free, but she dipped out of it and with great finesse threw it over a naked shoulder. Noonie wiggled back and forth with such abandon that the Carrigan boys moved so close their frozen breath made huge patterns of frost on the window. Their open lips were almost glued to the glass when suddenly there was a tremendous cracking sound. The platform began to move and shake and collapsed to the ground, and the Carrigans scattered like birds before an oncoming car.

"Are you okay?" Rosie was crying.

"Help me out of here." Noonie's teeth were chattering and there was a long red scrape, a ribbon of blood from her throat to her waist.

Rosie touched it with her finger.

"Ow!" Noonie pulled Rosie's hand away. "That hurts."

Rosie dipped her finger into the dripping blood and slowly, thoughtfully licked the finger.

"You're sick!" Noonie shouted. "Get away from me!"

"I'm scared. Ma'll hit us."

"Well, then help me clean up." Noonie put her jumper and blouse on again, and the blue cardigan sweater Elsa had knitted, and her socks and red tie-shoes.

"Maybe she won't notice," said Rosie, putting on her own clothes.

"Don't be so dumb." Noonie was no longer Natalie straight from Paris.

"Maybe," sighed Rosie.

By now, Mr. Mahoney was seated on the swirling stool in front of a white backdrop, his fire captain's hat in his lap, his navy tie straight.

"Now say 'cheese,' " Elsa said from behind her shallow curtain.

"Cheese," Mr. Mahoney said, seriously.

"Ma!" Noonie called. She knocked on the door.

"I'm busy, I'm working," Elsa sang, squeezing the dangling bulb. "Don't bother me when I'm in the studio."

"We had a problem," Noonie said, "but I think it's okay."

"Noonie broke the platform!" Rosie shouted.

"Shut up!" Noonie whispered.

"I'll be up soon," Elsa said sweetly, gesturing a small directional turn to the right for Mr. Mahoney. "Nice," she told him. "There's some cookies in the jar," she called.

"She was standing on the windowsill . . . !"

"I'll kill you!" Noonie screamed, grabbing Rosie around the neck with her hands.

"Mama!" Rosie called.

"Don't tease your sister, Natalie. I'll be up soon. Now, Joe, just a bit more to the right . . ."

Rosie crept into Noonie's cabin, crawled over to her bunk, shook her.

Noonie rolled over, her fingers splayed across Rosie's face, but she didn't open her eyes.

"Noonie!" Rosie whispered; she knew Noonie had seen her, heard her. (She was pretending Rosie didn't exist for a change.) "Noonie!" Rosie grabbed the flashlight from between the pages of the book Noonie was reading before lights out and shined it in her face. "Noonie!"

There was a loud chorus of groans, of "Shhh!"

"Whaa?" At first Noonie didn't remember where she was. (Overnight camp, what a relief: she slept in a room with seven other girls, but none of them was Rosie. Noonie was a Robin, Rosie was a Blue Jay.)

Noonie sputtered and shook her head like someone who was coming up from a deep dive. "Whaa?"

"I have to talk to you."

Noonie gritted her teeth and looked around. There was no choice (an encore of groaning was coming soon). She grabbed the flashlight out of Rosie's hand and led her out of the cabin onto the little porch where towels and suits hung in the night air. Rosie was wearing summer pajamas—they had been Noonie's and were pretty worn—and she was shaking.

"Jesus," said Noonie and went back and got one of those itchy camp blankets and wrapped it around her sister. "Now what's wrong?"

Suddenly Rosie was reluctant; she fell silent as a stone. She took her hand and placed it on her breasts and then her crotch, touched them with meaning, while Noonie, sleep in her eyes, watched in horror.

"Rosie," she said; she was shivering now and she grabbed Rosie's hand before she could perform this perverse pantomime again. "Tell me."

"He touched me," Rosie said. "Uncle Howie touched me there and there and . . ." And she ran away.

Noonie stood there a long time before she thought to move. She was very cold and frightened; she hugged herself. Rosie had the blanket. She should find Rosie. She thought of Uncle Howie, who with Aunt Alice ran the camp. Uncle Howie was a bald pudgy man in a sweatshirt with a whistle hanging from a black-and-red lanyard Noonie had actually made for him at the beginning of the summer. Now she imagined his bulging stomach bulging even more and his eyes popping out of the sockets, his tongue, red and wet, hanging out of his open mouth. She should find Rosie and bring her back here to sleep. She should find Uncle Howie and kill him. She started to cry; she should find him and tell him he couldn't do that to Rosie, but she was shivering and frightened and she didn't want him to touch her like that. So she went back to her cabin and wrapped her robe and a sweater around her and pulled her knees into her chest and cried until she fell asleep.

Was this enough to turn you from men? Noonie wondered years later when it became obvious that Rosie did not share Noonie's expectations. (Of course, Noonie never equated Uncle Howie with men, or Mr. Kleinert, or Mr. Horowitz. Men were movie stars, men were far away, men was a missing father.)

Noonie was a great believer in early Freudian heroines. She merely exchanged the Sleeping Beautys and Rapunzels of her childhood for Anna O. and Dora. Noonie thought that if only Rosie would acknowledge this—Uncle Howie—she would be freed like someone who had been under a horrible spell and learn to walk again. (She guessed Elsa just imagined Rosie hadn't met Mr. Right, but then, Elsa didn't know: Noonie couldn't get herself to tell their mother—or anyone else ever—about what happened that camp summer.)

Rosie remembered a thrilling girl at the Y, fifteen to Rosie's thirteen, with long silken haunches and legs—skin so smooth it looked poured on—and breasts that were high and brown-tipped. Once, this girl caught Rosie watching and very slowly, lasciviously, removed her towel. She lifted one leg onto the bench in front of the lockers and pulled the towel slowly through her thighs, then let it fall to the floor. Shaking a mane of dark hair from her rubber cap, she arched her neck, so Rosie watched openmouthed, her throat raw and parched.

But Noonie didn't know this, didn't have access to an entire history of moments, the grab bag of impressions and images that added up to a heart's desire; she had just one moment of trauma that she did not save Rosie from experiencing, and her guilt grew until it became anger—anger with Rosie for making her feel guilty, anger for denying them this final carnal connection in the adult world.

The next morning was like waking out of a nightmare. The next morning everything was fine and back to size. Rosie was in her blue swimsuit (Blue Jays had Swim first) jostling with her friend Phyllis in line, and there were powdered eggs and burnt toast and Aunt Alice was jolly in her apron and Uncle Howie was leading the morning songs.

When Noonie caught up with her, Rosie was laughing so hard she spat in Noonie's face.

"Rosie?"

"Yeah?"

"Last night . . ."

Rosie gave Noonie a fine, hard look. "I'll bring your blanket back after crafts."

And years later, they were watching someone on television, some fat clown, and Rosie said, "Oh, my God, doesn't he look just like Uncle Howie!"

She laughed when she said it. She seemed truly amused, so Noonie didn't say anything. Maybe Rosie really forgot. It seemed everybody had the capacity to forget except Noonie: pain took up permanent residence in her heart. She was the national repository for painful experience, as if her job was to remember every single bad thing that happened to everyone she loved so they could forget and get on with their lives.

When your options are small, when your world is defined by school on one side and the library on the other, and the yellow brick road is a dirty city street, you retreat to a world of your own making: Rosie slipped underwater,

Noonie read. Between the flat pages of a book, everything could happen but you could still be safe. These were the soft secret cradles for her imagination: her bed, a fat chair in the front room, a corner table in the library, the small back porch off the kitchen where morning glories climbed dime-store string.

Rosie's swimming talent, Noonie's dreaming talent: plenty of time to develop when your mother was busy working to keep things going.

(Where had it come from, this sensuality, this dreaminess? In Noonie's family, a parade of aunts, uncles, cousins, all the progenitors was marched forward to explain behavior, talent, hair color. Maybe Uncle Baby, with his big ideas. Rosie's swimming was harder to come by; a little golf, someone who danced with Isadora Duncan on the Continent, but long-distance swimming . . . ?)

Shortly after that camp summer, Noonie came upon a volume of Maupassant in the adult section of the library, just left out on a table. She pounced on it: a treasury of sexuality; here at last were the tales of seduction, passion, lust that Noonie had only imagined. Every night she hid it in the stacks (could she have persuaded Elsa to take it out for her?), every afternoon after school, shaking with fear, she retrieved it. By now, she wasn't sharing this with Rosie; she was not sharing much, their lives had taken on such different tones and balances. Every day after school now, Rosie went to the Y, to that tiled amphitheater of the damp, to swim butterfly with a coach. Like the little children carrying their violin cases or their Hebrew books, she clutched a small canvas satchel with a rolled towel, goggles, nose plugs, an orange.

Noonie visited museums: school trips, Mr. Horowitz; by the time she was twelve she went downtown on the

El by herself. She would moon around the Art Institute for hours, alone, the Impressionists mainly. What spoke to her again was the dreaminess, the lack of focus, the haze, the colors, the Frenchness. Outside it was gray and stone, granite lions stood watch on either end, but inside was a world that had nothing to do with El trains or snow mounds or steamy littered streets. About Chicago she knew really nothing, nothing of the great architectural treasures that grew on either end of the Loop. But buildings didn't matter to her, anyway; they were edifices and Noonie was obsessed with interiors, with the domesticity of the paintings: picnics and couples, women with flowers in their hair and ribbons at their pulsing throats and men in silky tall hats.

Imagining a mother's secret life. She didn't know that's what she was doing at the time, but it was. It was the connection to Elsa's life and the attempt to understand some of the comings and goings in the night.

Just the way Noonie once heard Tatiana say to Elsa, "But I don't understand. What do they do, these women?" and Elsa turned her face so that her broad profile hid Aunt Tatie's open mouth and Noonie saw the fine dark down on her mother's upper lip blow as she whispered into Tatie's ear.

What do grown-ups do? Hey, what do you do in there? Noonie would lie on her back in her bed and listen to occasional coughing, a name being called out like a bell ringing, the sound of water running, a toilet flushing, laughter.

Noonie was boy crazy, anyhow, that's what Elsa called it: boy crazy. But how could she have been anything else when they seemed to hold the key? They had the power to interpret the mystery, how to do it. Maybe if things were more like now, were outlined and explicit in books and movies, maybe Noonie could have gotten on with something else—geography or algebra or even French grammar, but everything paled in comparison. She was as stubbornly ignorant to the charms of anything else as Eve had been, and as determined. Men. There wasn't one in her house, obviously that was the reason that everything went wrong. (Sometimes the thing that is missing in a household takes up more room than the things that are in abundance.)

It was this wish, the desire for this knowledge that commanded her attention, her whole life, so that it was tracked from the beginning of the dirty games until the moment that she met Gus. What a relief! Now she could think about something else.

5

GUS

Noonie met Gus over a fence, across a net, the summer she was eighteen. He was the instructor at her neighborhood park where she, out of some kind of easy summer boredom and vague ambition, had decided to learn to play tennis.

Gus was tall and blond, and his long arms and legs were tanned. When he hit the ball, he seemed to be performing a primal male act—throwing a spear or reaching for the stars. But he was all business. Gus was nationally ranked; he was on the tennis team at the University of Virginia, in his senior year, an English major. He was living with his older brother in Chicago for the summer and going from city park to city park giving these classes. Gus thought this was a pretty mundane thing; he would have liked to be on the Junior Davis Cup team or teaching at a private club, but to Noonie he may as well have stepped out of one of those short but panting novels she had read in early adolescence over and over and over again. (Rosie never touched them, thought they were boring, dumb. She read biographies of great brave women, mainly fliers.)

Gus lined the group up against the net. There were Noonie and her friend Cheryl Ann, who couldn't stop giggling, and a few more of the local girls who didn't have the means or the imagination to be someplace else.

He stood in front of them and showed them the forehand grip.

"Just pretend you're shaking hands with the racket," he said, and went around, letting each of them shake hands with his racket (Cheryl Ann almost collapsed trying to keep herself from falling at his feet) and then show him on their own rackets.

When he came to Noonie, he covered her small hand with his big one and moved it a few inches and shook his head.

"That grip may be a problem," he said. "Let me see the racket."

Reluctantly, Noonie handed it over; she knew it was a problem. It was an old thing Elsa had found in a box in the studio. Noonie said that she would like to take tennis at the park; Elsa said no. Then she found the racket and said okay. It had been Uncle Baby's and was covered with a green mold and the strings were soft, like spaghetti, but Noonie knew asking for a new one was out of the question.

Noonie could never describe what happened then, but Gus gave her a look of such complete understanding that she felt totally naked, not her body, but her soul: the meagerness of her background, her hopes and desires for a better future (a future symbolized by tennis!). She grabbed the terrible racket and ran out through the gate.

Everyone stood and watched her run.

"Noonie!" Cheryl Ann shouted.

"What's her name?" Gus called as he took off after her.

"It's Natalie, but no one calls her that. Noonie."

Noonie hadn't gotten far: she tripped near the small zoo, which had a few dirty llamas and a goat, who was trying to eat the racket when Gus reached her.

"You okay?"

"My ankle, I think I sprained it," she said. (Those words just flew out of her mouth.)

"Can you put weight on it?" He held out his platter-sized hand and helped her up.

"Ow." She winced, and in a second Gus had lifted her up and was carrying her in his arms.

"Do you live far from here?"

Noonie shook her head. She was speechless. Her heart was in her throat, her stomach was hanging around there, too, so it was pretty crowded and all she could manage, as Gus hoisted her up, was to turn around and glimpse the locals in envious postures and Cheryl Ann in total disbelief.

"I'll give you a ride home," said Gus, stopping in front of his car. (It was a convertible!) Noonie put her head back.

"My God!" he said in alarm. "Don't faint."

"No, no," she murmured, smiling weakly, just barely seeing Cheryl Ann through her half-closed eyes as they sped away.

(The Beatles later asked us if we believed in love at first sight. They were certain it happened all the time.)

When Elsa saw Gus carrying Noonie up the stairs, she sighed deeply; she saw Noonie's dangling foot and sighed even more deeply. She did not approve much of activity out-of-doors. (Elsa thought Rosie's swimming was fine—very clean—until she did long distance in dangerous foreign waters.) When Elsa saw Gus, a tall, handsome boy dressed all in white, her sigh turned to a slight smile. And it didn't go unnoticed on Elsa's part that Noonie's young arms were draped around his neck, the way someone hangs on to a life preserver.

"Well," she said, giving Noonie a little dig in the ribs as Gus was lowering her into a wicker chair. "But you must have some lemonade and cookies before you leave."

Gus took a seat. He tried to explain about the class, but frankly the students didn't look too promising and he supposed they had all gone home. He hoped he wouldn't lose his job. Well, he was thirsty.

"You okay?" he asked Noonie.

"She's fine," Elsa assured him, pushing a large plate of home-baked almond crescents, her best, in front of him.

Slowly Elsa squeezed lemons, at least five, to make a glass, and watched Noonie peek at him. "I'd like to tell your fortune," she said to Gus, stirring sugar into the pale yellow liquid.

"My fortune? Well, I'm in kind of a hurry."

"It won't take long," she said, getting the cards from the drawer.

"Mother . . ." Noonie started, and then stopped because the look Elsa gave her was so extreme: it seemed life-and-death. Shut up, it seemed to say, I know what I'm doing.

Elsa told fortunes and made up horoscopes. She had learned from her mother. She had little cards made up that showed an annotated palm: MADAME ELSA, it said, and gave their phone number arranged on each fingertip and along the life line. Noonie was mortified. This was the same phone number she whispered to student-council presidents and football heroes. Elsa wanted Noonie and Rosie to hand out the cards on street corners and take a bunch to school. She slipped them surreptitiously into the boxes of Girl Scout cookies Rosie peddled and dropped them into unsuspecting trick-or-treat sacks. Once, at a school fair, Elsa had set up a booth and, wearing a lace tablecloth and using an upside-down goldfish bowl, had told fortunes and embarrassed Noonie greatly.

Now Noonie watched as her mother slipped Gus's driver's license from his wallet, which he had pulled from the pocket of his shorts when he sat down and was lying on the counter. Elsa straddled a kitchen chair and extended the deck to be cut. She played out the cards, dreamily.

"You are about to embark on a journey," Elsa began dramatically. Noonie rolled her eyes.

"Well, I am going back to school soon," Gus said innocently.

"You are from somewhere else, not around here," said Elsa contemplatively. "I see a field of shimmering wheat. You are Aquarius, barely out of the house of Capricorn." You were born on January twenty-first, nineteen thirty-nine, in Kansas."

"Wow!" said Gus. "That's amazing! Amazing!" he said, looking at Noonie for the first time in a while. "What else do you see?"

Elsa tapped the deck. He cut again. "You need glasses for driving," she said.

"True."

"Your middle name is Arthur."

"No one knows that! No one! How does she do this?" he shouted excitedly to Noonie, who merely looked embarrassed.

"I see a blond woman in your future," Elsa intoned.

"Yeah?" asked Gus, because it was relevant. "Kind of straw-colored?"

"No," said Elsa, opening one eye and looking carefully at the side of Noonie's head. "Darker. More the color of potato pancakes."

Here is Gus at twenty-two, the year he meets Noonie, standing at the crossroads of boyhood and manhood, a kind of American specialty. His father had been dead for fourteen years, his widowed mother teaches primary grades at the country school. Gus recognizes this theme from books but refuses to romanticize himself. (He will let others do it: women. Already, several years ago, the woman who runs the only restaurant in town began to teach this boy to expand on the classical aspects of his condition.)

This is the last thing Gus remembers about his father. His father is a teacher, too, the principal of the high school, but in the summers, when there is no school, he helps out at Grover's store, a kindness on the part of old man Grover, who needs Thomas Bentley in the summer in Kansas like he needs a blazing furnace. Summer is slow—busy in the field, slow in the town—but you can't ask the teacher to drive the tractor. It is a public gesture offered to this tall, quiet, educated man whose southern manners mark him forever as a stranger. The son of Virginia farmers and ministers, he makes his way west after graduation to follow the girl of his dreams—not the girl he marries, but the girl of his dreams, who has married someone else by the time he arrives.

(This is all the stuff of such American dreams, and this is the dreaminess that Gus inherits along with the height, the shock of gold hair, the slightly stooped politeness that is both vulnerable and vulnerable-making, something of the local sheriff tipping his hat to the town madam.)

The father is outside perched high on a wooden trestle, taking stock to the loft above the store, a neat pile of bolts of cloth at his side. As Gus approaches (with a note from his mother, a list of supper things), he sees his father suddenly salute, his hand touching his heart, his arm stretching in a graceful reach, and his body arching as it falls over the siderail, splitting it as he falls to the parched earth. Gus doesn't think he has fallen, however; he watches thrilled as if his father has executed an amazing leap, a slowed-down, slow-motion jump. Gus has been watching the local athletes preparing for the decathlon events at the county fair, and the final twist of their torsos as they take the bar is what Gus sees as his father suffers a heart attack and falls twenty feet to his death; he imagines his father has executed a perfect high jump.

Now he is the man of the house, the little man—they call him that, Grandfather Angus, the farmers and the teachers and the shopkeepers and the parents of his parents' students in the front parlor who touch him briefly on the head before moving on to touch the elbow of his mother locked behind him. His older brother, Thomas II, just Thomas now, is off at boarding school in the East (Gus will follow, and then follow again to the University of Virginia—always a limited imagination in such striving families, they lose their courage fast) where his mother, pious, ambitious, has found a scholarship for the worthy lads of small American towns.

Gus never learns how his mother found this scholarship; a contest established by a captain of industry who hails from these parts, found it for Thomas, then for him, at what a cost, too: the constant reminder of place, of poverty. His one suit, a blue suit inherited from Thomas, cut down from his dead father's (his best suit, not the one he is buried in; how Anna makes that decision is also unknown, a decision for the living before the dead), one pair of new shoes every two years even if your feet grow. In those days, they wear a coat and tie to classes, meals. And the Thanksgivings and spring breaks occasionally spent, by the kind invitation of a roommate, in some dark and austere Connecticut or New York mansion, or, more frequently, in the silence of the emptied dorms. No one imagines a lack of human kindness; the kindness is the opportunity for this kind of education.

(Is it any wonder that Gus, not given to hyperbole, identifies most closely, of all the English novels he reads in this school, in college, in graduate school, with Dickens? And that those are the ones—*Great Expectations, David Copperfield*—he finds, years later, the most difficult to teach?)

For five years, from month to month, Christmas vacation to summer break, what keeps him alive is his image of home, a mother's letters, occasional gifts (a handmade tie, a set of handkerchiefs embroidered with a large lumpy B), baked goods (cookies and brownies travel best). Once, early, eighth grade, a box of brownies arrives while he is at study hall, and the boys on his floor take the box and eat all the brownies so that all that is left are some hard brown crumbs, flakes on the bottom, a trail of powdered sugar. He remembers licking his fingers, with those terrible bloody bitten fingernails, to get up the crumbs that taste of home, his hot tears falling on the wax paper lining the bottom of an old shirt box. (He can almost see the wax paper roll hanging on the wire under the painted cabinets in his mother's kitchen.)

He survives, he even succeeds, he learns to play championship tennis, he makes some friends and meets some of their sisters and girl cousins, he wins the requisite scholarship to follow his brother to UVA, but he never forgets the cruelty of those boys. And when the time comes, he pulls away from their ambitions and examples to find the comfort, the ease that escaped him in those painful years.

(Gus guesses the only real equipment he might have to be a novelist is the sad childhood.)

"Hey, Gus," says Sugar Hansen, throwing him a wet cloth to wipe the table, "you can take me home tonight."

Gus turns sharply; he is a bronzed lad of eighteen, the summer before he begins college, the same summer that his own mother, anxiously scanning faces at eye level on the platform at the station in Topeka, does not recognize her own son, who has grown five inches between Christmas and June. He is a busboy at this dumpy restaurant with a dance floor. The instruments are always set up and ready, even though there is music only on Friday and Saturday nights; the bandstand, drums, pose like dusty ghosts in a wax museum during the week. But then who would dance during the week—the lunch crowd, the salesmen passing through on their way to another identical town?

So Gus takes his boss home (a euphemism if there ever was one). Like his own house, it is a square-frame structure with a front porch and two bedrooms. In one is sleeping her small son (at no time does Gus notice the sameness, the analogy, the single woman and her single sleeping son), and Gus does what thousands of boys have done. Not necessarily in this silent breezy bedroom, although by the time Sugar, as fussy as a great ballerina or diva, calls it quits at fifty (when she is getting, as she says, "long in the tooth,"), she will have seduced over sixty of these boys, she figures.

So Gus, hands shaking, heart pounding, a slice of moonlight in his fair hair, will kneel down against the edge of the mattress, his jeans around his knees, as Sugar laughs an easy laugh (not too loud, her boy is sleeping) and snaps the elastic of Gus's briefs; he has forgotten to take off his tennis shoes.

She reaches for him, her breasts are soft, the nipples small and hard and the color of dark cherries, cerise, a color more suited to fabric, and indeed he will never see them this color again. And so this woman, not uncomely, but turning slightly, like milk left out in the sun, lies down in a small square room, with lace curtains blowing and the slip of moonlight in the window and the high bed with a carved mahogany headboard, an old dresser covered with a slab of marble and a linen cloth—all she takes from a bad first marriage. And a rectangular mirror, where later she will inspect her face after making love, the young man's sleeping profile in the corner of her own reflection. She touches her face lightly, her lips feel slightly bruised, she pushes back a few stray hairs, touches her mouth with pleasure and self-congratulation, catching the last smile of lazy pleasure as she ties her robe and goes into the kitchen barefoot to wash the dishes that sat in the sink unwashed all day.

(There are some events that are absolutely lacking in originality, unless they are born of violence or dismay. For all of us, they require a sameness that we assume is unique.)

Gus goes home that night to find the door to his mother's house is locked, the light in her room is off, her door shut. Another boy might have noticed that she usually waited up for him, that her door would be ajar, the front door unlocked, but he was too much in love with his own experience, his own pleasure.

Gus's mother: what he remembers is the long drape of black hair—ominous, its rise and fall signaled morning and night like a stage curtain. In the morning, it hung to the backs of her knees, swept the floor in front of her like a mop when she bent forward in an attempt to brush it. In the mornings he stood, handing her dozens and dozens of U-shaped pins, solemn as an altar boy assisting mass. Each night, he stood as she let this hair down, plait by anxious plait, gathering the pins in his fist, releasing them in a single blow, like a game of pick-up-sticks, into the glass bowl on her nightstand.

His mother, Anna, sharp-jawed, straight-eyed, eyes the glassy blue color that can be transparent or black, the color that takes on the temper of the moment. She is the descendant of honest Scottish and German farmers, and she finds the Virginian on the front porch, like a gift, wrapped in a raccoon coat, a ukulele under one crooked arm, some poetry books (Swinburne, Matthew Arnold) hanging by a worn leather strap from the other. He is straight from the sting of rejection, so the warmth of her parlor, the apple cobblers cooling on the round pine table, the schoolteacher daughter of the old man who owns this land and runs the school board, are particularly inviting and he trades adventure for security, an occurrence not unusual, even in the twentieth-century heartland.

Truth is, Anna would have given him the money home, she loves him that much, loves the smell of him, to be frank—a man who smells good. Years later, she will still bury her face in his shirts at night.

Luckily the father is not simply taken in by the scent, eau de toilette, the spicy aroma of 4711, but he duly notes the trembling spinster daughter, recalls the need for a teacher of classical languages, botany, geography at the higher levels, and extends a place at his table.

(Isn't this like Elsa observing her daughter Noonie's flaccid arms around the stranger Gus's neck? How willing the generations are to repeat themselves, these patterns of courtship and marriage, in odd ways. Gus has always been suspicious of the story of his parents' meeting, told even more frequently after the untimely death of his father; he feels his practical mother would have had to lift it direct from the pages of a dopey women's magazine. But of course the story is true, they are always true, these trite stories of our lives; they are trite only in the telling, not in the doing of them.)

"Mother," said Gus, bold, his first night home from college the Christmas vacation of his senior year. "Mother, I've met a girl . . ."

And he began with warmth to describe his girl Natalie, Noonie: her fairness, her humor, and the wet sister, the quirky mother, the tennis lessons, the fortune-telling . . .

"Gypsies!" his mother started, and then shouted, almost immediately, "Jews!"

Gus stared. He had never heard that word in his house before (in church they are referred to as Hebrews or the people of Judea); he would never have thought of that himself.

So this was the second time Gus's mother cried herself to sleep, and if he were a different kind of boy, he would recall the first time, and the door strangely locked in the middle of the night.

Gus resisted his attraction to Noonie—she was very young, just graduated from high school. She would begin college in the fall, at Navy Pier, the Chicago branch of the University of Illinois, she told him sheepishly (she was unhappy about it, ashamed of its location, lack of prestige, but there wasn't any money and she hadn't studied much in high school). But he had to see her twice a week at the tennis class and he began driving her and her friend Cheryl Ann home (Cheryl Ann hanging over the front seat from the back, breathlessly looking from Gus to Noonie, watching their moist open handsome profiles) and then somehow he mentioned the name of some movie he wanted to see and Noonie wanted to see it, too, and he took her to a fancy restaurant and she wore a pink sundress and he heard about a place with good music and dancing.

Noonie never learned to play tennis; she was too busy looking at Gus to watch the ball.

"Turn, step, hit!" Gus called across the net.

"Turn, step, hit," said Noonie obediently, but she could not perform them at the same time she said them. She remembered a cheerleading routine: "One-two, three-four, who-are, we-for?"

"Noonie!" Gus shouted, waving his racket.

"Sorry." She smiled, assuming the ready position.

"Let me see you go through the forehand," Gus said encouragingly.

Noonie turned, stepped, hit.

"Perfect!" Gus shouted enthusiastically. "Don't forget the follow-through."

Noonie smiled again, although she knew that she wouldn't be able to hit the ball.

If Gus didn't teach Noonie how to hit a tennis ball, he did teach her how to drive a car and make a pie crust and one wet rainy November day, with the few remaining yellow leaves lashing the windowshield of his brother's car, Gus, visiting for Thanksgiving, began to teach Noonie how to make love. Noonie caught on quickly to this; she felt as if her life had been a rehearsal for this, that she had been learning the lines and gestures and directions for this moment, and now the curtain had gone up and her life could begin.

So this is the boy who came to Noonie, this mix of dreams, a pack of mythic memories, but it isn't what Noonie saw. Gus was four years older than she and four years was a big chunk of her life, so he was a man to her. For Noonie, Gus was the missing father. And for Gus, Noonie was the woman reaching out in the moonlight on that high rumpled bed.

6
WET DREAMS

"There are some things you should know about Noonie," Rosie said to Gus, in ominous tones.

Rosie and Gus had been sent to the grocery store. There were so many guests coming in from out of town. Noonie was having a fitting.

His heart dropped, he lowered his voice. "What?" What could it be? Some man? He knew it! He should have guessed something: this pretend innocence layered with a cagey knowledge he had been hard-pressed to figure out.

"She reads all the time," Rosie was saying. "You know, books—her nose is always in a book."

"Books?" said Gus, hanging on to the shopping cart.

"That line looks empty," said Rosie, guiding Gus. "Yeah, she doesn't have any feel for life. In fact, I'd have to say she doesn't have much interest in it. Fiction, she only reads fiction. I've tried to get her interested in some good biographies. Oh, she does like letters, she's snoopy like that. And she's not observant, know what I mean? Not the little things—she's very involved with detail, minute details—but the big picture, forget it." Rosie tossed him a loaf of white bread like a basketball player handing off a shot. Rosie had the kind of ease and spontaneous grace Gus had noted in real athletes before, this kinship of bone and muscle, while most people wore their bodies like heavy overcoats.

"Also, she almost drowned once," Rosie said as an aside. "Of course, so did almost everyone I talk to. Evidently, it's not so unusual."

"I never drowned," said Gus, concerned about poor little Noonie.

"Where did you grow up! What were you going to do, drown in a field of corn! Ha ha!"

(Noonie's family found Gus's geographic origins hilarious; Kansas to them was the setting for a movie, and indeed, one time when Noonie and Gus were in the back seat of his car, making out, Noonie leaned back after a particularly long embrace and sighed. " 'Toto, I've a feeling we're not in Kansas anymore,' " a line she would regret forever.)

Gus opened the car door for Rosie, who settled in appreciatively, stroking the upholstery. "I do like this car," she said. "Noonie drowned in the lake, not around here, for God's sake, too damn shallow even for Noonie to accomplish, but up in Michigan or something when she was three. I don't remember it, of course. Aunt Tatie's husband, our Uncle Tootie, had to pull her out."

"Did he put out his cigar first?" asked Gus, shifting gears. (If Noonie's family found him funny, he found them more exotic than all the inhabitants of Oz.)

Rosie laughed. "Anyway, that's the story, so she won't swim anywhere except in a pool now and along the edge, you know, the sides of the pool. She has to be able to reach out and touch concrete as she swims or she can't do it. Boundaries," she emphasized. "Noonie needs boundaries."

Rosie squinted into the mirrored visor, stuck on the sunglasses of Noonie's she found on the dash. "Goldfish expand in direct proportion to their environment, did you know that, Gus? If you stick them in a fishbowl, they never get any bigger, if you put them in the ocean, they grow into full-grown fish. They realize their potential." She turned and stuck out her tongue at him. "See what I mean?"

This was the happiest day of Noonie's life, but Noonie was as white as her dress. She was in the bathroom of a room in the small hotel downtown where she was going to marry Gus in a few minutes. Elsa was chain-smoking and Aunt Tatiana was weeping and Cheryl Ann was talking about penises, penetration, something, and Rosie kept jabbing Noonie in the ribs (white satin ribs) and saying she had to tell her something. They were all in the bathroom with her. (Someone had opened a bottle of champagne and Cheryl Ann was already drunk, but Noonie just felt sick.)

Noonie's hands were shaking. She wasn't afraid of marrying Gus, she was afraid of not marrying him, afraid if they didn't hurry up, move right along, something would get in the way, something as extraordinary as the thing that allowed her to meet him in the first place.

"You look like a ghost, Natalie. You look as if you're going to your grave," Elsa said, inspecting her face. "Put some makeup on. Tatie, where's your purse? Do you have some lipstick . . . ?"

"Raunchee Red," said Aunt Tatiana, handing it over. "Here, you look like death."

"Well, she's supposed to be nervous," Cheryl Ann giggled. "I mean, when she sees what's going to happen to her . . ."

Elsa ignored her, opened the gold case, pushed the little lever until it was all the way up, offered it to Noonie.

Noonie's hands were shaking badly. Gus could leave, he could change his mind; certainly his mother didn't look overly secure when she first met the Gluck family yesterday, when Aunt Tatie hugged her (there was so much Arpège in this room, Noonie could barely breathe). Maybe she would kidnap him, take him back to Kansas; maybe he would trip over a chair, break his leg, die . . .

"Noonie," Elsa said.

Noonie tried to grab the lipstick from her mother, almost dropped it down her dress. They all watched in amazement as the red cylinder flipped from the case. Rosie caught it and handed it back to Elsa.

Elsa clicked her tongue disapprovingly, took the tip of her pinkie and fixed Noonie's lips, spreading some color on her cheeks. (Actually, by now, Noonie's cheeks were plenty red—they were burning.)

"Well," Cheryl Ann was saying, "it was this big . . ." and spread her hands apart like someone telling a fish story.

Elsa focused on her, took her shoulders. "Would you, please, um, find Noonie's Uncle Tootie and tell him we are ready to begin."

Cheryl Ann left with a wink and a sigh. "Good luck," she called.

Noonie smiled wanly. She followed the others into the elevator. Several total strangers smiled at her, but she didn't smile back. She was staring at Rosie. Why hadn't she seen that before; Rosie looked ridiculous. Her maid-of-honor dress made her look like a pink cabbage with its big pouf skirt; little straps bissected her bare, developed shoulders and wide tan lines.

"Noonie," Rosie whispered as they stood in the doorway to the ballroom. (They were waiting for Uncle Tootie to finish his cigar.) "Noonie, I have to tell you something. You know what Cheryl Ann was talking about, I've done it. I mean, I think I like women."

"Women, what?"

"I mean, I like them . . ." Rosie was looking down at the rapier toes of her dyed-to-match high heels. "I like them, you know . . ."

Noonie's mouth was open as a great surge of music, a violin and a piano doing Mendelssohn, swelled.

"I'm a dyke, Noonie," she whispered as Elsa signaled from the front row for Rosie to begin, and that was the last thing Noonie heard before she walked down the aisle to marry Angus Bentley.

These days Rosie lives in Key West with a woman named Madge Cook, who is her lover and her coach when she isn't teaching domestic science at Key West High (mascot: the conch). Sometimes Rosie works at a restaurant with a huge aquarium behind a long bamboo bar. The aquarium has women in it, women and a few tired sea creatures, and once Noonie sat at that bar for hours drinking strawberry daiquiris and watching Rosie, in a tiny bathing suit, gyrate back and forth among the mammoth sea turtles and eels. Rosie claims she shouted obscenities to Noonie and the other customers but it all came out glug, glug, glug.

Noonie had come down to watch Rosie train for a difficult and previously unattempted Caribbean swim (forty miles, connecting several islands) and sat in the motor boat with Madge, who conversed with Rosie through an old-fashioned megaphone. She used a small chalkboard to write messages to Rosie, although by the fourth hour Rosie could see only large numerals and, after that, she was almost blind in the water. Noonie held a large square jar of Vaseline on her lap, in case it grew colder. Noonie watched her sister, the short black hair pulled tight under three rubber caps, her head sleek as a seal's. Rosie's lips were white and swollen, and opened and closed with wordless advice.

"What is she saying?" Noonie asked.

"We all begin life as swimmers," Madge informed Noonie solemnly.

On the wall of the bathroom was a huge calendar, marking dates of a female nature. Once upon a time, Rosie and Noonie were synchronized like the moon and the sun in an old chiming clock; they rose and fell together each month. Now Noonie has had a child, and Rosie was in such good shape, it seemed, that she no longer menstruated regularly.

"Ho ho," said Noonie, happy at last to have something to contribute to this underwater adventure. "You don't believe that old stuff about not swimming with your period, Rosie?"

"Sharks!" said Rosie.

"Sharks!" said Madge. "We are talking about sharks! Sharks pick up the scent of blood"—she snapped her fingers—"like that!" She jabbed Noonie's shoulder with a friendly fist. "Sharks *love* blood!"

Three months later, Rosie was sixteen hours into this

swim when the people in the boats lost sight of her. She was missing several hours more when Madge obediently sent someone to telegraph Rosie's family and Elsa called Noonie.

Noonie was lying next to Gus at a swimming pool in Guadeloupe when she got the phone call from Elsa.

Noonie was a free-lance writer; she wrote a weekly column for the local newspaper, and she was an assistant editor of the alumni association of the university. Her columns had to do mostly with memory, nostalgia: the first day of school, the smell of cookies baking, Halloween. Sometimes she wrote an article for the alumni magazine about research into women in the Middle Ages or the effects of DNA research on public safety. Recently she had convinced the editor of the Sunday *Times* travel section to let her write about their family vacations; it would pay for some of the trips and allow her to sharpen her writing skills. This was all a start, but none of it was what she wanted to be writing anyway.

Noonie thought of these free-lance pieces as her pornography, like Anaïs Nin writing erotica to support herself. Of course, they were not at all like the delicate short stories she carried around inside. They had been there for so long she could almost taste them: perfect samples of puff pastry, crisp but layered with buttery complexity.

"I want to write as if with a painter's palette," Noonie had confessed once long ago to a teacher in college, "little Vermeers."

Instead she sat at the pool and wrote: "The Parc Naturel has the best hiking grounds in the Caribbean." (As if she would know a thing like that!)

"You've got a cutie pie next to you," Gus whispered conspiratorally, raising his greased body.

Noonie looked up, expecting to see Sarah in her new flowered bikini, only to stare into a pair of large breasts, oiled the color of a well-used handbag.

"Ooooh," sighed Gus as Noonie's name was being announced over the loudspeaker. "Oooooh, there goes another one. I feel like I'm fifteen," he confided. "It's just one big wet dream."

Noonie thought about Rosie all the way to Florida, flying in a tiny prop plane, over palm trees, beaches, rocks that looked like a continual travel poster. Noonie thought about Rosie, but she didn't think about Rosie today, Rosie afloat in a sea of sharks; she thought about the day Rosie was born. She was not thinking about it from Rosie's point of view, of course, but her own: what happened to Noonie that day.

Aunt Tatiana had taken Noonie to play in an empty lot and they had picked flowers, clovers, and dandelions for Elsa in the hospital. Then they went to a toy store—Noonie must have been in the big high-sided rattan stroller—and bought a present for the new baby sister, a squeaky toy, a duck, probably. (Could she really remember this or is there a snapshot—Noonie in the stroller, Tatiana squinting in the sun behind her?)

And Noonie was thinking about the day Rosie came home from the hospital. She remembered they made her sit in one of the stuffed chairs in the waiting room and told her to put her arms into a bow and they put Rosie's head in one elbow and wrapped the blanket over her bare toes that hung over Noonie's other elbow. (Another photograph?) Noonie remembered the weight of Rosie's head, its roundness, and all the wet black hair around the spongy soft spot and the pool of sweat in her own crooked elbow.

There had been a blood incompatibility and Rosie was still jaundiced and her arms were long and thin and her nails were translucent and sharp. What Noonie thought was: This person doesn't look anything like me, but she does belong to me.

That was totally ridiculous, how could she remember it, maybe a sense of it? Probably she thought this years later in another context. Actually, everything was ridiculous, the palm trees and the plastic cup in her hand and she was in the air and what she was thinking was, What if Rosie is dead? But she didn't say that. What she said was, "Are you serving a snack on this flight?"

By the time Noonie arrived, Rosie was lying on a dock in Key West. She was flat on her back and her skin was white and puffy, like a canned lichee or another rare tropical fruit, and she looked as if the skin would break if you touched her and something unsavory, bluish, would ooze out. Her eyes were puffy and red and running and stuff was pouring from her nose. She couldn't be alive.

Noonie stood over her for several minutes. Rosie opened her eyes and then lifted her shoulders and arms straight forward, as if she were bench-pressing her own weight. Noonie knelt down and Rosie took hold of her shoulders and pulled her close, so she was right over Rosie. Then, like a man, like a lover, Rosie pulled her forward and kissed her square on the mouth. Salty snot poured from Rosie's nose, spreading onto Noonie's face, and Noonie pulled back repulsed, then embarrassed by those feelings.

"That's how I remember you," said Rosie faintly. "You were a big pink face in my carriage and you leaned over and licked the stuff from my nose."

"Don't be ridiculous," Noonie said, irritated but relieved. "You're confusing me with a cat," said Noonie, straightening up. "You're thinking about the cat at Greenbaum's store, the box with the kittens."

Just like Rosie to claim this act of feline intimacy as her own. This was what Rosie remembered: the mother cat and her kittens curled on a faded flannel blanket in a wooden crate at Greenbaum's grocery store on the corner. They would go there with Elsa every day. Noonie could see Rosie squatting in the corner, swinging back on the heels of her white sandals, her dark damp curls, the bow tying the back of her sundress, almost in the box with the kittens as the mother eyed her and finally bit her on the face.

Madge drove Noonie back to her house. Madge was sunburned and exhausted (she had acted as Rosie's pacer, getting into the water with her every three or four hours to swim for half an hour alongside her for encouragement, companionship), but she seemed more concerned about Noonie's welfare. Towels and a little wrapped bar of motel soap and clean flowered sheets were on the narrow bed in the room Noonie was shown to, Madge's sewing room.

"Do you need anything?" Madge asked, sticking her head around the corner.

"No, I'm fine," said Noonie, shaking her head, shifting under the sheets. And she meant it; in a way, she was fine. Madge made her feel, strangely, like a cherished child.

She knew she should have been solicitous of Madge, but she really couldn't deal with her at all. Madge was like many of the women Rosie had lived with over the years: somewhat heavyset and energetic and good-natured. She was hearty and perfectly pleasant, and took good care of Rosie, making her herbal teas and giving her long, swell massages, and today she had probably saved her life. But there was always something, some confusion, disappointment that Noonie had to fight; she always felt uncomfortable. (Noonie tried not to think too much about the women in her sister's life, never thought they might have something to do with the way Rosie loved her.)

The places Rosie lived were a bit shabby and often too pink. Here flamingos were peeling from the shower curtain and speckled mirrors framed the hall so you looked virulent with smallpox, and the plants needed water, and there were few pictures or hardcover books and the TV was on most of the time. The china never matched and the glasses were from fast-food places, and hugely fat cats left hairs on the sofa cushions.

(Sometimes Noonie thought she and Rosie were like two sisters in an awkward modern fairy tale, where one sister had been turned into a strange unhuman animal and the other sister was supposed to rescue her.)

Once, when Rosie was living with a sculptor named Alison in Boston, they had taken her for a drive to see some of the big old houses in the surrounding area, large formal gracious homes, redolent of a pleasanter era. Alison had given Noonie in the back seat a running commentary of what the lives of the normal middle-class people who lived in such houses might be like, as if they were foreign or ancient or fiercely exotic.

"I live in a house like that!" Noonie wanted to shout. "I am one of those people!"

In the morning Madge was gone and Noonie poked around: Rosie's swimsuits hung limp and lifeless on the backs of chairs and over banisters and from the rope line on the patio, like skins shed by snakes or aliens in a science-fiction film. Noonie looked around the bathroom, feeling the folds of Madge's pink gown and robe hung neatly on a single hook, her electric curlers, bath salts and powders in floral scents. All very feminine, something that continued to confuse Noonie, even though she understood it was pathetically narrow on her part.

There was an old-fashioned razor on the bathtub rim, the double-edged blade kind, the kind she hadn't seen in a long time. Noonie picked it up, unscrewed the bottom so the blade was exposed, remembered the thin stiff papers the new blades came in. Her fingers would shake as she unwrapped them, imagining the sharpness of the edge.

She remembered the first time Rosie needed to shave her legs and arms; some coach had suggested it. Elsa made Noonie do it; she was afraid Rosie would cut herself, but she couldn't have been more nervous than Noonie was. Noonie remembered Rosie's leg across her lap as she carefully applied shaving cream some man of her mother's had left behind, and very carefully scraped it off. Rosie's hair was darker and coarser than Noonie's, but her legs were so similar that if she dared close her eyes, it would have been like shaving herself. Noonie screwed Madge's razor and put it back on the edge of the tub.

She went into the bedroom; the bed was neatly made, four pillows fluffed at the head. ("What do they do, these women?" No answers here.) The room was full of charts navigating the course of Rosie's aborted swim, a stack of self-help books: meditation. On Madge's side, there was a basket with knitting and a cookbook from the Junior League of South Florida. In a drawer, Noonie found a notebook, a journal in Rosie's angular handwriting, but she closed it without reading anything; she had relinquished her rights to Rosie's secrets years and years ago.

Then she went to the hospital to visit her sister. Rosie's blood pressure and temperature had stabilized, and they said she could go home the next day, the day Noonie was leaving.

"How's Sarah?" Rosie asked. "I'd really love to see her. And Gus?"

Noonie mumbled something, poured herself some water from Rosie's blue plastic pitcher.

"How long has it been? A couple of years, I think. I remember we went to a fair at her school and Gus was in the dunking booth. I remember I kept knocking him into the water with my curveball," Rosie chuckled.

Noonie remembered Rosie and Madge were wearing matching loud pink sweatshirts with sequin flamingos that day. "You can come any time, you don't need an invitation," she said gruffly.

"Maybe Sarah could come down for part of her vacation at Easter this year."

"She's very busy," Noonie said, picking up a magazine and flipping quickly through the pages.

Noonie knew this was not pretend interest on Rosie's part. Rosie loved her child, loved Gus; the four of them had spent a lot of time together. When Sarah was born, Rosie had come to live with them for several months.

Noonie and Gus's first baby had died at six months, crib death, although she hadn't been in her crib. Noonie had taken her for a walk in her big blue buggy to the pharmacy to have a prescription filled—Enovid, of all things! she had weaned her that week—and when Noonie had come out five minutes later, her baby was cold, dead. Then she had lost another baby, another girl, miscarried; then Sarah was born eighteen months later.

(Noonie had dreamed of eggs, baskets of eggs, cartons of eggs, angel food cakes, meringues, towering and fragile. She understood the dreams: she had put all her eggs in one basket. She had her tubes tied after she gave birth to

Sarah, something that she was told she would regret, and she did regret it, although she didn't think she could have risked that much again.)

Noonie didn't really want Rosie there. She wasn't helpful; mainly, Rosie and Gus hung out together. Noonie wouldn't have let anyone help, anyway, but in a weird way, it seemed right: Rosie being there—in the way.

"We'll talk about it," Noonie said gruffly as the end to afternoon visiting hours was announced over the loudspeaker system.

"Hey, Noonie," Madge called to her as she walked in the door, "come keep me company in the kitchen."

Noonie sat on a stool in the corner, a piña colada in her hand, while Madge cooked their dinner, vigorously banging pots and pans, stirring things, tasting them with a huge wooden spoon. She was making, in Noonie's honor, and out of the kind of energy women have when they are relieved, when they have survived something large and domestic and terrible, a *picadillo,* a Cuban stew with meat and olives and yellow rice and black beans. She let Noonie taste from the blackened tip of the spoon, then banged the lid onto the pot and wiped her hands.

"Let me read your tarot," Madge said, untying her apron and lighting a long cigarette. She took a deck of worn cards from the drawer with the knives and string.

"My mother tells fortunes," said Noonie uneasily.

"Rose never told me that," Madge said, clearing a place on the kitchen table with the flat of her hand. "I think you're the Queen of Cups," she said, looking at Noonie straight on, "fair, dreamy, pretty responsible, usually well-behaved."

Noonie laughed. She didn't feel well-behaved. She felt strange, light, unreal almost; maybe it was the rum.

"You know, I used to be a high diver," said Madge, filling Noonie's glass from the dripping blender. "Oh, years ago, of course."

Noonie stared at Madge's large soft form in her trousers and cotton sweater.

"It's a bit of a stretch, I know." She grinned. "But I was and I will always remember what scared me most, scared the hell out of me, was whether I would have enough air to get back up. Not the jump, I mean, we all fear the jump, but what really consumed me was not going down but coming back up," she said, and turned over the cards carefully.

That evening, they walked into town to see a movie, something arty and English, but more violent than either of them had anticipated. At one point, Madge turned her face from the screen, pressing it into Noonie's shoulder and reached for Noonie's hand, slipping her fingers through. Madge's fingers were longer and bonier than Noonie would have suspected in that fleshy frame. Her hands were cool and silky, a mother's cherished hands in the nightmare of a childhood fever.

Is this what Rosie likes about it? Noonie wondered, feeling the soft weight of Madge's hand. Is this the attraction, this familiarity? She sat very still, breathing evenly, watching the pictures on the screen carefully, but she felt relief when Madge took her hand back.

There was no need for this guilt, Gus tried to tell her when she returned to the hotel in Guadeloupe after this visit to Rosie.

Sarah was snoring on the roll-away cot in the alcove near the hallway, her mouth open and wet with sleep. Noonie covered her with the tangled sheet.

Gus took Noonie's suitcase out of her hand, and helped

her undress and led her to their bed in the strange air-conditioned room. With her eyes shut, Noonie imagined she was underwater performing a slow, cautious breast-stroke; her legs slapped in and out with the frog kick; Gus was the water and her body seemed to match Gus's move for move.

"Rosie wants to visit us," she said sleepily. "She misses you and Sarah and me, but I can't have her around to remind me . . ."

"Noonie," Gus said again, before he fell asleep. "You haven't done anything wrong."

"Natalie," Elsa would shout from an open window down to the street, just as she made it to the bottom step, "take your sister with you. Noonie, did you remember Rosie?"

7

NOONIE AND GUS

It is the first morning of your marriage and you are nineteen years old and the toast is in a silver rack and there is a real rose in the bud vase on the rattling cart, and the napkins are folded back on the plates so their backs are arched like whitecaps on a busy sea. The winking jolly bellboy (a man past fifty, actually) pushes the rattling cart, smiles broadly at the telltale signs: the filmy peignoir thrown over the bed-end, the fading bouquet of white roses, lilies of the valley, baby's breath tied with white streamers, tied in knots—love knots, the florist calls them—the empty bottle of champagne, which he tilts, then turns definitely upside down and whisks away the ice bucket past the grinning groom, who somehow knows to extend the hefty tip.

The cart opens magically, chairs are pulled up, and Noonie is seated opposite Gus, her husband, Gus. (MRS. ANGUS ARTHUR BENTLEY, announce the hundreds of engraved ivory note cards, a gift from Aunt Tatiana. Noonie works harder at these thank-you notes than she ever did for an assignment in school: "Thank you so much for the teacups. We'll spend many happy hours sipping from them." "Thank you so much for the Corning Ware casserole. I'm going to learn to cook really soon." "Thank you so much for the tablecloth. Green is my favorite color.")

Gus is starved, he says, ripping into the toast with his handsome white teeth; Noonie can't eat a thing (although it is the first meal she remembers being able to order whatever she likes). All she can do is look at Gus (her husband!), this large blond man in striped pajamas and a plaid bathrobe and slim leather slippers (a gift from his mother), a real man, reading the newspaper and eating toast and holding out a white china cup for more coffee, which Noonie, in a white lace gown (a gift from her mother), her golden hair bouncing on her shoulders, pours from the metal hotel pot as if she has been doing it all her life.

Soon they will go back to bed, soon they will have to pack up and leave this room (not before Noonie takes the rose from the bud vase on the cart and presses it into the box with the thank-you notes, blurring a few on the top). Soon they will go to Gus's brother's house for a week before they leave for Europe to begin their married lives in an unheated bed-sitter on the fringe of Bloomsbury, near the University of London, where Gus reads literature on a Fulbright for a year and a half.

Noonie will base much of her future repertory on this year and a half in Europe; it will take on mammoth proportions, like a slender novel read over and over again. At the time, she was cold, frequently lonely, disoriented, the days were almost continually gray, but never mind, the wonderful thing about remembering is what we forget.

Europe: "When Daddy and I were in Paris," she would

say to Sarah (years ago or just last week). "I bought these marvelous espadrilles, they laced up to here." Or they ate the most wonderful ravioli in Rome or saw the most beautiful castles in a valley called the Loire. A year and a half to make up for what happens ever after.

Noonie has been married to Gus for almost seventeen years when he walks in the door one night and announces that he has been having an affair with a teacher at his school (the JV lacrosse coach), a big-boned very young blonde called Pigeon. (Her name is Priscilla.)

"Two years?" It is all Noonie can say at first.

"Off and on." He isn't proud of himself, he feels raw and tired and he wants his dinner, which he doesn't suppose Noonie will give him after this.

"Why now?" Noonie asks, trying to catch her breath. "Why are you telling me this now?"

"I think I want to leave. I think I want to live with her."

"Why now?"

Gus looks out the window at the leaves piling up on the lawn. He should rake them before he goes, but he thinks Noonie will laugh at him, make some crack about his cleaning up after himself or something. "She wants to leave her husband; it's a really unfulfilling relationship."

Noonie stares at Gus in disbelief. Is she supposed to feel sorry for this woman, feel generous, make a donation?

"She wants me to move in with her. She doesn't want to be alone," he explains patiently.

"What about me?" she screams. "What about me being alone!"

"Things haven't worked out exactly." He shrugs so that his new glasses slide on his nose. "I thought . . ."

"What?" Noonie shouts.

"I don't think we have as much in common . . ."

"Huh?" Noonie opens her hand to include the house, the furniture, a picture of Sarah. Even tonight's dinner, a leg of lamb with garlic, seems touched by mutual growth and consent.

"Do you think this is what I imagined I'd be doing with my life? I wanted to write novels, so here I am teaching English at a private school. 'Coming of Age'! Seven fucking years of *The Catcher in the Rye*! I need a change."

"Change! Grow a beard, take up skydiving, buy a sports car, isn't that what you're supposed to do?"

Gus isn't listening, he's annotating his disappointments. "And I coach the tennis team, I mean, more promises I didn't keep . . ."

"Gus, who comes this far without a trail of broken promises?" Noonie goes up behind and touches his sleeve. "I'm not disappointed in your life. Do you think I am?"

He turns and throws his arms around her, hugs her very hard. "I have to do this, Noonie."

The next afternoon, possibly the last afternoon of their marriage, Noonie and Gus go to the supermarket together, a rare event. Theirs has been a traditional arrangement; an orderly affair, with divisions of labors, tasks, amenities: income (his), housekeeping (hers), child care (hers), sexual advances (his), complicity (theirs). It makes Noonie think of a wedding present an aunt of Gus's had sent, a set of fringed guest towels: HIS, HERS, YOURS, it had prophetically announced in flaky gilt thread.

Gus is moving into Pigeon's apartment about five miles away and wants to pick up the groceries.

"Oh, I have to get some things, too!" Noonie shouts

immediately, grabbing her coat and car keys so quickly he has no time to protest. He follows her meekly to the car. In the car, she hands him the keys.

Noonie knows it is a way of prolonging her pain, but it is also a way of prolonging his leaving. In the car, she reaches out surreptitiously and touches the sleeve of his sweatshirt, lightly, so he can't feel it. She withdraws her hand as he pulls into the parking lot.

As he opens the door for her, Gus presses his hand on the hollow of her back. She assumes Pigeon must like it and he is trying it out on her. In retrospect, Noonie realizes she knows this other woman's preferences in bed, too: Noonie and Gus have become like a pair of Arthur Murray dancers following the steps for two different routines: a Charleston and a waltz, perhaps.

"Shall I drive?" Gus asks, selecting a silvery cart from a row, bouncing on the balls of his new running shoes.

"No," says Noonie immediately. "I can't shop if I'm not pushing the cart." Whenever Sarah accompanies her, Noonie wanders aimlessly as an armless Nike.

"Who's going to eat those?" she asks Gus when the Mallomars hit the cart. "Sarah's trying to give up chocolate. Pimples."

"I am. I am going to eat them. I thought I was doing my grocery shopping."

"I forgot," says Noonie.

"Would you rather I got my own cart?" he asks politely.

"I don't care."

"Look, I'll put my groceries up here and you can have the whole bottom, okay?"

His and Hers, thinks Noonie.

"What are you crying about?" asks Gus.

Luckily, they are in the paper goods aisle. He picks up

a box of tissues from the shelf, tears it open, hands her one.

"It's not the brand we buy," Noonie sniffles.

Gus flips the box into the cart, pushes off; Noonie follows him.

"You can't really make any predictions," she says. "Wait, I need milk. I mean, look what people said about Martin and Lewis."

"Who?"

"Dean Martin and Jerry Lewis. When they broke up, everybody said Lewis had all the talent, but they weren't quite right. Or Simon and Garfunkel. I liked him a lot in *Carnal Knowledge,* didn't you?"

"Noonie," asks Gus, "what are you talking about?"

"Me," says Noonie, heading for the checkout.

She sets their piles on the checkout belt. Gus puts his arm between them to emphasize the separation.

"Hi, Emma," says Noonie to the checkout lady. "This is Gus." Don't bother to memorize his name, she wants to add.

While packing their groceries, Emma describes a program about Lapland she watched on TV last night. "Did you catch that, Mrs. B?"

"I'm afraid I missed it," Noonie says, rescuing her eggs from the edge.

"I'm putting your ice cream in here," says Emma. She tells them the program showed how the Laplanders had to drive their herds of reindeer across dangerous and frozen tundra each winter to find grazing land.

"This is the last time they're going to have to do it," says Emma, counting out Noonie's change. "They've been doing it for centuries, but they won't have to do it anymore."

"What are they going to do instead?" asks Gus.

"Airlift," she replies. "The Swedish government is going to airlift all the reindeer. Progress."

Noonie notices that Gus's new checks show a tiger stalking something into an albumen sunset.

Eighteen months' separation, reads the law, the way to civilized divorce (the marital equivalent of painless dentistry, Noonie assumes). Sometimes she thinks it must just be her turn. Like getting engaged or having babies, she is following the rhythms of her generation. Only this time there are no glossy magazines with four-color promises or parties or presents with shiny wrappings.

This time there are days when Noonie lies on her bed all day until Sarah comes home from school, staring at the ceiling as if it contains a brilliant rococo painting or reveals a screen replaying the story of her marriage. She lies fascinated but detached, like a patient in a twilight sleep watching her own eviscerated heart laid open for examination.

But then the gaudy scenes give way to nothing, a totally blank screen. Noonie feels like one of those cartoon characters who is flattened by a speeding truck and then lifts off the pavement and waddles away, but is still flat as a pancake. Noonie, who lived such a rich life of the imagination as a child, who wrote dialogue for the imaginary men in her life, who drew a picture of her wedding dress when she was eight, who could tell you with startling candor that she would marry a prince, cannot imagine what she will be doing tomorrow, except lying on her back on her bed or fixing Sarah dinner or talking to her mother in the hospital on the phone.

Every morning when Gus picks up Sarah to drive her

to school, Noonie hears the engine of his big old Chevrolet. She puts the pillows over her head (she has them all now, of course).

Some days she goes out for walks, so many walks she wishes she had a dog to rationalize them, but she doesn't feel capable of caring for another single creature. The public library is a short walk from her house, and she wanders in and searches the stacks. (She looks up divorce in the card catalogue.) She doesn't take out any of the books but sits cross-legged in the aisles reading. She even reads the plethora of books in the children's department, although she knows Sarah would disapprove of public sniffling. (Sarah does her crying alone, at night, in her room.)

Creative Divorce, Inside Divorce, Divorce: The New Freedom, Divorce Without Victims, Uncoupling; everyone seems in such a hurry to share his or her story, give advice, solace, statistics. (These days it is the unhappy families who are all alike.) Personal journalism was part of the great unzipping of the sixties; we are history. In earlier times, one turned events into art, or left behind letters or journals to be published, posthumously, if at all. Noonie remembers a button Rosie wore in the early days of the feminist movement: CHOOSE OURSELVES. Evidently, everyone has.

"You had a good man and let him slip through your fingers," says Elsa defensively when Noonie arrives to visit her in the hospital in Chicago. "He came to see me. He flew in specially. Three hours he was here. To see me."

Noonie notices that her mother has painted her nails again and there is a slender ribbon from a box of chocolates tied through her thinning hair. In fact, she offers Noonie a candy from a large golden chest.

"No thanks," Noonie snaps.

"Someone wasn't minding the store," Elsa says, turning up the sound on the television so loud she cannot hear Noonie's confused denial.

"Gus says he's disappointed. I know he's disappointed; life didn't turn out the way he hoped it would," she says to her closest friend, Lola, as they jog along the golf course.

"Yeah, I know the feeling," says Lola, "every time I pick up the vacuum cleaner."

"I don't know if I feel disappointed. I never had any serious expectations. If someone had asked me what I wanted to be, I suppose I would have said 'bride.' "

"Well, that's lucky, Noonie," Lola says as they run in place madly at the stoplight, "because now you get a chance to be one again."

"I'll kill him!" says her old friend Cheryl Ann when Noonie calls her in San Francisco with this news. "Let me at him! I'll put a knife in his heart!"

Noonie laughs. She is enjoying this. "He keeps referring to her as 'a professional woman,' 'a working woman.' My God, she's a gym teacher."

"Ah," says Cheryl Ann, wisely, "you remember what we used to say in high school: 'Those who can't do, teach; those who can't teach, teach gym.' "

"Gus has left my sister," Rosie tells Madge at dinner. She waves his postcard ("*Greetings from New Jersey: Scenes of the Revolution*"); Noonie has not told her anything.

"Hm," says Madge, lighting a long cigarette. "This is what you should tell Noonie: a voodoo woman here in town—oh, yes, I know you don't have patience for it," she says, seeing Rosie's smirk, "but listen. A woman came to her with the same problem and she said to get some strands of hair from her husband's—hum, from below his waist—and tie the hairs into tiny knots and put that hair in some receptacle he has to walk past a lot, like the flour bin or under the napkin holder on the kitchen table, and it worked. He was rendered immediately impotent. Of course," she says, grinning widely, "it worked so well he was like that for the wife, too."

"Shhh," says Noonie, watching an old movie on TV as Sarah gets into the bed with a plate of Oreos and a big glass of milk.

"What's happening?"

"She's leaving with her husband."

"Rick isn't going?" Sarah shouts in disbelief.

"No," says Noonie in a choked voice.

"Hey, are you crying?"

"You have a milk mustache," Noonie says to Sarah.

Sarah pushes her mother's hand out of the way. She pulls out a huge book. "What are these things in your bed?"

"Oh, a few books," says Noonie, embarrassed. Unable to sleep, she has piled volumes A to P of the *Britannica* on Gus's side of the bed for weight, for ballast, for company. At least, when she rolls over in the middle of the night, with her eyes closed, it feels as if someone is there.

Every morning Gus awakens and is startled to see the long stretch of Pigeon's tanned body, her tangle of blond hair, next to him. She wears pink frilly shortie gowns or baby-doll pajamas (Noonie sleeps in long underwear from Swiss army regiments or in T-shirts or nude) and wonders where he is. He knows this is less about lust than about change.

Everything about Pigeon is so regular, so predictable, so relaxing. She drives the kind of car she is supposed to (she subscribes to *Consumer Reports*), she orders her bright and cheerful clothes from the catalogues Noonie makes fun of, she doesn't wear men's clothes (Gus's).

He goes to bed late and gets up early, as he always has. He greets Pigeon's dog, a young retriever, male, who needed to be locked out when they first made love in her house. (Noonie had guessed right about motels; they tried motels first. There was a whole string of them out on the highway, although he guessed they'd be gone soon, in a few years crowded out by corporate headquarters and shopping malls. He wonders where all the noontime couples will go, but maybe adultery will be phased out, too.)

He makes the coffee in Pigeon's harvest-gold machine and eats his cornflakes with half a banana and drinks a large glass of Tang—and thinks about Noonie.

Being away from Noonie allows him to think about her all the time. He remembers reading that the American writers who went to Paris in the twenties had suddenly been able to write about America (he teaches *The Nick Adams Stories* in COA). Freed from the place, they became obsessed by what they had left; geography gave them permission. (This is about space and distance, too.)

Every morning, when he picks up Sarah on his way to their school (Pigeon drives herself), he pulls into the driveway, up to the garage, so he can back out of it. That way Sarah can think everything is normal on her way to school. (That is what all parents want: change for themselves and continuity for their children.)

Sometimes when he isn't thinking just about Noonie,

he thinks about Rosie or about Rosie and Noonie, how unalike the two sisters are: one imagines herself a princess, the other a fish.

Rosie has one passion, her swimming; all she needs is someone to take care of her. She is unbelievably clever to avoid men and pick maternal women who make her good things to eat and wash her towels: what more can we ask from the beloved? (This is Gus's secret assessment, that Rosie is being clever, because there is no way in his maleness that he can imagine her preferring women sexually.) Noonie, who grew up in the same house, the same neighborhood, acts as if she has been handed a set of engraved instructions about style and life (she confuses the two). She is full of airs and la-de-dahs—look at all that sleek white German kitchen equipment. She has imposed a set of invented visual standards on herself. People are always telling him that Noonie has such good taste, as if that were a talent or something important, for Christ's sake. What is she going to do with all that good taste—open a gift shop?

The things he thought Elsa had tried to teach her daughters, her very real skills of hard work and survival, they took for granted in others, ignored completely in themselves. Rosie had focused on Elsa's basic eccentricity, her lack of a conventional role in the community. Noonie had selected her flirtatiousness, her ability to fantasize, the outward lack of seriousness about anything important.

Both daughters thought they had circumvented their mother's life completely. Rosie had a weakness for women who were efficient and playful, domestic, but who would bark at her—a combination of softness and gruffness. Noonie had a weakness for men like that. They had both grown up looking for someone who would take care of them, when the message Elsa was flashing all those years was: no one will take care of you but yourself, take care of yourself. (So much for the influence of mothers.)

On Saturdays, Gus picks Sarah up about ten. One Saturday he rings the bell and Noonie answers. She usually avoids him, goes to an aerobics class or the store or hides under the covers.

"Sarah's sick," she says through a crack in the door.

"Oh, no."

"She would have called you, but she hoped she'd feel better."

"Can I see her?"

"I think she's asleep," Noonie says, but she opens the door and lets Gus in.

He feels very uncomfortable, but it is his daughter, too, isn't it? He hadn't just lent his sperm for the occasion. The one thing he and Noonie agreed on one hundred percent was this child!

"It's okay, Daddy," Sarah says, leaning over the banister, her eyes bright with fever. "I'm up." She is wrapped in his old flannel bathrobe (that's where it is) and furry slippers shaped like tomatoes; a cashmere muffler of Noonie's is wound around her neck.

"Get back into bed," he says gruffly.

"I'm sorry I can't come today. Are you very disappointed?"

"Sure. But I think you should stay put. Maybe you can come over tomorrow, if your fever's gone." But he looks at Noonie as he says this.

"We'll have to see." Noonie frowns. "Gus, do you think you could pick up a few things at the store for me, so Sarah isn't alone?"

"Wouldn't you like to get out? I could stay here with her."

"Go ahead, Mom, it's Daddy's day."

Noonie balances on one foot for a minute, then shifts to the other; she stings with rejection. "Yes, thanks," she says, grabbing her bag and slamming the door hard behind her.

Gus sighs; that was a little hard on Noonie. "Do you want to play a game? I really think you should get back in bed," he says gently.

"A game?" Sarah giggles through her wheezy cough. "Like checkers or go fish?"

"Whatever you like," he says, coming up the stairs. He averts his gaze so he won't look into the bedroom he shared with Noonie. (Has she been with someone else?)

"You don't have to treat me like a little child," Sarah says, getting the Monopoly set, an old one, a hand-me-down from Gus's nephews. "Can I be the dog?"

"Of course. I'll be the racing car," he says, settling on the corner of her bed. (Gus made this bed—well, put it together from a kit the day Sarah graduated from her crib and they put it in the attic, a final act.)

"Were you asking Lola out for a date?" she asks, sorting out the money.

"What?"

"Well, I saw you talking to her when you came here this morning."

"I saw her on the street," says Gus, surprised. "I haven't seen her for a while and I was just saying hello."

"Oh. Remember that Thanksgiving Mommy got sick and you and Lola had to fix dinner?"

"I think so," says Gus, confused.

"Well, Rozie and Danny and I were playing I Spy in

the kitchen and I saw you kissing Lola. But don't worry," says Sarah, shaking the dice, "I never told Mommy."

"There was nothing to tell, Sarah," says Gus.

"It's your turn."

"I was just saying hello. Why would I ask Lola out on a date? She's married," he jokes.

"Well," says Sarah, moving her game piece. "So are you."

8

HISTORY REPEATS

When Elsa comes home from the hospital, Noonie stays with her for a week. They are reversing roles in such a swift, frightening way, she feels like Alice tumbling down the rabbit hole. Maybe it is necessary, natural, this process by which one becomes one's parent's parent. Noonie feels so responsible and conscientious these days that once, at the Hi-Lo shopping for dinner, when they announced over the loudspeaker: "Would someone please open the back door for a delivery?" she obediently marched there to do it. Only when she met the butcher in his bloody gown did she realize they were not addressing her.

She begins to fantasize moving here with Sarah and taking over Elsa's studio (why had her mother never bought her even a Brownie camera?). Sarah could go to their old school a few blocks away.

But then she would run out to get some kaiser rolls at the corner store and discover it is an Indian grocery: musty spices and dried fruits, sticky candies on waxed, rolled papers. Farther down Devon Avenue, a storefront theater shows Indian and Pakistani films (not the ones from the New School Indian Film Festival, either), exotic restaurants are called the Taj Mahal or the Delhi Deli. At the Sari Palace, gilt-patterned sheets wrap the dummies with Nordic features, as inappropriate as when it was Rosenthal's Dress Shoppe. Here and there a kosher butcher, a Chinese restaurant, a French cleaners survives.

The library is gone; Noonie's library—replaced by a neo-Georgian savings and loan. And where is Kaplan's Shoe Emporium, where she and Rosie faithfully stopped every day on the way home from school to watch their bones wiggle in the X-ray machine (as voluminous and forbidding as an iron lung), and the bakery, where a small buttery cookie in the shape of a fan with a trail of chocolate sprinkles was always waiting when she went to buy a rye bread or pumpernickel? Gone, all gone.

Noonie begins spending one weekend a month in Chicago, sometimes bringing Sarah with her. Like urban roommates, they share the Hide-A-Bed in the dining room, living out of Le Sportsacs, swapping clothes, sleeping in T-shirts, whispering in the dark after Elsa goes to sleep. As soon as their plane lifts from the tarmac of O'Hare on Sunday afternoon, they resume their domestic battles like the ancient Greeks returning to their city-states after the Olympic games, but here in Chicago Elsa is the mother, Noonie and Sarah mutual children.

By now, of course, the past is beginning to take over, that yellowing foggy haze that happens to old photographs and newspapers and even the best complexions.

Noonie and Sarah are on the front-room floor with a carton: Noonie's yearbooks, prom bids, brittle corsages, diaries. Noonie is amazed that so many years, so many hours and hopes for happiness can be compressed into one ordinary soup carton from the grocery store. She accuses Elsa of having thrown things out (which Elsa, from the sofa, trying to rest, vehemently denies), but every time she thinks of something else: the program from the play she starred in junior year (*The Skin of Our Teeth*), the tassel from her mortarboard—she fishes through the carton and finds it. So she guesses this is the sum of her young life.

Looking through these mementos, Noonie thinks that everyone in her high school longed to be somewhere else. The science teachers were frustrated doctors and researchers; Miss Clinton, the best English teacher, had a long unfinished novel in her bottom drawer. Even Noonie's favorite teacher, Dawn Murphy, the long-legged and sweet-faced French teacher ("Oh, how I'd like to wake up at the crack of Dawn!" whispered Noonie's boyfriend Frankie Malone), wanted to be married and standing in her total-electric kitchen. All of them, teachers and students, were simply biding their time in that public high school. Like the village in "Sleeping Beauty," covered by vines, overgrown with thickets and brambles, Noonie and her friends were waiting for the prince to come with his machete and hatchets and wake them from their lethargy so they could go out into the world and be what they were really meant to be.

Noonie had vague and artistic ambitions: writing, painting, singing, being on the stage; wearing beautiful clothes, and having tall handsome men in love with her. An alternative image presented her with a tired but affectionate husband in a tweed jacket with patched elbows (a doctor, a professor, *Father Knows Best*) and a houseful of loud happy children and sloppy dogs. How to attain either of these fantasies was equally obscure to Noonie, but she guessed school had nothing to do with it. She thought she might make it on sheer desire, energy, charm; she knew her attributes: even white teeth, good legs, piles of golden hair.

Sarah simply wants to do well. She doesn't want to become something bright and shiny, she wants to be a lawyer, she wants to join the Peace Corps. She doesn't want to be on the cover of magazines or make movies or be seduced in the back seats of limousines by men with foreign accents (all sincere ambitions of Noonie's when she was about thirteen). She wants to have at least three children: boys.

"It's not easy, being a lawyer and raising children," says Noonie, suddenly the voice of reality.

"My husband will stay home."

"Oh?"

"Yeah, I'll marry someone like Daddy," says Sarah, "who'll be home a lot."

"I never noticed Gus staying home," Noonie points out.

"You never went to an office," Sarah snaps.

"Well, good luck finding that man."

"What man?" says Elsa. (She is supposed to be napping.)

"Sarah's going to marry a man just like Gus, who stays home with the children while she embarks on her fabulous career."

"Sounds smart to me," says Elsa.

"Gus was never home, he was always drinking coffee at some dump."

"Gus was at home a whole sight more than any man I ever knew," says Elsa, yawning. "You never treated Gus properly."

"Oh, I see," says Noonie, "at this late date in the feminist struggle, if a man doesn't stay home, it's his wife's fault."

"I don't think you give Daddy a chance," says Sarah from behind a magazine.

"Oh?" Noonie answers coolly. (What does anyone in this family know about it, anyway? In an attempt to protect them, Noonie has packed her hurt, her rage, in so much cushioning that, like some tiny fragile crystal lying in a box of Styrofoam bubbles, it appears to have been misplaced.) "Well, I think we have about five thousand years of grace left until we have to be sensitive to men's feelings," she says.

"That is your problem, Noonie," says Elsa, shifting her weight easily. "Attitude."

"Oh, I forgot, I'm with the president of the Angus A. Bentley Fan Club," she snaps.

"I like men," says Sarah.

"Of course you do," says Elsa, soothingly.

"Oh, excuse me," Noonie shouts, "it's my fault. Men have changed."

But what has really changed? Here is Elsa lying on the sofa, dying of the disease that claimed her mother and will probably continue its ravage for several more generations. And Noonie is imitating Elsa's life to some extent now: a single parent, a working mother. The only thing that seems different is the vocabulary: Noonie is chock-full of self-knowledge, very self-aware. Elsa never subjected herself to this kind of self-criticism; plenty of people out there to tear you down, she tried to tell her girls, no need to do the job yourself. But Noonie hadn't listened, she was that intent on improvement.

Another difference is that Elsa has real domestic skills. She is an accomplished cook, a talented baker; she can knit and sew with great competence. She doesn't view any of these things as being creative or self-expressive;

she can't imagine opening a restaurant and cooking for strangers. If Fate had dealt her a winning hand, she would have lived like her sister Tatiana, with cooks and maids. She says she hopes in her next life not to be able to tell the difference between a rolling pin and a safety pin. People without options have to learn to do these things, the way you had to work if you had two little girls to support. Lifestyle, liberated woman, single parent—Elsa would have never used words like that. Noonie is the romantic; she sees her life in capital letters—Mother, Dumped-Wife, Lover, Columnist. Noonie may have studied literature (for a while) in college, but her ideas come straight from the magazines she wants to write for.

"Future Homemakers of America!" shrieks Sarah, looking through Noonie's yearbooks. "Aprons!" she shouts at Servettes, a girl's honor club. She howls with laughter at the Synchronized Swim Team. "Is that Aunt Rosie?"

"Let me see that!" Noonie says, snatching the book from Sarah's hands. "Yes." She stares at her sister in a rubber helmet with floppy flowers, the apex of the formation, one arm delicately dragging through the water in the murky high school pool.

"Why don't we ever see her?"

Noonie hears her mother's heavy sigh as Elsa sneaks out of the room. "She lives in Florida."

Sarah sighs—wow, Noonie must think she's dumb. "It's not that far away."

"Look," says Noonie. "We had to wear these horrible gray cotton tank suits. The minute they got wet, they sagged down to your knees." It wasn't easy to swim with your hands on your breasts, Noonie remembers. "I could never get my hair dry in time for the next class. Oh, I hated Swim."

"Why didn't you bring your hair-dryer to school?" Sarah asks reasonably, leaning over her shoulder.

Noonie snorts in a superior way. "What hair-dryer?"

"Oh, oh, look at you!" Sarah suddenly cries, unable to catch her breath, at the picture of Noonie in a ponytail, holding gigantic pompons over the appliqué megaphone on her chest. "Oh, Mom!" Sarah is rolling on the floor.

Noonie likes to laugh, too, but she likes to be in charge of the laughter. It surprises her how much it hurts to hear her own daughter make fun of her teenaged self. Suddenly Noonie and her friends look so vulnerable and hopeful to her, innocent in a way Sarah could never believe. They had grown up in a black-and-white world, had been tossed mere crumbs of information patched together with hearsay, layered with daydreams. No one had outlined and diagramed and Xeroxed life for them.

Last fall, in Sex Education, Sarah's teacher had assigned, as homework, the drawing of a penis. The whole male body, actually, but Noonie had imagined Sarah had to draw just a penis. Noonie knows that, at that age, she probably would have sketched the Washington Monument.

" '*Sex Change in Fish Found Common,*' " Sarah reads to Noonie from the *Science Times* several weeks later at home. " 'When a school of fish loses its single male, the largest female begins acting like a male within a few hours and will produce sperm within ten days.' Yick." She sticks out her tongue. "Do you suppose they have a choice?"

"Who?"

"The fish. Can they decide if they want to change or not?"

"What's this sudden interest in fish?" Noonie is pounding chicken breasts; she is fixing them with lemon. (Gus's favorite dinner.)

"It's not sudden," says Sarah. "I've always liked science."

"That's a good thing for a girl," says Gus, coming in the back door. (Noonie wishes he'd knock.) "Lots of opportunities for women in science."

"I'm writing a term paper about fish," says Sarah. "I'm calling it 'Wet Dreams.' "

"Where did you hear about that?" asks Gus, not amused.

"Sex," says Sarah. "We have that the year after we do Drugs, remember? Ha ha."

"Do they still call them wet dreams? Don't they call them nocturnal emissions?" Noonie asks, interested.

Gus looks away, uncomfortable. He does not consider male sexuality an appropriate topic for women and children at all. He can only imagine what Sarah and Noonie talk about when he isn't around; he worries how he can keep Sarah as an ally. The separation is his idea, but he is trying very hard to be civilized, accommodating. (Dinner once a week is the idea of their family therapist, Dr. Schnabel, who considers it a nugget of continuity in a troubled time.)

"Did you know goldfish expand in direct proportion to their environment?" says Gus, changing the subject. "If you put a goldfish in a tiny bowl, he will remain small. If you put him in the ocean, he will grow to be a huge, full-sized fish."

"A different species, surely," says Noonie, stirring rice.

"Rosie told me that," Gus says softly.

"What would Rosie know about fish?" Noonie asks. She wonders if Gus made that up.

"Rosie lives underwater," says Gus.

Noonie gives him a dirty look; Sarah laughs and says, "Brett and I have been keeping fish in our locker all semester."

"For science?" asks Gus, bewildered. (He hadn't meant anything mean about Rosie.)

"Oh, Sarah, how could you?" says Noonie, alarmed. (When did Rosie tell him that? Have they been in touch?) "How could they breathe in there?"

"They don't need air, they're fish. They breathe in water, remember? We thought it would be cool, like having an aquarium in your office. Ichthyosis did the best. Mes . . . uggen . . ."

"*Meshuggeneh?*" asks Noonie. "Do you know what that means?"

"It's Yiddish for crazy," says Sarah, chewing her nail.

"Did Brett teach you that?" Noonie jokes, handing her a fistful of silverware.

"It's on the Word-A-Day calendar Daddy gave me for Christmas last year. So's 'icthyosis.' "

"Is that a real word?" asks Noonie.

"I believe it pertains to fish," says Gus, picking undressed lettuce from the salad bowl with his fingers. "How's Elsa?"

"Her chemo begins next week," Noonie says, signaling Sarah's presence with a thumb. (She isn't sure how much she wants to burden Sarah with.) "She liked your flowers."

"Well, I like her," he sighs. "I'll open wine. Where are you keeping the corkscrew these days, Noonie?"

"There's an open bottle in the fridge," she says.

"What are we drinking?" He pulls his new half-glasses from a breast pocket and inspects the label carefully. (Gus has become very serious about wine—he and Pigeon have recently returned from a wine tour of New York State.) "I think I'll open mine."

"I think I'll go to my room until dinner," says Sarah.

"Sit down!" commands Noonie. "I think we can eat."

Noonie wishes Dr. Schnabel could be made to attend some of these family dinners, the way she used to wish all pediatricians had to breast-feed and all gynecologists menstruate. Seeing Gus at the head of the table he abandoned makes her feel like a boxer who gets up for the twentieth time only to be knocked down again. Actually, she's heard enough about Dr. Schnabel's eclectic domestic arrangements to guess he's put in his time. But then, shouldn't he know better? ("Physician, heal thyself!" is what Elsa said when she heard all this.)

To celebrate the end of a bout of treatment, Noonie and Sarah take Elsa to lunch at Marshall Field's.

"What are you going to have?" asks the waitress, balancing on one hip.

"I'll have a hamburger, fries, and a Coke," says Sarah, snapping shut her menu. (She always orders this troika of American adolescent cuisine.)

"At Marshall Field's!" Noonie cries in disappointment. Sarah sighs: a warning.

Noonie orders her favorite, the Special Sandwich: turkey breast, iceberg lettuce, covered with Field's Special Dressing.

"Frankly, I never knew what you saw in this place," Elsa says, waving a soggy bacon slice, bits of dressing dribbling on the white cloth.

"Mother," says Noonie, "this place is like a shrine! Don't you remember the Christmas tree in the Walnut Room and how we took the escalator up to visit Aunt Holly and Uncle Mistletoe. There was this huge maze they erected each year, a labyrinth of parents and children waiting to see Santa," she tells Sarah, who is picking a scab on her wrist. "And the goldfish in the fountain in the Oak Room," Noonie reminds Elsa.

"Well, I certainly do remember the fish," says Elsa, abandoning the mountain of lettuce and lighting one of her filterless cigarettes (Noonie wishes the doctor would make Elsa quit; she guesses it doesn't matter and he doesn't have the heart). "Rosie caught one once and we were asked to leave."

Sarah perks up.

"Do you remember the clown cones?" Noonie asks Elsa.

"You would have thought it was one of the Seven Wonders of the Ancient World, the way she carried on," Elsa says, puffing.

The ice-cream ball sat on a plate with a doily ruff. Candied fruit served for the nose and eyes, raisins stuck to the cone hat; a concept so simple in design, so original in execution that it simply took Noonie's breath away each time it was served to her.

"An ice-cream cone upside down." Elsa shrugs, exhaling.

"All around the room women and little girls sat in picture-book hats and white gloves and leggings that fastened beneath your Mary Janes . . ." Noonie looks around. Only one hat: a leopardskin baseball cap on an eccentric housewife. "Marshall Field's was a kind of civilization, a bulwark of culture."

"Mom," Sarah sighs, licking ketchup from her fingers. "Why don't you write this down and put it in one of your columns?"

Once, as Noonie and Sarah are walking down the street, headed for the El station to visit Elsa, who has to stay over in the hospital, Noonie thinks she sees Rosie coming toward them. (It is certainly a medium-height woman with curly dark hair, dressed in jeans and a down jacket, her hands stuffed in the pockets, with a kind of loping walk. But it can't be Rosie, she wouldn't be here.)

Noonie isn't sure, she grabs Sarah, pulls her across the busy street. "Hurry," she says.

"What's the matter?"

"Don't turn around!" Noonie commands. "I think my sister's over there. No, hurry."

She pulls Sarah along the street and up the street steps to the platform. "Whew!" she says when they get inside the train. Then she starts laughing. "That was close."

"I don't think it's funny," Sarah says, rubbing her arm where Noonie grabbed it. "I think it's sad to run away from your own sister. I wish I had a sister. If I had a sister and I saw her on the street, I wouldn't run away from her. I'd be glad to see her."

"Oh, come on," says Noonie, "it was funny. It's like a scene in a movie." (Noonie is laughing, but she is also shaking; she has just run away from a woman she thought was her sister.)

"I think you're crazy," Sarah says. "First you get rid of Daddy, now you're getting rid of Rosie. You're going to find yourself alone," she says darkly.

Noonie knows most people would feel that way. She knows people who have kept constant touch with siblings who are prisoners, paranoid schizophrenics, Hare Krishnas, not just a woman who loves women and swims long-distance and doesn't dress properly. What has Rosie done except not grown up to be Noonie?

Noonie looks at Sarah's profile locked to the train window, a fine scatter of blond hair over her jacket. They are seated on a train Noonie might have sat on with Rosie on their way downtown together. (Maybe they are buying Elsa a Mother's Day present: stationery or sachets.) Out of the dirty clouded windows, Noonie can see backyards and staircases, clotheslines and wooden porches, boarded-up windows, so close she thinks she can reach out and touch them. At the station stops, the neon signs are already bright in the darkening afternoon: movie marquees and dry cleaners, liquor stores and pizza parlors (with many missing bulbs). Nothing romantic here, grim and grubby dailiness; what an effort it must have been for Noonie to pretend she was someplace else. (What an effort for Noonie to get someplace else.)

Shortly after Gus left her, Noonie imagined she had hit a neighbor's dog who was always running into the street. She was so shaken that she drove ahead two blocks, dazed, before turning around to see if he was all right. But the dog wasn't there when she got back. And when she rang her neighbor's bell, there was Polo, frisky and yapping, so she must have imagined a dog lying whimpering and hurt. So she imagined her sister this morning, her stooped shoulders, and funny walk, her aloneness.

She hasn't talked to Rosie for weeks. She hasn't told her about Gus or about Elsa's progress. She just called after the surgery to report things in the most perfunctory way; she didn't say how truly sick their mother is and that she is going to die.

Noonie knows that if that had been Rosie on the street, if Rosie had seen her running away from her with Sarah, she would have been wounded. Rosie loves Noonie in a way Noonie cannot believe, because she feels she treats Rosie so badly: resents her, ignores her, rejects her. But Rosie continues to love Noonie (it is such a habit by now!) and Noonie's power over her is dependent on Rosie's fear that Noonie will slam a door in her face, won't play school with her, will run wildly across a big city street, pulling her child along, to avoid facing her.

Sarah is doing her homework at Elsa's dining-room table. "Time me," she orders, handing Noonie her digital watch, a gift from Rosie, a little robot that can be removed from the strap, its tiny arms and legs opened like an insect.

The robot stands in front of Noonie. "Ready?" she asks.

Sarah takes a deep breath, as if she were about to dive. " 'The Myth of Demeter and Persephone,' " she introduces. "Demeter had a daughter, Persephone, who was young and beautiful and good. One day while Persephone was sitting in the fields sniffing the narcissus, the earth opened and Hades appeared in his golden chariot, with the black horses, you know, and took her away to the underworld. Persephone's cries of anguish echoed through the hills—that's a quote—and Demeter could hear them, but no one would tell her where her daughter was. Finally, she left Mount Olympus—did I say she lived there? Oh, well, and dressed as a feeble old woman, she wandered the earth in mourning. That year, no crops grew, the earth was barren, there was no food to harvest. Hence . . ."—Sarah blushes (another quote, evidently)—"there was no food to eat . . . How many minutes is that?"

Noonie holds up two fingers.

"Oh. So, Zeus finally had to come and plead with Demeter, and Hades said he would allow Persephone to return to her mother. But before she left he made her eat four pomo . . . poma . . ."

"Pomegranate."

". . . pomegranate seeds, so that she would have to return for four months, one for each seed she ate. That's kind of sneaky, don't you think?"

"Extremely," says Noonie, but she is also deeply moved. (Has Sarah selected this myth or was it assigned?)

"Anyway, Hades brought Persephone up to the earth

in the golden chariot and she leapt into her mother's arms . . . Hey, are you crying?"

Noonie shakes her head violently, neither yes or no. "I like it a lot," she says to Sarah hoarsely.

9

AFTER GUS

After Gus leaves, the repairmen arrive. Perhaps they heard Noonie was in bad shape, rotting away, in need of buttressing and a fresh coat of paint, and were hastened by some magic shining beacon to her door. She feels as if a large sign declaring, in the subtle way of the local realtors, AVAILABLE has been planted on the front lawn. (This is all true and she is grateful for the company.)

Noonie has always been overwhelmed by this big drafty house Gus insisted they buy when they moved here seven years ago after Gus accepted a position as head of the Upper School English department at the Day School. It is hard to keep clean and expensive to maintain and has vague historical pretensions: a Revolutionary War headquarters, home to a signer of the Declaration of Independence, a stop on the Underground Railway. She liked to make jokes about it, point out to Gus that the signer was also buried in the local graveyard, maybe he'd like to order his cemetery plot, but now that it is the only thing she has, it has become important for her to take care of it. Perhaps she hopes Sarah will inherit it, or maybe she imagines a little bronze sign with her name and dates on the door next to the others.

The arrangements with the repairmen were made years in advance, of course; good craftsmen are fiercely pursued in this little town, whose sophisticated citizens frequently resemble French peasants with their obsession with real estate. After all, you can't quibble with such minor things as divorce and separation, unhappiness; these are fleeting. What matters, what survives, are floorboards and moldings and rose ceilings and leaded-glass windows. Long after the unhappy inhabitants have fled and have been replaced by others, the houses stand.

Noonie has never understood the title housewife: married to a house! But she knows a lot of women like that; her friend Lola always becomes a little flushed and dreamy when discussing wallpapers or new kitchen cabinets or carpeting for the playroom. Now that Gus is gone, Noonie has become passionately interested in the house. This doesn't surprise her; her attention span has always been short. When she was in school, she would fly around all semester until the very end, the final exam, when she would discover a sincere involvement with the subject. If only she had paid attention the very first day . . . but it is no use. Noonie isn't interested in beginnings, only in endings.

So, like a good student, she begins to read the historical society books and relevant biographies that Gus had purchased and displayed on a wobbly antique table in the front hall. She inspects the crown moldings and the banisters, the wide pine boards upstairs, the marble fireplaces (seven of them!). Gus arrives to pick up Sarah one day and finds Noonie polishing the brass front-door knocker and handles.

Noonie imagines herself in period costume conducting a group of tourists through the house as she discusses how the signer and his family would gather 'round the piano in the front parlor or how he composed his memoirs in the paneled library on the left. What about some boarders, a bed-and-breakfast? She worries about money all the time.

(Sometimes there are real groups on a tour of the town's historic sights. Noonie can see them through the filmy curtains of her bedroom windows: families with toddlers or an occasional lagging teenager, older couples led by one of the sprightly gray-haired ladies from the Historical Society. Noonie sees them look up at her beautiful old house, symmetrical and gracious, can almost hear them thinking: If only I could live in a house like that, I could live happily ever after. Well, why not? That's how she thought too; Noonie had believed that this house could protect her happiness.)

Noonie has always been an obedient tourist, and that is how she has come to view her life here. She feels as if Gus is behaving like a disappointed traveler; he seems to be treating their marriage like an unpleasant Caribbean holiday, in which the weather has been unpredictable and the food mediocre and the natives unfriendly, and so he vows to try a different island next time.

The Grabowskis come shortly after Gus has moved the last of his things out. They always arrive without too much advance warning, just pull their blue van into the driveway and dump sanders and bags and buckets of polyurethane into the mainstream of your empty life. Although Noonie had not exactly known when they were coming, she has to let them in. Even though they were booked years in advance, there was no order to their selection of needy floors. If you hesitate, cite other plans, they will be gone and not be seen again. After all, who are you? They are the Floor Kings, Anthony G. Grabowski and Sons. They know where the need is sitting. They do entire gymnasiums; Noonie's floors will be like biting into a cream puff for these giants.

On the other hand, once they come, they stay and stay. It is slow going; handwork. And they have to leave early; their mother has just died and they are taking turns sleeping with the old father. Noonie likes to imagine them, Nick and Mickey, big and knobby as oak trees, lying on either side of their fragile father, who snores as soundly as Snow White.

Although they tell her just to leave the key (in a flowerpot on the sidewalk; stick it in the dirt, burglars never look there, they tell her), Noonie stays around to watch. Their presence is comforting. She makes them tea from China with rose petals mixed into the black tobacco-y leaves, she bakes them granola cookies, she makes sandwiches, she reads to them from her latest column (dating services). They, in turn, tell her about the bad floor habits of her friends, who are referred to by a single initial, as in a story by Kafka.

Is she aware that when J. moves her furniture, she just pushes it willy-nilly?

Or that Mrs. P. lets her children ride their tricycles in the upstairs hallway?

And has she ever, Mickey asks rhetorically, seen K. lift his dining-room chair when he wishes to exit the table? Never. He merely slides it back. Scrape, scrape.

The gist of this is that these ungrateful people, Noonie's contemporaries, then have the nerve to call the Grabowskis and complain about the wisdom of their methods, the strength of their polyurethane. After this, Noonie is very careful; she practically leaps from wall to wall. She tells them about a Great House she has written about, in Jamaica, where she was given small quilted pads to skate across the antique floors. The Grabowskis like that a lot.

Eventually they discuss her desertion. (Like most of the town, they assume it is the folly of daily contact, the fallout of ladies' lib.) Because Noonie knows the Grabowskis operate somewhat like Homer and that whatever she says will become part of their repertory for years to come, she always tells the truth. Why not let her hurt become part of the public record? It is Gus's fault, not Noonie's, after all; she had been driving Sarah to a cello lesson the day Gus and Pigeon bedded down for the first time. She is the leftover. Every time she tells the story, though, it is like taking a deep breath for the doctor examining you for a heavy chest cold. It hurts. Mickey has to lend her a succession of soft plaid handkerchiefs, one of which she squirrels away for future reference.

After that, they become perceptibly kinder. They advise Noonie to have an alarm system installed. Nick teaches Sarah, home with the flu, to do cat's cradle with the long shoelace from his big high-topped boots.

Down on their hands and knees, breathing the fine dust, they peel off layers and layers of wax, like layers of dead skin, other women, black and white, have applied. Don't let us ever hear that you put wax on these floors, Mrs. Bentley, they make her swear.

They tell her about their father (Anthony G.) who had come to the United States as a young man and who came home from the first day of work and told his wife, "Mary, I will be a millionaire in this country. Every day I get paid a dollar. A million days, a million dollars!"

"Ha ha!" laugh Nick and Mickey.

They spread white paint over the floors and wipe it off immediately. Even though they disapprove of bleaching floors, they do it for Noonie (who had requested it last year; another life). Down on their hands and knees, Mickey brushes it on; Nick, following him, wipes it off with clean rags, so that it leaves the palest whitewash on the natural pink of the oaks. The floors are beautiful, like paintings of sky, like frescoes or the *faux* marble at Versailles.

"Are they still here?" asks Gus, required to use the back door.

All the rooms have been divided into vertical spaces, all the furniture pushed to one side, so that Noonie, rolling over in her sleep, alone in her great bed, flings her arms dangerously into walls and windows.

"What is this going to cost me?" Gus yells through an open window to Nick and Mickey, who are doing their strange dance on the living-room floor. He doesn't even want this done. They ignore him.

"Who's sleeping with Pa tonight?" Nick asks Mickey at the end of a day.

I will! Noonie thinks. Let me! She would have gotten down with all of them on those beautiful bare floors, rubbed pink and raw, tongue in groove.

The carpenters are an entirely different experience; another generation. They have come to repair the sleeping porch, which Sarah has begged to use since they moved in and has not been allowed—Noonie could see Sarah and her friends and all the rotted boards come tumbling down like that unsuspecting baby in its treetop cradle.

"Wow!" say the carpenters. "How old is this thing?"

Noonie is used to this; often she has to take repairmen

through the house while they slap their thighs with glee or chuckle that such things still exist: coalbins, kitchen fireplaces, copper plumbing with porcelain chain pulls, dark back stairs for servants, but especially idiots who would buy such a monstrosity.

The carpenters are counterculture heroes, leftovers from the early seventies, college dropouts; they have expectations. They are victims of the media: they make assumptions about housewives of a certain age, divorcées, based on films and the soaps. They wear their tools on thick leather belts slung low on their hips, like western sheriffs. Tiny running shorts peek from underneath. Although it is only April, they immediately remove their rock-concert T-shirts to reveal bronzed and developed pectorals. Only their feet seem adequately covered: they sport high suede hiking boots with thick orange wool socks. They tie bandannas on their foreheads before beginning work, as solemnly as if they are participating in a Cherokee puberty rite.

There is no need to ask if they want a cup of tea. They are up-front with their desires: imported beers, springwater, the toilet, this morning's *Times*. Sarah, home because of a school holiday, hangs out in the adjoining hall. Noonie is afraid to leave Sarah alone with them, imagines all of them lying on the precarious porch, smoking dope.

Coming home from the magazine or from doing errands, as she pulls into the driveway, she watches them balancing almost naked behind the faint torn screens, like geishas in an old print, slightly hidden and made more beautiful by it. Although she finds herself taking frequent peeks, they don't tempt her for a minute. They are too young, too obvious; they anticipate her interest. They blow smoke in her face, rub close to her backside while opening and closing her refrigerator door or using her phone, and they do a lot of posing before they hammer and nail.

In a dream, they swing their shoulder-length blond hair and shout in disbelief at Noonie's refusal, "Hey, don't you know the song? We're workmen . . . we're carpenters, and you are a lady . . ."

It is Gus she continues to dream about, the wishful dreams of mourners and the terminally ill. In one dream, Noonie comes to clean Pigeon's condominium. She arrives in a taxi with mops and a pail, the hose of her Electrolux wound around her neck like a snake in a sideshow. Gus is wandering around in an old bathrobe. He keeps motioning for her from the platform bed, patting the foam mattress.

"Honey," he keeps saying, as Noonie tries to clean. "Honey, sit right down and give me a big kiss."

Occasionally Noonie is coerced out to dinner to meet someone, a man. Lola will call, breathless: some accountant has moved in across the street with custody of his three lovely children, or a classmate of Marty's, recently divorced, shows up on the same train on his way to the city. According to Lola, Noonie should be grateful: single, heterosexual, employed men are not in ample supply.

Noonie has some knowledge of this. Recently she interviewed a woman in East Orange who gives dinner parties for middle-aged divorced people as a business; she charges fifty dollars. They are all supposed to pretend they are friends who have just been invited for dinner. At the party Noonie meets two dentists, a painting contractor, a high school guidance counselor and the usual assortment of neglected, attractive, and intelligent women she meets by the dozens. Over cocktails and dinner they exchange stories of deception and daring. No one seems particularly surprised by the chain of events that has landed them in this strange dining room, none of them wishes to be here, everyone is sad. All of the men ask Noonie for her phone number (she appears to be even more popular than in high school), but she declines on a professional basis: she is only a reporter, she says, it wouldn't be fair. (Whew!)

At the dinners Lola invites Noonie to, Marty picks her up at her house (three blocks away) so the man will have to take her home. Everyone seems to understand the rules except Noonie, who finds she can barely breathe, let alone speak, and when she goes to swallow her food (and Lola is a very good cook), it remains whole in her mouth, so when she opens it to sip some wine or answer a question, it catches in her throat.

"That's an original approach," says Lola in the kitchen, where Noonie has escaped with some dirty plates, "getting to know a man while he's doing the Heimlich on you."

Noonie opens the dishwasher, begins to stack.

"Get back in there," Lola commands like an anxious coach. "Go sit down," she orders, handing Noonie the dessert plates.

"Noonie just interviewed the most amazing woman," Lola says, slicing a Sacher torte, "who makes things out of eggs. Hollows them out and puts things in them or something, right, Noonie?"

"Yes," says Noonie, looking at her lap.

"Noonie, what was that funny story you told me about the convention, the 'eggers' convention,' you called it?"

But Noonie finds herself telling a story about Gus, something he did years ago or something Sarah told her about him last week.

"So, how long have you been divorced?" asks this evening's hero, a lawyer in his early fifties whose name is Sol.

"I'm not divorced," says Noonie, almost knocking him down as he attempts to open the car door for her. She catapults from the front seat. "We're separated."

They stand at her front door.

"Would you like to come in?" she sighs.

"I thought you'd never ask," says Sol, smiling.

"Would you mind removing your shoes?" Noonie asks. "The floors have just been refinished."

"Uh, no," he says, slipping out of a pair of handsome tasseled Loafers; his socks are nice, too, silk lisle with a small, tasteful design. (He might have had a hole in the toe.)

"Would you like a drink or some coffee?"

"Do you have decaf?"

Sol follows Noonie into the kitchen where she grinds beans. He sniffs the bag appreciatively, then thoughtfully chronicles his Life and Times for her. He likes jazz and he loves Mozart, he bites his nails (he used to smoke cigars and still misses them with brandy after dinner), he collects Japanese prints, he loves Irwin Shaw's early stories, one of which he outlines as Noonie watches the coffee drip slowly into the glass pot. The story seems to involve a man and a beautiful unattainable woman, a wholly anachronistic notion. He lists the women in his own life: students, fellow attorneys, a stockbroker, housewives, a minor English film star whom Noonie has never heard of, an army nurse, his ex-wives Kiki and Marie-Claire; they march across Noonie's kitchen table like the women in Leporello's aria in *Don Giovanni*. (He sings a few bars for her.) "I always thought marriage was like one of those large dinner parties where you got to change partners at the dessert course."

Noonie steps back as if she has been stabbed.

"Ah," he says wisely, "you loved your husband."

"Of course I loved him. For your information, I still do."

"I see," says Sol. "You're still wearing your rings."

Noonie looks down at her fingers as if she had been doing something very naughty. "I can't get them off."

Sol helps himself to some cookies in a package on the counter. He looks at her skeptically.

"Look," she says, twisting them painfully up to her knuckle.

He is walking up to her, coming so close Noonie can feel the crumbs on the side of his mouth.

"This is happening a little quickly," she says.

"I don't know what you're used to," he says, putting his hands on her waist.

She puts her head back and laughs.

"It's an act," she says, moving out of his embrace, gathering the coffee mugs and cookies and going into the living room. "The shoes, the dress; I'm just your average frightened American woman."

"I suppose you've never slept with a man before."

"Not quite like this."

"So are we going to do it or not? Noonie," he says seriously, leaning closer, "I want you to know that I haven't been involved with a woman like you in years."

"What does that mean, a woman like me? Do you mean middle-aged or overweight or what?"

"I mean a woman who needs so much persuading, attention, preliminaries."

"Oh." (They have been in her house about twenty-five minutes.)

"I feel like I'm back in high school. Do you know what it was like to be a boy in high school in the fifties? Oh,

God, you had to be so clever, I mean, if you weren't a football hero. You had to find a reason for a girl to do something she wanted to do very much, but she wasn't supposed to do, so you had to find a reason for her to do it. And the zippers, the hooks and buttons, oh boy, you had to be Houdini in those days. And every unfastening was accompanied by tears, by promises . . . Earth to Noonie," he calls, waving a hand in front of her face. "Have I lost you?" he asks sweetly.

"What about these new women? What do they do, attack you on the street?"

"They don't need a lot of chatting up," he admits. "What's that sound?" he asks suddenly.

"Oh," Noonie says, smiling broadly, "that's my daughter, coming home from a party. Hi, sweetie," she calls gaily, "I'm in here!"

"Would you like a sandwich or something? I was going to make some lunch," Noonie asks.

There is only one workman left, a cabinetmaker named Tommy who was hired to build a bookcase for Gus's study. Noonie is surprised to see him leaning against a stack of raw fresh boards reading a book of poems from a pile Gus didn't bother to take.

"Sure," he says, startled, "that would be great."

He has been standing there a long time, and Noonie has been watching him a long time, his head bent gracefully, leaning on one leg in a sunny corner.

"Is egg salad okay?"

"Fine."

"I wasn't sure, so many of you young people don't eat . . ."

"Lay off, Grandma," he says.

"I'm sorry."

"I'm probably not that much younger than you are."

"Let's not put it to a test," says Noonie.

She watches him wash his hands carefully, first unclasping his wristwatch and laying it on the windowsill above the sink. It is a gesture that reminds her of Gus; it was often the last thing he would do before turning to make love to her. Tommy is at the table across from her, in jeans and a T-shirt and an old lumberjack shirt (which Sarah had particularly admired), his hands spread in front of him, the nails so wide and smooth they look like spoons. Noonie has always liked hands; people's hands seem such a key to some piece of themselves, not the soul piece, but the doing piece, the action. She takes his hand and turns it over, tracing the lines in his palm.

"My mother used to tell fortunes," she says, dropping his hand.

It is his turn to look surprised. "Was she good at it?"

"Sometimes." Noonie smiles.

"So what do you see?" he says easily, reaching across the table and touching the side of her face, letting his fingers trace, down to her throat, the bones at the base.

"My mother's dying," she says, letting him touch her.

"I'm sorry," Tommy says.

"She's been sick a long time."

"I'm still sorry," he says, reaching out to stroke her hair.

Why is she telling him this? She pulls away suddenly. "I don't need to do this," she says. "Another sandwich?"

"It's great egg salad."

"I've had lots of practice."

"Why do you do that?'

"What?" She can feel him coming up behind her as she stands at the sink scraping the plates.

"You know, put yourself down. I watch you all the

time, you seem like a smart woman, attractive, you're reasonably young . . ."

"Thanks a heap. Coffee?"

"Do you have any herbal tea?"

"Sugar or honey?"

"Honey, but I can get it. Sit down."

"Look, Tommy," Noonie sighs, putting her hand on his shoulder; they are almost the same height. "My husband, whom I love very much, just walked out on me and I'm a little sore right now . . ."

"The walking wounded . . ."

"Yeah. And I'm a little afraid to risk anything else that might hurt."

"I'm not going to hurt you."

"It might not be something you mean to do . . . it might just be me. And I have a child, who's probably closer in age to you than I am, and I'm not sure I want her to be your next candidate."

"You give me a lot of credit, don't you?" He slams his cup on the counter. "I'm going back to work."

"Wait, I'm sorry. I just, I don't know what you're after." She thinks of Sol. "I mean, girls were brought up, in the fifties, at least I was, to imagine all men were after was sex. It's taken me a long time to learn that men and women can be friends, too."

"Are you serious about her?" Noonie asks a week later in Tommy's bed as he hangs up the telephone. She runs her fingers over the furrows in his brow.

"About Gail? Serious, do you mean like, am I going to marry her?"

"Yes, I guess that's what I still mean by serious." Noonie runs her hand down the side of his face, his smooth jaw.

His skin is warm, flushed, freckled, bone and muscles, a man's healthy young body. Noonie has been in love with all this before; it is a second chance, a return visit. How beautiful he is, with all the simple beauty she had possessed, too, and taken for granted or dismissed when it had been hers.

How crazy to deny this, she thinks, but it is not the kind of thing she expected or planned and so, this morning, when she met him in the hardware store and he offered her a lift home in his van, and when he suggested they stop at his apartment for some drawings he needed, and when they started touching in the van and when they started embracing in the kitchen as he was making tea and started undressing; when he took her hand and walked her into the bedroom, she was still saying, "I can't do this."

"So?" she asks, placing her hands on his shoulder blades.

"That's what my mother means by serious. 'Are you going to marry her or is she just one of your little roommates?' "

All the plurals make Noonie flinch, and anyway, she doesn't want to share the bed with Tommy's mother, a woman with whom she imagines she has more in common than with his girlfriend Gail. "What time is it?"

He yawns and rolls over to check his watch on the floor near the mattress. "Two-thirty."

"Oh." Noonie sits up, reaches for his worn robe. His name tag is sewn in the collar.

"Are you hungry?" he asks.

"I don't have time," she says, sifting around to find her jeans, shoes, bra.

Wrapping the robe around her, she looks at her face in the old framed mirror balanced against the large oak dresser. Behind her she can see Tommy, stretched out on his back, his arms raised, his long hair on the pillows, the sharp slice of jaw that really separates her generation from his.

The sheets are a striped pattern she owned many years ago, at the beginning of her marriage to Gus. Noonie has just spent several hours in this bed. She wonders where Tommy has learned to do this so well, but then the times have changed (all that sex education) and, well, so has she.

Although she would not have guessed it, she is not much of a sexual adventurer. Conversation is too important for her and sex is too tied up with history, her history with Gus, her first guide in these matters, the man who will provide the watermark forever. It is too dangerous to sleep with strangers, to take off your clothes in front of them and trust them with your ancient feelings. She wants to be in Gus's bed, she wants to talk to her daughter, she wants to be five years old and asleep with Rosie in her mother's house.

10

FLESH AND BLOOD

Noonie travels back and forth between her home outside of New York and Elsa's in Chicago: a commuter/daughter. Elsa is home, she is in the hospital, she is home again. She has chemotherapy, then radiation, followed by another round of chemotherapy. Elsa must enter the hospital early Monday morning for treatment; she is still too sick to go home until Tuesday. Wednesday, as she is beginning to feel better, Noonie leaves to pick up the pieces of her newspaper column, her household wars, dinner at Lola's, an afternoon with Tommy. But on Sunday night, Noonie must return to Chicago to be sure Elsa makes it to the hospital on Monday.

Weeping, Elsa begs Noonie not to force her to go, resorts to the tricks and excuses Noonie as a child had tried with her. Now it is Elsa, in bed with the covers up to her quivering chin, who plays the sound sleeper, Sleeping Beauty, rolling over with a loud snore when Noonie calls her name and tries to shake her awake. Elsa will tell Noonie they have the wrong day or that she heard on the radio that the hospital burned down in the middle of the night (this is reported with a faint smile). When the phone rings with a wrong number, Elsa announces that it is the doctor's office telling her not to come in that day. (Noonie has taken to picking up the kitchen extension, the way she does with Sarah.) On her knees, with locked fingers above her head, Elsa prays—out loud—for a blizzard so they will not be able to get to the hospital. (It is the mildest winter in the recent history of the city.)

Getting Elsa ready for the trip to the hospital is difficult, too. She is rather weak and has lost a great deal of coordination. Her bladder has been affected and Noonie must remind her every fifteen minutes to go to the bathroom. As soon as Elsa is finally dressed and ready to descend the stairs, she tells Noonie she has to tinkle. There are strange hollows in her dress, too, where her breasts had been. The prostheses are heavy, she complains, something to do with the nerves that had been cut. They don't resemble breasts, anyway; who were they kidding—they feel like two heavy corsages stuck to her chest.

The doctors, Gus, Aunt Tatiana, all try to convince Noonie that she does not have to perform this traveling act. She can hire someone, call for an ambulance; certainly Elsa will give in to common sense, survival. It is pure selfishness on Noonie's part; out of sight, Elsa might do anything (she might die, for instance), although it is her docility, her willingness to obey and trust Noonie that frightens and saddens her more than anything that comes after.

(At one point Noonie had bundled her mother in a big shawl and, splurging on first-class tickets, dragged her to New York, to Memorial, a cancer factory. She was certain in all that silence, that marble and glass, they would find what to do, but some things were truer than architecture.)

It is evidently in the hands of God, although Noonie cannot imagine any of the taciturn, brusque surgeons using that kind of expression, so she must have made it up. Elsa has given Noonie both a vivid imagination and a sense of literalness, so that she can actually see her mother, weak, thin, her wispy soft gray hair, like an aging poodle's, curled up in a pair of massive hairy hands with buffed fingernails.

Although they are frequently accused of it, the doctors seem not to confuse themselves with God; they are soft-spoken, impatient, somewhat bowed by Elsa's condition and Noonie's ferocity.

"Why should she keep doing this! Why are we putting her through this!" Noonie screams, catching one of these green-draped, tired men in a corridor. She outlines the routines, describes the anguish of getting Elsa here on Monday morning.

(Things have moved from organ to organ, not a stately march, a solemn progression, but a scattered array of disorder, though a predictable one. When the doctors talked to Noonie it made sense, like plotting a good strong novel, but then she'd come home and realize it was Elsa's liver they meant. The radiation was worse and better: five days a week, but only for a month.)

"But she isn't getting any better!" Noonie shouts.

"We're doing what we can, Mrs. Bentley. We're prolonging her life."

"For how long?" Noonie demands.

They stop and sigh and perhaps polish their glasses on the end of a smock or put a soft papery hand on Noonie's shoulder. "That's all any of us does for our patients, just prolong life. None of us is immortal."

This is the stuff of nightmares. Noonie has no outlet

for this confusion, these feelings; perhaps Shakespeare could have done it justice. She looks for something to do. She would like to take up smoking again, but spending so much time in hospitals has stripped some of the glamour from it. She goes to a yarn shop near the hospital and selects a difficult pattern for her first sweater: a fisherman's cardigan from some northern country, and buys eighty dollars' worth of rough natural yarn.

"Look!" she says to Elsa, dropping all the skeins on the hospital bed.

Elsa actually rises from the bed, a smile forms on her lips. "Ha ha!" she chuckles.

"I'm making Sarah a sweater," Noonie says. "I thought you could give me a hand."

"Oy, Noonie," says Elsa, covering her mouth. Laughing makes her nauseated.

"The saleswoman said it was very simple. The neck is a little tricky," she admits, "but basically, it's knit and purl."

Elsa rolls her eyes. "I feel terrible."

"I know," says Noonie briskly, "but you'll feel better soon. Now, first, I have to unwind this yarn and make it into balls. Can you put your hands up, like this . . ."

"Use a chair . . . I can't sit with my hands up."

Noonie goes into the hall, drags back a straight chair. "Now, the woman said it was very important to find where the yarn starts . . . Oh, damn!"

"Give that to me, Noonie," sighs Elsa, pressing a hand to her abdomen. "You look as clumsy as a man in high heels. Give it to me before you mess it all up."

Elsa, the patient, manages to knit Sarah this sweater, a vest, and matching mittens, and (on the sly) makes an afghan with embroidered American eagles for Gus, but

Noonie does nothing but hold her breath. She walks up and down the corridors of the hospital, smiling and waving and eavesdropping, making up little stories about the patients and their families (she writes none of it down; it is too sad) or turns the pages of the glossy best-sellers Elsa has been sent by her sister Tatiana: generational novels about Jewish families in the garment or newspaper business, snappy columns about the joys and pitfalls of being a housewife, softbound books of cat cartoons, although Noonie can't imagine Aunt Tatiana expressing affection for any animal that cannot be made into a coat or a handbag. There is a lot of fruit to eat, too.

"Take Sarah some oranges," Elsa says, as if they were still the exotic items of Dickens's London.

Noonie ends up doing what she imagines most Americans end up doing: she watches television—game shows and the soaps, although she has to miss entire episodes and is always consulting Sarah.

"Why can't Vanessa get into her apartment?" she asks long-distance late on a Tuesday night, after she has settled Elsa in.

"Todd threatened to change the locks after he found her in bed with Geoff."

"Oh," says Noonie, trying to remember Geoff (the Australian who runs the disco, she thinks). "I thought that was a metaphor." She can hear Sarah's gum cracking across the wires; she wonders if she is wearing her retainers.

"Mom," says Sarah, "these are real-life experiences. It could happen to you! How's Grandma?"

"Better. I'll be home about five tomorrow. Okay? Stay at Daddy's until I get there."

"Can I stay an extra night? Pigeon said she'd take me shopping. Please."

"Okay," says Noonie, disappointed.

"What are you eating?"

"Mallomars," says Noonie, digging into her box.

"You don't eat junk like that."

Noonie has started eating childhood things, not really from her childhood (Elsa baked every other day, was an early skeptic of packaged goods) but from Sarah's; chemicals and cardboard suddenly speak to her. In the past year, the hospital cafeteria has been replaced by an army of stainless-steel machines. Noonie selects her meals from metal shelves, zaps them in microwave ovens; her coffee tinkles in a slow steamy stream into a wobbly Styrofoam cup. Elsa's dying has pushed Noonie into the mainstream of American life.

One night in Chicago, alone, lonesome, Noonie does a dangerous thing: she calls her old boyfriend Frankie. There are six Francis X. Malones in the North Suburban phone book and she has to call three of them. There is absolutely no reason to believe he will be home or he will come, but he is and he does.

"Oh, please," Noonie prays in the mirror, combing her hair, "don't let him be fat or too bald." She doesn't expect him to look like the returning hero in a romance novel, but she hopes he doesn't look like the Pillsbury Doughboy.

Frank seems a little shorter than he used to be, and he has traded his traditional white T-shirt and black leather jacket for a pair of neatly pressed designer jeans (he has gone into the family dry-cleaning business) and a V-neck sweater, so Noonie can see an enameled saint's medal resting in the chest hair.

They stand in the hallway holding hands, swinging hands slightly. Noonie gives him a peck on the cheek, smells Aramis, sees silver in his sideburns.

"Um, would you like a drink?" she asks finally.

"Sure." He smiles. Other than an occasional beer in the back seat, it is not a part of their past activities. He follows her into the front room.

Noonie searches for something to drink in the cabinet under the television set. She remembers the tall clear bottles with porcelain stoppers that Otto kept his slivovitz in. No slivovitz, but an assortment of fruit liqueurs in fancy bottles: strawberry in a plump valentine, pineapple in a yellow scaly cylinder. These were souvenirs from winter cruises Tatiana treated Elsa to over the years. They didn't intend to drink them, of course; they brought them back as gifts and then forgot all about them.

"Did I ever tell you that my mother was in Havana the day before the revolution? She and Aunt Tatie were on the last tourist boat out of Miami. She said it was very quiet, all the stores were empty." Noonie laughs. "I always wondered what Castro would have done with Elsa." She fills two metal shot glasses.

"I'm sorry to hear about your Mom's . . . health," says Frank.

(Noonie and Frankie on the sofa; is this not a thing of Proust, of déjà vu, of second chances?)

"Do you remember . . . ?" Noonie begins, and moves closer, boldly.

"Oh, Noonie, you had the loveliest breasts," says Frank, unbuckling his wristwatch.

"Did I?" she asks. She cannot remember. "They're a bit saggy," she admits, concerned. She is quite familiar with her breasts, actually; since Elsa's cancer was diagnosed, Noonie has spent many hours fingering her own breasts, examining them, imagining them.

Frankie puts his thimble of papaya liqueur on the coffee table, turns to Noonie.

Noonie suddenly giggles, chokes on her drink, sputters, spitting a fine shower onto the front of Frank's sweater. "Oh, God, I'm sorry . . ."

"Well, I think it should come out if we act quickly," he says, looking unhappy.

Noonie runs into the kitchen for a paper towel and water.

"Cold water," Frank calls professionally. "Hot sets stains."

Noonie hands him the wad of paper towel. "I'm really sorry," she apologizes, "that was a terrible thing to do."

"It was just an accident, I don't think it will stain."

"No, I mean laughing," she says, staring at Frank. He has taken off his sweater and is applying the paper towel carefully, like a sponge, soaking up the stain. She stares at his back (there is a small bluish mole he might want to keep an eye on). Have she and Frank ever seen each other completely undressed? Their relationship took place in small tight spaces in the dark: back seats of cars, backstage at school, closets, sofas, Elsa's darkroom: hastily pushed-down panties, an open zipper, one breast escaping from its white cotton hammock, a surrealist landscape. It had very little in common with what Noonie later knew to be sex, which usually involved beds, birth control, and breakfast. This was fumbling, it was furtive. No wonder it was called puppy love: they were like two young animals tumbling over each other with excitement and enthusiasm, but unsure of what happens next.

Following Frank's directions, Noonie blow-dries the spot he has created over his sweater with her portable dryer. "Come on," she says gently, helping him pull it over his head. "I think Katz's delicatessen is still open."

Over coffee and a sweet roll, Noonie and Frank establish

a new relationship, this time based on adult disappointment and adolescent children.

"My kids! My kids are going to kill me!" moans Frank, but he pulls out his wallet and displays a veritable album of middle-class family life: baby pictures, midget sports teams, the veils and white bibles of first communion. ("That's my sweetheart!" he confides.)

Noonie manages to find a single snapshot of Sarah: a school photo taken against a cloudy background that makes it look as if Sarah is standing in heaven with her braces and long dangling earrings and a sweatshirt that announces, I AM A DEAD HEAD.

"She has her mother's pretty face," he says.

Noonie blushes slightly, whispers thank you, although it is Gus Sarah resembles completely.

Frank and Noonie trade stories, stories of daring and tragedy, horror stories that parents of teenagers tell each other, supposedly to comfort themselves. "You think that was bad . . . listen to this . . ." As with combat soldiers, there is a degree of competition, too: whose kid drank the most, drove the fastest, has the most sexual experience. Noonie is pleased Sarah comes off as innocent, gentle, studious.

"Do you think they're really worse than we were?" asks Noonie. "Sometimes I just think we didn't have the opportunities, the temptations. We couldn't fuck up our lives quite so dramatically, so young."

Frank laughs, agrees, then tells her some amazing stories about Ginny, his estranged wife, Noonie's fellow cheerleader. Evidently, Ginny has learned to turn more than cartwheels. Noonie tries to be a sympathetic listener; she clicks her tongue, pats his hand.

For some reason, Noonie doesn't tell Frank about Gus

and Pigeon. She doesn't mention Tommy. She makes fun of her career, which is in good shape. She certainly forgets to remember Rosie. ("Yes. Still swimming!") She doesn't tell him that one day she was in such pain she drove through the automatic car wash three times so she could scream at the top of her lungs as the brushes and streams of water hit her car. She decides to paint her life as one of good humor and swift dedication to order, like the mother superior of a convent school.

And nowhere does he catch the irony: what Noonie and he are talking about and the somewhat daring and naughty kids they had been. O taste and see! was Noonie's motto in those days, and the fact that they are sitting primly across from each other at Katz's deli, instead of rolling around Elsa's double bed is lost on Frank. Noonie is lying, but she has salvaged his feeling and escaped having to go to bed with him.

Like the solid city they are in, surprise and irony are not the chief rewards of Frank's life. He is concerned with family and dignity and hard work and simple pleasure. This is Chicago, second city in her childhood, now the third, a city of neighborhoods, neat ethnic boxes designed along symmetrical lines, a grid numbered consecutively, north and south. East is toward the lake, Noonie had learned as a child, a not universally useful direction.

"I don't like to interfere," Madge says to Rosie one Saturday morning as they are doing errands: groceries, cleaners, hardware.

"Good," says Rosie, backing out of the drive-in teller. "I treasure that about you."

"But . . ." Madge grins.

"I knew it couldn't last," sighs Rosie.

They are comfortable together, both good-humored women. It was not always like this; when Madge met Rosie, she was a tight, tense, wired-up young woman, very thin when she was training, jumpy—well, six years ago, when she was first here with her lover Alison, who had taken a house for the winter months in Key West.

She was standing across the room at a crowded party in the black jeans and slogan sweatshirt she wore everywhere (this one said HURT, PAIN, AGONY, AND ECSTASY) and a pair of expensive moccasins, the kind Italian drivers wear with rubber dots on the bottom, but Rosie's were worn all the way down so she slipped a lot. She was standing in the corner alone, twisting the stem of a large goblet with something frozen and alcoholic in it.

"Come meet Rosie," the host said to Madge. "She's a swimmer, she did something very fabulous, something famous . . . what was it?"

"The Channel?" Madge asked politely, always a good guess.

"Yes, she was the youngest American woman to swim the English Channel." He didn't look so impressed anymore.

But Madge was. Madge had been a diver, almost Olympic caliber, and she gave lessons besides teaching domestic science. She sized up Rosie as the real thing from across the room: the broad shoulders and chest (although she didn't have much sympathy for the sentiment on her shirt), her hips and legs narrowed into an arrow, a small neat head. There seemed a kind of smartness to her, too, an urbane eccentricity that Madge, a girl from southern Missouri, was able to recognize but not quite place.

"She's living with that woman over there with the thick gray ponytail, Alison Barrows. She's a sculptor, huge metal things, but it won't last long I hear . . ." (He didn't mean the metal things—they would last forever, they were made to rust.) He was whispering as they crossed the room.

Rosie had heard some of this drifting over the music and noise; her neck snapped painfully as she turned to see where this information was coming from and noted the soft plump woman walking over with this magpie Rolf . . . Rolf something, who ran a gift shop in town. Who didn't? Rosie had never seen so much junk in one place in her life; in most towns it occupied a few streets, but all of Key West was a gigantic monument to T-shirts, funny hats, obscene posters and postcards, running shorts, bathing suits, flamingo prints, and ice cream. It was all junk shops or restaurants.

"Rosemarie Gluck," she said, and nodded shyly.

"Well, this is Madge Cook, and I just knew you two had to meet. Madge is our local diving coach and Rosie . . ."

"Rosie is a swimmer," Madge said quietly, giving Rosie a look of friendly conspiracy.

"Okay, say it," says Rosie as they sit in the car in the McDonald's drive-through. It is backed up.

"When did you last talk to your sister . . ." Madge is not completely comfortable with her name, any more than Noonie likes to use hers.

(How strange, Rosie thinks, this assumed connection between complete strangers because they share one thing—a person; how amazing to think we will have a relationship just because of this, this melding of strangers, in-laws in a more conventional world than theirs, people who are supposed to fall into each other's arms; no wonder everyone drinks so much at weddings. But she had felt something real for Gus, she knows.)

Madge really likes Noonie; she remembers with fondness the overnight several years ago. She has never met Rosie's mother, Elsa, and Rosie doesn't talk much about her childhood. (Madge hasn't spoken to her own family in so many years she couldn't tell you. There seems to be a universal lack of patience among certain families for this kind of deviation.) She guesses Rosie has been hurt by Noonie, so she doesn't talk about her anymore, either. She just remembers one remark by Alison, the former lover, who stood at the door as Rosie moved out her duffel bag and boxes, her tall heavy form slouched into a question mark in the lighted doorway. "She'll never find her sister in you," she said. Oh dear.

Noonie has kept Rosie informed with abrupt medical bulletins. Assuming no real interest on Rosie's part nor an intention to do anything about it, she has taken over as usual, and Rosie learned long ago not to battle Noonie for her assumed position of superiority. Rosie is afraid of Noonie. She has always been. Rosie, from the pieces of information she has of her mother's illness—both breasts, spreading to the liver—has talked to a doctor here who said they never should have removed her second breast; if it had already spread, it didn't matter at Elsa's age and she could have been spared that. But Rosie doesn't pass this on to Noonie; she guesses she can't do anything at this point, and Elsa has made it clear she doesn't want to know about Rosie's life or opinions. She wishes to remember Rosie as a cheerful, lively, dark-curled girl-child, quick-footed and obedient and, perhaps, dead.

Rosie has always done what was expected of her; even when she wasn't really equipped to do certain things, she did them anyway because there was a basic quiet obedience to her, a belief that it was easier to do what people expected of her in the small things so she could get on with the grand chaos of her life. It was Noonie who made a moral issue of minutiae—everything from setting the table to coming home on time for dinner—while harboring the most conventionally repressed soul imaginable. (This was the basic difference between Elsa's daughters, and no one could have guessed it.)

When you are doing something unusual, deviant, different (and no matter how natural it feels to you, it is always that), it is important that you feel comfortable, trust your partner. Madge and Rosie both think this way. Neither of them really cares for short-term relationships—Madge, as she gets older, hates them; Rosie flirts with the idea of change (and with an occasional somebody at a party) but basically rejects it. Her last lover, Alison, was thrillingly difficult, imaginative, greedy—oh, how Rosie adored her at first, or maybe simply adored the fact that she had picked Rosie from a field of better educated, equipped, beautiful lovers. (It was that *frisson* in the schoolyard when you are playing Farmer in the Dell and the farmer picks you first, that heady mix of fear and anticipation that everything worth having possesses.)

Madge and Rosie share the water, an even temperament, an appreciation of foreign films and easy music, a taste for frozen tropical drinks and Cuban beans and rice. And in bed, well, they like the same things, too.

"Did you remember the rubber hosing?" asks Rosie, swinging into their driveway. They are trying to arrange a better outdoor watering system and give some respite to the hibiscus, gardenias, poinsettias, all exotic things to Rosie, who doesn't know a maple from an elm. Madge had grown up in the midst of farmland, flowers, a mother's treasured vegetable garden, wild berries for the ice cream every Sunday, peaches for pies and preserves.

Even now, Rosie can safely identify only one bird, the male cardinal, the Illinois State Bird. She remembers how, in the third grade, Noonie was selected to draw the cardinal on the blackboard in the main hall. She can still see her sister standing on her toes, her long gold braid filling the hollow of her back, her forearms streaked with red chalk as she strained to reach the top of his red round head.

"Oh, you know what a turkey looks like," jokes Madge.

"Is that a bird?" Rosie asks politely.

(Would Noonie acknowledge the similarity of Gus's Kansas childhood and the Missouri childhood of Rosie's lover Madge? Is this mere coincidence or was it a means of seduction for these sidewalk-bred girls?)

"Call," says Madge, pushing Rosie toward the phone.

Rosie stares at her toenails; they need cutting. "No answer," she says triumphantly, hanging up.

"Call again later," says Madge, "or call Chicago."

Rosie picks the tip of the nail, yanks it. "Shit." It will be ingrown.

"You shouldn't pick at your toenails, Rosie." Madge sighs. "Let me see it."

Rosie lifts her foot gingerly, balances it on Madge's bent knee. "I don't want to talk to them," Rosie says. "It hurts."

Madge presses the toe. "Well, I think you can save it if you soak religiously." She goes off to get the gauze and tape, leaving Rosie holding her foot and staring at the telephone.

Elsa is lying in bed in her hospital room, remembering. It is a weekend Noonie is not coming, although she has already heard from her and Sarah, and from her sister, Tatiana, and her neighbors the Wolfsons, who said they'd pop in this afternoon. She is remembering how some summer mornings, years ago, after the fat kaiser rolls and the Sunday papers the girls went out early to get, they would load into the car and drive out to the country. It was her father's old car, a solid squat Chevrolet with the curves of ladies of that period after the war, when the first cars began to be manufactured again. There were seats woven from cane and a steering wheel of pale agate and a tiny window in the back like the porthole of an oceangoing ship. Rosie's and Noonie's faces could not both fit in this window and there were fights about this.

She drove. Otto had not officially left the car to her, he had simply left the car in a good parking spot in front of the building and died. Elsa was the most likely candidate. She remembers one of her suitors, Mr. Kleinert—that fool!—taught her after the shock of her father's death wore off. She remembers leaving Noonie and Rosie to play in a field of flowers while they circled the country roads nearby.

Now she was at the wheel and her mother was next to her in the front seat. In the back, forming a natural frontier between Noonie and Rosie, was the lunch: a large tin box with handles, containing deviled eggs, tart plum tomatoes, some kind of luncheon meat on thin crustless bread with a frilly lettuce slip, or, if they were really lucky, Mama had made her special chicken, flattened and fried in butter and wrapped in a huge dinner napkin, the ends tied up like a babushka. That chicken was the best thing to eat in the whole world; by the time you got to where you were going, it was exactly the right temperature. (Elsa makes this chicken to this day, when she is well, of course, although she has not been able to teach either of her daughters: Rosie simply can't cook and Noonie doesn't let it cook long enough—no patience.) She had to turn around several dozen times to remind the girls not to open the box!

They were on their way to the cemetery to visit Otto's grave, Otto, and the little brother Noah, born late in the marriage, unexpected, who died when they moved to the city. Elsa remembers the day he died, sick from diphtheria, whooping cough, some long-ago childhood disease, and her mother took to her bed. But what she remembers (she was fifteen) was how Otto, in tears, got into bed with her mother and how the sounds of lovemaking followed their sobs. (Her mother corroborated this many years later—how she loved her mother—but it is only now that Elsa understands the need for renewal, for life after such a death.)

The cemetery was country, it was out past all the buildings and the city as her children knew it. Maybe you had to spend your life walled up in crowded urban conditions, but when you died you got to live in the country.

They drove in through big stone gates, as at a massive estate, only with stars on the tops, and up a winding road and down a series of other roads. Even though they went several times a year (and considering nobody there moved), there was always a lot of discussion of where everybody was.

"No, Ma," she would have to say as soon as she turned in the gates, "that's where the Kauffmans are."

"No, I think they're in the Pansy section with Aunt Ida."

Most of the family was in the Rose section, although there were no roses in sight—maybe a few succulents and tiny American flags among the tall weeds. (Rosie collected the flags. Of course she had to put them back, and frequently extended military honors to old women and mere lads.)

"Ach, they said they'd put begonias on the graves," Mama would exclaim in dismay. "I told them pink begonias for Noah, white for Otto."

"Ma, you know the guy's a crook," Elsa always said with satisfaction, putting out her Chesterfield on the heel of her shoe.

(That was why you went, to make sure they planted the things you paid for: the annual fees. Noonie won't be able to do this. She'd better tell Gus, Elsa thinks.)

Elsa had brought plants anyway, a flat of marigolds purchased from a greenhouse located conveniently across the road, and a trowel. She clipped the tall grass around the headstones with a pair of big shears from the darkroom. She took care of nothing else green or living or planted in the earth except these graves, her one foray into farming. She did this not out of a great belief in the afterlife or the power of the Almighty but for her mother.

While she was gardening and Mama was wiping her eyes, Noonie and Rosie walked around looking at pictures on the headstones: those sepia oval images of immigrant faces: wide-eyed, wide-cheeked, with thick lips and fat ties, high tight collars or lace jabots. Were these death photographs or had the family selected a favorite snap of their loved one? (There was an album of death photographs Poppa had taken when he first came to this country, of the farmers and their families. Infants, too! So many dead children; Elsa was always fascinated how they were dressed and held as if they were alive, only their tiny eyes were closed.)

There was writing on the gravestones, the squat design

of Hebrew letters and distant dates and foreign places—you did a lot of arithmetic here. (Rosie liked to find someone exactly Noonie's age and then let out a big scream—which always caused Mama to shriek—falling on the grave and sobbing conspicuously.) There were tiny graves, like Noah's; he had lived two years and had a lamb carved under his picture. Noah stared out of pale watery eyes; he had ears like the handles of a sugar bowl, and his fair hair was cut straight across like a haystack.

Old men, stooped and bowed, thin from lack of regular eating, their prayer shawls handy, worn fedoras on their heads, traveled these paths, too, like peddlers. For a fee you could have a prayer, the Kaddish, the mourner's prayer, said over the grave, for those who were incapable of performing this function themselves (or unsuitable: women). They fingered the soiled fringe of their tallithim, the frayed soft pages of their prayer books; they swayed back and forth.

Even though Otto would have preferred a sprightlier number—the Andrews Sisters doing "Bei Mir Bist Du Schoen" had been a favorite—her mother gave the men something and let them perform.

Elsa always lit up during this and rolled her eyes at the end. It was not from lack of faith, but the strong sense of irony: in this life, Otto and God had not been a winning combination.

Back in the car, and on the way out, not far, just past the gates, there was a flat truck and a grinning black man in a cap, barefoot, selling watermelons from huge blocks of ice. There was a sign with a price, but some haggling went on. Elsa remembers he always plugged one for her.

"He won't do it for everyone," she liked to inform her girls, the sharp red flesh on her teeth.

It went into the back seat, under Noonie's feet, and

then they drove a little farther on to a picnic spot and they cut wide slices of it for dessert, and their mouths were full of cold summer sweetness and smooth black seeds.

"You'll grow a watermelon in your tummy!" Elsa remembers she used to warn Rosie, who swallowed them by the handful. In a strange way Elsa really believed that it might be true.

Rosie! Elsa thinks, something sharp stabbing in her chest; it hurts to think of her. Damn her! She wants to spit, doubling up with pain in her side, but she doesn't call the nurse.

How could she have let it happen, how could she anticipate? It was like a descent, the steepness of which you don't know until it is too late, the steepness and the length of the fall, how far to the bottom of it. That damned woman, that coach: Marie Marks. Elsa remembers she telephoned one morning, all friendly, wanted to talk to her, wanted her to come to the Y for a little chat. Rosie was sixteen at the time, she had been swimming with Marie for a long time. Certainly Elsa knew her name, Marie, a part of Rosie's own name, she thinks with regret, thought each time she heard Rosie say: "Marie says this . . . Marie says that . . ." Before Marie, Elsa had no rival.

Elsa remembers the warmth, coming in from a wet winter day, snowflakes the size of quarters, her face flushed red from the sudden heat, in the short Persian lamb that had been her mother's. (This was not long after the death of Mama, she remembers.) This woman, Marie, was padding around in rubber slippers, a pair of gym shorts, a man's skivvy shirt pulled taut across her flat chest, a whistle dangling between what should have been breasts, just two tiny nipples, her graying-blond hair feathered (my God!

She can describe this woman to this day!), a kind of swimming Doris Day: bouncy, friendly, but sinewy, not soft, in a day when few women aspired to look like that.

Marie found a folding chair for Elsa, pushed it into the doorway of her tiny office and started to talk about potential. Rosie had real potential. She wanted to push her out, it was time; she thought the Channel first. Here was the good news: she had found financing for this, a company was willing to sponsor Rosie, but there was the problem: Rosie was underage and she needed Elsa's permission. Here, she extended a soggy sheaf of papers, a fountain pen.

All this time Elsa sat, a pool of sweat collecting behind her knees where she crossed them in her stockings. She felt suffocated in her furs; her hat had a veil and a long feather that threatened to jab Marie Marks in her eye.

There was this cloud of moist heat that enveloped her, made her think of the Turkish baths her mother was partial to, had taken her to years before. She had hated having to look at the other women's bodies, gone to fat and ripples, lumpy as the heavy white dough mounds for *spätzle*. Towels were wound around their tiny heads like wimples from a medieval illustration. Elsa would look away from them, with a modesty they didn't share: they laughed at her, made fun of her shyness, teased her. But it was something that frightened her, it was something that held no promise. She understood that her body, her lovely smooth firm body, would turn on her like this someday and she would become one of them.

(She had seen her daughters; Rosie's sleek muscled back and arms, Noonie's soft round curves, tiny waist. A woman lives on in her daughters, given half a chance, Elsa knew.)

All this time, Marie was talking, a farm flatness to her

voice, a monotony, not unpleasant, but difficult to focus on in the heat. Elsa wanted to pull Rosie out of the water, bring her back, but she signed, signed Rosie away.

Every mother has a favorite child, every mother knows this; not that she loves one more than the other, but only one is the direct descendant of her soul, her dreams. Noonie would always belong to the big world, but Rosie had been hers.

Rosie was the spitting image of Victor. It hurts to think of loving him, her hands shake to think of touching his chest, thick black hair like a carpet, so thick. Noonie could have been anyone's child; they said she looked like a fairer version of Tatiana. She had the kind of pink good looks handed out to thousands of American girls, but Rosie was the picture of the man Elsa lost. (Twice, lost.)

She tried to share, she thinks, she really tried. She went to practice, certain events, she smiled for the camera, she handed out a towel, but it hurt too much. Marie was always right there, in the front; her hug, her words. Sometimes it is more painful to have a part of something than not to have it at all. At least, that's what she had thought at the time.

11

SAYING GOODBYE

Gus goes to Chicago to visit his mother-in-law. He sits in Elsa's hospital room and holds her limp hand. He reads to her from the newspapers (today's horoscope: now is the time to solidify all plans). Like skating lovers, holding fast to waist and arm, they go up and down the bleak corridors. Gus does these things because when he isn't doing something, when he is just sitting on one of the hard, turquoise Naugahyde chairs, he feels like burying his face in his hands and weeping. He wants to weep for Elsa, for Noonie, for himself. He weeps because he knows he has let this woman down.

What can he say? There is only so much weather in the world. So he talks about himself, his classes, his projects; or he talks about Sarah, her classes and good grades and cello lessons, aware that she is the repository of affection and hope—she is the future—for all of them.

"You had better tie a red ribbon around your wrist," says Elsa gruffly. "That's what my mother might have said, with all these good things happening to Sarah, all these prizes."

"I beg your pardon?"

"To ward off the evil eye," she explains, waving her hand weakly. "Not my mother, she was an American, but further back, I'm sure. Pagans!" She almost spits. "Primitives, like those headhunters in New Guinea."

How interesting, Gus thinks, all the things I don't know about Elsa's people. He wonders if Noonie knows, but she's never shown much interest in them, either.

("The Chosen People?" Noonie had asked politely of his mother's pastor on her first visit to Kansas. "Chosen by whom?" But Gus means in Hungary, Poland. In the great hurry to assimilate, Noonie's family probably lost the only things that had been uniquely theirs.)

"One minute you look at them in the cradle, the next you're looking down at them in the grave," Elsa mumbles now.

Gus looks up quickly. Elsa has already turned her face to the other wall.

"What?" he asks softly, under his breath. He knows there is a dead brother, but he has never heard her talk about him before. He wonders if she is talking about Rosie.

But it is his baby she is talking about, their first child, dead almost fifteen years; Gus has to pull that number out because he doesn't think that way, doesn't want to think about the dead—that is Noonie's territory.

Of course he remembers, of course it is all there: the hysterical phone call from Noonie, the ambulance ride, the doctors, the funeral. Noonie refused to deal with anything, left it to Gus, Gus and this woman, who is dying in the flat bed here. That time it was Elsa who came to him and held his arm and made decisions he couldn't begin to make because of the dryness of his mouth: he could open it, but nothing would come out. Noonie wouldn't pick out the tiny white coffin or identify the body; Noonie lay on her back, in her bed, for days and days. It was Elsa and Rosie who rode in the undertaker's limousine with him, followed the body and watched as it was lowered into the ground, a thin rectangle barely three feet long, and Elsa who, on the eighth day, slapped Noonie on the face and said she had to eat.

(What could you say about someone six months old—that she had reddish fuzz and they loved her?)

"Emily?" he asks, louder, in case Elsa wants to say something else, elaborate. Let's just shout it out, he wants to say, get rid of some of the pain, but Gus is not a courageous man in the arena of human feelings, so he looks down. When he looks up again, Elsa is asleep.

Gus leaves Elsa and walks around the streets for a while. He feels lonely. Finally, he gets into a taxi and goes to her apartment. He has promised to pay bills for her—she is worried about the continuation of things: electricity, insurance. (There is a solidity to Elsa that he likes, admires. His own mother is a woman of the earth, too, both feet planted firmly on it, and he has grown up believing in the strength of women. Maybe that was the deep attraction: Noonie was a cream puff, a wisp, a snowflake. Her slender ankle in the soft sock and white gym shoe, lying on the pavement in Chicago, many years ago, was a sight he never let go of in all the years of their lives together. He fell in love with that weakness.)

Gus looks out the window of the cab. He doesn't know Chicago very well. He thinks about the summer he was here, the summer he met Noonie; he remembers how lonely he was then, too. He was living with his brother in a suburban development northwest of the city, split-level houses with wall-to-wall carpet and barbecue pits in the backyard and carports. Oh, how grand Gus thought it was, how pleasant he found Thomas's life. He wished it to be his own as quickly as possible (he was one year away from graduation, from an M.B.A. program or a corporation recruitment), and he would have had exactly that life if it hadn't been for Noonie. It was Noonie who believed he could be a writer, when she was the one with the talent and the desire, the classic projection left open to women of that peculiar day and age, and when that didn't work out it was Noonie who said he should be a teacher, lead a life of high purpose; Noonie who wanted to travel and experience things.

Well, it hadn't mattered: his life has ended up approximately like his brother's, anyway. Bathrooms, cars, vacations; it was just the numbers of these things. Few American lives held the uniqueness, the beauty, the imagination that Noonie could almost taste but had been unable to describe adequately or pursue. A life of such original proportion had never been his desire really, but he couldn't confess it at the time.

Gus had slept on a pull-out bed in the rec room; the bed was frequently stuffed with plastic guns and toy trucks, and his nephews would awaken him early every morning to watch Captain Kangaroo on TV. He remembers wrestling with them on the floral sheets, their small round heads and fierce limbs. He was in love with his sister-in-law, Beth, her long bowed legs and heavy breasts, her freckled bare arms and the sweet pads of flesh peeking from her summer shorts.

Gus opens the door to Elsa's apartment. He has never

been here alone before. Noonie is right, it does smell of coffee, like certain European cities. It is easy to find things—they are in order with notes slipped under the broad elastics. Elsa has prepared for her own death; he should tell Noonie. (Would this give her comfort?) There is a slender leather photo folder in the checkbook; he wonders if Elsa left it for him. It is a picture of Noonie and Rosie he doesn't remember seeing before: Noonie and Rosie on a large carousel horse. Noonie sits tall in the painted saddle, her feet splayed in the stirrups, with Rosie tucked in front of her, back to belly; Noonie's arms surround Rosie as her hands grope for the reins. They are laughing, two little girls at Kiddieland on a summer Sunday afternoon. (He misses Rosie.)

Maybe he was in love with both of them, the light sister and the dark sister, maybe he loves the mother, too, all of them, Aunt Tatiana and Elsa and Noonie and Rosie. Once he had gone along to the airport to pick up Tatiana and had walked behind them, carrying the aunt's conspicuous luggage. From the rear, the women in his wife's family had looked like a set of fine mares, their broad haunches covered with printed silk, their slender ankles and feet balanced on high shoes, their lovely heads turning slightly in profile, then lifting to the sky with a high whinny of laughter and delight.

He takes the folder with the picture of Noonie and Rosie on the plaster horse and slips it into the breast pocket of his coat.

Noonie holds Elsa's hand loosely; she isn't sure if she is awake or asleep. She has forgotten how smooth, satiny really, her mother's hands are, the last outpost of her vanity. (Noonie knows just where the large bottles of glycerin and rose water are, how Elsa smooths the lotion over her hands, caressing each finger; where the rubber gloves are hanging for printing photographs and washing up and the old white cotton gloves Elsa slept in once a week after smearing thick cold cream on her famous hands.)

How long has it been since she held her mother's hand, pulling on it, hoping to be free? How old was she before Elsa let her cross the street alone, and then she had stood on the other side shouting instructions like a football coach on the sidelines: "No! You didn't look the other way. Now!" she had called.

Elsa rolls her head on the pillow, opens her eyes suddenly. "Is it night, Noonie?"

"No, it's ten o'clock in the morning."

"Where have you been?"

"I've been here, Ma."

"You've been with a man," Elsa says, angrily. "Week after week, like the hide-and-go-seek. You never learn," she sighs before closing her eyes again. (This is the last thing she will say.)

Noonie sits in her mother's hospital room, imagining how she will die. She has envisaged heavily costumed scenes; Elsa is pretty dramatic under normal conditions. She waits for another pronouncement. (There is a lot of equipment, and in our accepting way we begin to believe this dying will go on forever, the way we previously thought living would; we take it for granted.)

People don't die that way, of course. Noonie went out of the room for a cup of coffee and Elsa died. She had been unconscious for three days.

Noonie dreams she is sorting out things—her mother's things. She is in her bedroom when Elsa enters, dressed for work: an old pair of serge trousers, rubber gloves dangling in one hand as the other is untying her smock, a smoking cigarette hanging out of the right side of her mouth. It is Elsa of twenty years ago.

"What are you doing here?" Noonie asks, amazed.

"Hm," says Elsa, not entirely pleased, squinting into the smoke. "I wanted to see what you were going to do with my things."

Noonie awakens a few hours after Elsa's death, still in the egg-shaped plastic chair, to find her sister standing in front of her, muscled and slim, in black jeans and a University of South Florida sweatshirt. Rosie is carrying a duffel bag and her nose is running. Noonie has been trying to get in touch with her since Elsa became comatose.

"She's dead," Noonie says coldly, forgetting Elsa is Rosie's mother, too.

Rosie sits down quietly next to Noonie, takes her hand. Noonie sees her nails are dirty and she is still wearing a silly beaded bracelet Sarah made her in day camp years ago.

"Did she say anything about me?"

Noonie snaps to attention, furious. She said you must behave! she wants to spit, but says instead, "Where have you been?"

Rosie pulls her fingers through her curls, yawns. "It takes a long time to get here. I took the bus. Anyway, I'm starved. Do you think we could get some breakfast?"

"You took the bus!" Noonie is shouting. "I don't believe you!"

"I don't have the kind of bucks you do, Noonie."

"I would have given you the money, or Gus or Aunt Tatiana, certainly."

"I like to do things my way, you know that."

"I'm surprised you didn't swim here."

Rosie grabs Noonie, wraps her arms around her, hugs her, so that Noonie sobs. Then Rosie starts to cry. "Did it matter?"

"I had to do this alone, dammit!" Noonie says, pushing her away.

"I mean, you weren't counting on my bringing her back to life, were you?"

Noonie raises her hand to slap Rosie across the face, Rosie grabs it. "You know, she's my mother, too, my mother just died, Noonie, okay. You still see the whole world as happening to Noonie."

"Mrs. Bentley . . ." A nurse tugs gently at Noonie's arm. "Can you tell us what to do with the body?" She coughs quietly. "I'm afraid we need the bed."

Noonie looks into the room, her mother's form is still there. In death, she seems to have regained her original size, the mound under the sheet seems full and robust; her face is covered, but Noonie expects her to shake off the covers and pull them back in the teasing way you play peekaboo with a baby. "It's me!" she'll shout. "Just joking!" she'll laugh.

Noonie remembers the first play she was taken to see—*Medea*—remembers her own widemouthed wonder when all the little children returned pink-cheeked and bowing for a curtain call. No such luck here.

"Yes, of course," she tells the nurse, hoarsely, "we'll make the arrangements."

Aunt Tatiana arrives at Elsa's apartment, crying and carrying several shopping bags: Blums-Vogue. "Here, darlings," she says, embracing Rosie and Noonie. "I brought you some things to wear, black things. I suspected you wouldn't have anything proper." She sighs, sizing up Rosie's jeans, Noonie's wrinkled dress.

(Later, Noonie and Rosie unpack the bag: several knee-length black crepe dresses with four-inch shoulder pads and pleated bodices under the long pointed pique collars, a collarless three-quarter-length black jacket with even larger shoulder pads, a quilted silk bolero jacket, piped and frogged, a velvet pancake hat with a wispy veil, a large crushed velvet saucer with bows. There are elbow-length gloves with box-stitched fingers and open-toe suede pumps with thick high heels and another pair with stiletto heels. There are even handkerchiefs with black borders.)

"I brought a little something to eat, too," Aunt Tatie says, as her son, Richard, unpacks a few dozen bagels, tosses onto the counter long flat packages of Scottish salmon, purple onions, avocados, tomatoes, cheese.

"We made a little stop before we came," says Richard, giving Noonie a small wet pursed kiss on the mouth, the family kiss.

"You must eat to keep up your strength," Aunt Tatie is saying.

Rosie is starved; Noonie nods, wonders if her mother was alive the last time she ate.

"Sorry, Noonie, I loved her, too, you know that," Richard says, a solemn man in his thirties in Harris tweed.

(Did Richie love his Aunt Elsa? Did he think about her for more than twenty minutes in the last twenty-five years? She was the only one who managed to discipline him, little male child. Once she locked him in his room for an hour while he screamed and kicked the door. The only male grandchild—dimpled, pudgy, angry Richie. Tatiana had almost died in childbirth, that was true, but the story had acquired such mythic proportions that it made Athena's birth seem pedestrian, or, as Rosie used to ask on Christmas, "Isn't this Richie's birthday?" Little Richie Rich, they had called him when they visited in California, rooms full of toys: electric trains, stuffed bears on wheels, the Erector Set Ferris wheel delivered and set up on the twenty-fourth. Sent off to Swiss schools and California universities, he had acquired a law degree, a pipe, and did something in the movies.)

Noonie knocks on the door to Elsa's bedroom. Rosie has been in there a long time, and she giggles slightly and adjusts the veil as Noonie opens the door; she is painting a small black mole next to the corner of her mouth.

Noonie stops in amazement: her sister's image in the vanity mirror, Elsa's lipsticked mouth and magic mole. She can see her mother on this worn backless tufted seat before the triptych of mirrors complete with a necklace of lightbulbs. How many times did they watch Elsa make herself up for a date, drawing that mole, rouging her large tough nipples before harnessing herself into one of the lacy steel brassieres Noonie aspired to fill.

"Rosie, you can't . . ."

"What?" Rosie raises her thick brows.

"Gus and Sarah are here," she says, and closes the door.

Just as they are about to get into the limousine to go to the cemetery, Aunt Tatiana licks the palms of both her hands and slaps them vigorously up and down Noonie's back, a mother animal cleaning her young. "Hold still," she admonishes as Noonie wiggles, "there's lint all over your dress. And you—Rosemarie—wash your face. This isn't a circus!" She wipes a tear. "Thank God, Baby didn't have to live to see this terrible day."

Elsa is buried next to her parents and her tiny brother, Noah, the four spaces in the cemetery not quite contiguous but arranged head to foot, like acrobats in a balancing act. They take up all the spaces, too, there will not be room for Noonie and Rosie, they will have to make other arrangements, real estate not being a high priority for either of them. Noonie remembers the Sunday trips to this cemetery, now swallowed in urban sprawl, wall-to-wall mall. She wonders if Elsa had been here recently, if she would be disappointed.

Noonie glances at Gus. He is being supportive: he seems truly shaken, solemn. He sits on one side of Sarah, whose hand Noonie is holding. Rosie is sitting next to Gus. The others rise for the Kaddish, surely the saddest sound anywhere, a male chorus of sadness, though there are not many: a few hired hands, the rabbi, Richard humming. Noonie wonders if Gus feels left out. There is a mysticism to this that he is unable to understand, something ancient and musty that is completely foreign to his white-bread handsomeness, his wholesomeness; his blondness shines, Sarah's too, with her straight long legs, her pale straw hair parted on one side.

(Noonie's blondness is an old gold hue—"Goldilocks," Poppa called her—gold mixed with pink, an old-world gold, the color of Grandma's brass candlesticks. If she could have them, she thinks now, tears crowding into her eyes, she would light them every Friday night, she swears. She wouldn't say anything, of course—what could she say, she didn't know what to say, but she would light them and let them burn down, and faithfully light them again, she promises. A little late to make deals with God.)

"Are you okay?" she whispers to her daughter.

"Are you?" Sarah snaps.

"Of course." She smiles and squeezes her hand, the kind of gesture children recognize immediately as dishonest, so Sarah takes her hand back and folds it into her lap, leaves her head on Gus's shoulder.

Noonie thinks she has spotted everyone she knows: Mr. Kleinert has passed on, but Mr. Horowitz, dreadfully thin and snaggletoothed, is here, and Elsa's attorney (a more recent admirer); Chick O'Connors has sent an obscene wreath balanced on a black easel. How neatly the phases of life are assembled at an event like this. Of course it's a complete waste because Elsa isn't here. Noonie clutches Aunt Tatie's arm.

"Yes, darling," Tatiana says, "hold on to me."

Back at the apartment, Noonie can eat nothing.

"Eat! Eat!" admonishes the rabbi, pastrami sticking from both sides of his wide mouth as he passes, interrupting a discussion of the virtues of buying condominiums in Tel Aviv. "You know, Natalie," he begins sonorously (they had met this morning after Richard hunted him down in the yellow pages), "in the Jewish religion, it is called for the mourners to eat."

"Where?" she snaps.

He seems confused. "Where what?"

"Where is it 'called for'?" she says cruelly, in just the way Elsa imitated Noonie's teachers.

"Why, mmmm . . ." he continues, unabashed. "And it is a custom to serve eggs at the meal following the interment, for the egg symbolizes the continuation of life." He hands Noonie a hard-boiled egg, peeled. "Excellent chopped liver," he concludes.

"Thank you," she says, handing back the egg. "Katz's catering service."

Who is this man, this stranger, telling her to eat, talking

about her mother this morning? In the service, he mispronounced her name ("Ilse," he called her, as if she were a German film star), included Richard among her children. Rosie laughed out loud, but Noonie is unforgiving. Who are all these people, eating sandwiches and drinking coffee and schnapps, kissing Noonie on the mouth with their papery dry lips, their sour breath in her ear, smiling at her sadly as if she is a little child? She wants her mother back! And where has Rosie disappeared to?

Noonie runs to the bathroom, locks the door, presses her head into the black-and-white ceramic tiles. Where the hell is Rosie again?

The first child gets the best a family has to offer, was Elsa's belief—it was a way of excusing Rosie's bothering Noonie—so maybe she gets the worst, too, thinks Noonie.

Where is Rosie? Noonie again feels disappointed, let down. Rosie can't be serious; her failure to escape the dangerous eccentricities of their family is a constant reminder to Noonie of past errors and pain. Noonie has tried so hard to be conventional, respectable, normal, to make a family in the style of her childhood readers.

She suddenly remembers once when she volunteered to have some Girl Scouts from another troop stay with them, a troop from a fine North Shore suburb. She had met them at the meeting downtown and they had come home together. She recalls how their faces began to change as they left the El station and walked into the building where her mother's studio commanded the bottom floor and Noonie started, naturally, up the stairs.

"Where are we going?" one of them asked, confused.

"To my house, I live up there."

"You live up here?" she asked, and began to roll her eyes at the other girl.

And Noonie was able to see for the first time how strange

it was to live upstairs from your mother's work (to have a mother who worked!). For the first time, she smelled the soiled chenille runner up the stairs and the odor of strange food clinging to the dark flowered wallpaper; she saw the small square rooms, the economies of their fatherless lives. The girls were polite, but they might as well have been plopped down in an African village or a dude ranch—that's how far the distance between their lives and Noonie's was. Elsa liked to pretend they were like everybody else: Scouts, good winter coats and party shoes (paid for by Aunt Tatiana), tickets to the ballet. But those girls weren't fooled for a minute.

"Where's Sarah?" Noonie asks, coming into the kitchen. Gus is there, with Mrs. Wolfson from next door, washing up, his sleeves rolled, a flowered apron of Elsa's tied around his waist. (Oh, how Noonie loves him from the back, she wishes to put her arms around his waist, squeeze the silly bow, touch his broad planed back.)

They both turn around, look at Noonie with sympathy.

"She went for a walk with Rosie; just before the rabbi left, they cut out," says Gus. "Rosie said she was going to take her to see your old school."

Noonie walks to school, the six blocks she walked four times a day (they came home for lunch) for eight years, past the tidy square lawns and chain fences, past trees whose leaves and bark she had collected each fall for the assigned Tree Books, through an alley to avoid a famous growling dog, certainly dead by now. She had forgotten there would be only gravel in the schoolyard (all those scraped knees!), none of the bright jungle gyms and hanging tires of Sarah's experience, but the mottled high slide still stands in one faraway corner and next to it the swings with their lethal wooden seats. Near the swings, Noonie sees her sister and her daughter on a seesaw, each clinging to a handlebar, the seats pressed tightly between their thighs; their heads are thrown back as they go up and down, back and forth, and they are talking, at least Rosie is, but Noonie cannot hear a word they are saying.

"I wanted to talk to you before you leave," Gus says to Rosie later that day.

"Okay," says Rosie. "Wait, I'm supposed to be really pissed with you. I mean, I am really pissed with you. I'm not going to be very sympathetic, Gus," she says, sitting across from him in a booth at Katz's. "Noonie really smarts, I can tell that just by looking."

"How's Madge?"

"She's fine, nice of you to ask."

"Well," says Gus, looking down at the place mat, "I do know about her, about the two of you . . ."

"So does Noonie, but she can't ask how she is. You know," Rosie says, her voice straining, "I used to think it wouldn't matter if my mother was dead, I had so little to do with her, I lived so far away. I know she went around for years telling people I was dead."

Gus looks away, he had heard Elsa do that; why hadn't he stopped her? But he felt her pain, too. "I'm sorry. I can't believe she's gone, either."

"The cheesecake's pretty good," Rosie says, "or it used to be."

"I'll have carrot cake," Gus tells the waitress, "and a cup of coffee."

"Tea," says Rosie, "and a piece of cheesecake. Is it sex, Gus? Is that it?"

Gus looks away from Rosie, out the long plate-glass window at the street (it is the intersection where Noonie caught the bus to high school, but he doesn't know that). There is a place like this near his school, where Gus likes to go and sit at the counter and eat a piece of carrot cake before going home sometimes. The stools are filled with construction workers and computer programmers and accountants and it possesses a friendly anonymity he assumes men must need more than women because both Noonie then and Pigeon now just knock the weak coffee and sugary cakes. Gus can't explain the need for a public life for a man, a life of clubs or cafés or coffee shops or saloons. He looks at Rosie across the counter, so small and slender except for her shoulders and arms.

"Well, sure it's sex, it's always sex, isn't it?"

Rosie stiffens slightly. "Is she very pretty?"

"No one's prettier than Noonie," he says brusquely, realizing he doesn't wish to discuss sex with his wife's sister, after all. He is curious, but not really (Gus doesn't really want to know!), and he would never be able to explain to her or anyone how he felt the first time he saw Noonie undressed or the first time he made love to her or how he would come in while she was taking a bath just so he could watch her in the pink steaminess. Noonie will always possess a kind of female perfection for him, but that isn't it, either. "Noonie's still waiting for her prince on his white charger," he says defensively.

"But you're the prince, Gus. Oh, how she fell for you, she couldn't see straight, I remember. Her hands shook so much on her wedding day, she almost dropped a lipstick down her dress."

He shakes his head, irritated. "Noonie as the heroine of some silly novel."

"Thomas Hardy," says Rosie.

"Yes, Hardy," he says, "and I'm not up to playing the

hero." (He doesn't confide in Rosie, although he suspects she might understand what it is like to make love to someone who views it as natural and uncomplicated as a good jog around the block.)

"Well," Rosie says, smiling, "I did warn you how she lives through books."

Gus reaches across the table and squeezes her hand. "I miss you," he declares. "I don't know what happened between you two. We used to see you a lot. Remember the summer you worked at Johnson & Johnson?" (Rosie had worked as a Band-Aid tester down the highway from where Noonie and Gus lived. The scientists plastered bandages all over her body and all day she dived in and out of a sickly green tank to test the sticky stuff.) "And after Sarah was born?"

Rosie thought she would come and give Noonie a hand. ("Big help," Noonie liked to say. Gus and Rosie would stay up all hours playing blackjack and poker and drink Rolling Rock out of tall slim bottles.)

"Remember how we would sit Sarah up and put some cards in her fist, so she looked as if she was playing?" Rosie asks.

"I have pictures of that," Gus laughs. Noonie was such a wreck, walking around with her long hair flying, in a thin blue nightgown all day and night. Rosie was comic relief.

"I think what happened," Rosie says seriously, "is Sarah got bigger and maybe Noonie decided I wasn't the best influence to have around, you know . . ." She pulls at the tag on her tea bag. "I remember when Uncle Baby and Roland used to come, two skinny affectionate men, and I'd watch my mother and Aunt Tatie and Grandma all skip around the issue. A grown man traveling with his buddy, come off it. Noonie and I didn't know what it was, we couldn't have given it a name, but we were happy to accept them as they were. They were so good to us and to each other and it showed, so maybe I wasn't afraid when the time came and I knew it and it didn't seem strange to me. Anyway, men were strange. I'd never lived with any of them. You're the only man I've ever really known, you're the man I've been closest to. Even my coaches turned out to be women." Rosie is twisting the tops off dozens of sugar packets (state birds) that now lie scattered on the table. The waitress eyes them disapprovingly, swipes at them with a sponge before slapping the check on the wet top.

"I'd like to know Sarah, Gus. I don't have any kids and I don't suppose I will." She laughs in a funny bark. "And, in a way, she's my only family."

Rosie is speaking softly, and Gus feels very close to her. He reaches out and takes her hand again, covers it with his; hers is a small tight fist.

"Once I went to stay with the uncles—that's what we called them—in California. Noonie had gone off with Mother and Aunt Tatie to a fat farm or something in the desert, and I stayed with them alone. I had a little cot in the hallway, and I remember when we went to the grocery store they pushed separate carts. I always remember that. I don't know if it was for the sake of appearances or if they kept separate accounts, but it was funny. Of course, I thought it was because they each liked to push a cart. I liked to push a cart, but Noonie never let me. Maybe that was it, maybe they had decided when they grew up they could push a cart. But what I really remember is how close they were. They were like brothers—they always went shopping together, and they died within weeks of each other, Uncle Baby first, then Roland, of a heart attack, you know, the way you hear about great lovers, devoted couples. Isn't there a name for that? Maybe in Japan?"

"I don't know." Gus sighs, bouncing the coins in his pocket, looking for a tip.

"I always wondered how my mother could deal with that, her brother, you know, still love him and she couldn't stand it in me. I guess"—she smiles sadly—"it's because he was a man. Men got away with murder in our house."

12

THE COMFORT OF WOMEN

Noonie knows she should go through her mother's things but she cannot. She had just locked the door to the building in Chicago and fled. But everything reminds her of Elsa, she cannot escape that; she finds herself thinking and sounding a great deal like her. She has started using her expressions—"Ach!" and "Ho ho!" are the main ones—and she does a great deal more eyeball rolling than previously. Maybe it is a simple indiscretion of middle age, sounding like one's parent, but when the parent is dead and was mysterious, you feel as if you may have become the repository of her soul. So every now and then Noonie finds herself saying something (usually in the interrogative), and slaps her forehead—another Elsa-ism—and sighs to anyone who is around: "Now, did I say that?"

She spends more and more time with the handful of friends who had met Elsa. "Did you ever meet my mother?" she finds herself asking Tommy more than once. And she looks for excuses to call Gus so she can talk about her.

"I feel as if she's perched on my shoulders and whispering in my ear," says Noonie as they wait for the curtain to rise at Sarah's eighth-grade musical. "Wouldn't she have loved to be here?"

"Hmm," says Gus, an expression of sympathy. He reads aloud, " 'Golde, his wife, played by Sarah Bentley.' "

"Do you remember how we met?"

"Of course," Gus sighs. "Elsa was reading my driver's license and I thought she was telling my fortune brilliantly."

"She always said, 'For all his sins, Gus is a believer.' "

"Nice," Gus agrees, although he doesn't think for a minute Elsa said that.

"Where did you get that awful shirt?" Noonie asks, suddenly noticing Gus is wearing a pink spandex ski shirt with yellow wildflowers, the kind of thing he never wears.

"Shhh," says Gus as the curtain rises. "Elsa sent it to me for my last birthday."

(It is Rosie she should call, Rosie who shares her sadness, memories, and probably has the same need to talk, but the habits of the past are difficult to overcome. Maybe Noonie is just being loyal to her mother by not calling Rosie. It is a powerful part of her legacy, this misunderstanding about Rosie.)

Going through the winter things, Noonie finds a voluminous down coat she bought several years ago but rarely wore. She felt like a mattress in it, an unmade bed bouncing up and down the street. She always thought of her grandmother's traveling eiderdowns or of Japanese prints of prostitutes carrying their skinny futons on their backs. She remembers when Elsa first saw this coat. She rolled her eyes, rubbed a slender pinch of slippery cloth between her fingers and thumb, and sighed, "Have the geese stopped flying south for the winter?"

Noonie is not really a believer in warmth without weight,

either. She is always following Sarah around with a sweater or a pair of mittens, so she doubts she will survive with just some memories of Elsa, without her fleshiness, her frequent phone calls and admonishments.

Noonie is waiting for Sarah to wake up so they can go shopping for a Halloween party Sarah is going to that night. Sarah has been talking about her costume for weeks. (Noonie wishes she would spend one-tenth the energy on her time-line of the Middle East or the *passé composé* of *être,* but she knows enough not to say that.) Sarah has been deeply distracted since they came back from the funeral in Chicago. Her studious pose is changing, she seems angry, something Noonie would simply put on adolescence—those shimmering hormones—but she guesses it has to do with Elsa's death and seeing Rosie and the fact that it is almost a year since Gus left. Sarah has to believe in it now. She spends more time with Pigeon. So Noonie is glad to be included in Sarah's plans today.

(Sarah is including her mother because she needs entrée to her wardrobe and access to her pocketbook. Once she has a driver's license and a money card, she will no longer need Noonie for anything.)

After rejecting going as a Hawaiian (a sarong, plastic leis, and flip-flops), Sarah has decided to be a French spy. She will borrow Noonie's trenchcoat, tall black boots, a slinky dress, fishnet stockings, and sunglasses. She refuses the loan of a small purple hat a man at a dinner party told Noonie reminded him of the costumes of women in porn films, an entirely fatuous remark; Noonie thought it made her look like an organ grinder's monkey and never wore it again. She appears to have misplaced her cigarette holder over the years.

"I love Halloween," says Noonie dreamily, licking an

ice cream in front of Thomas Sweet. "One year I went as a bride. Then I was Betty Hutton in *The Greatest Show on Earth*. Elsa sewed two long white scarfs for a cape, and I wore a leotard and lipstick. In the third grade I went as . . ."

"Little Bo-peep," yawns Sarah.

"Have I told you this before?" Noonie asks sincerely. "What blend-ins did you get?"

"What did Aunt Rosie go as?"

"I don't remember. Can I try?"

Sarah sighs, extends her dripping cone. "Reese's Pieces and Oreos. Why don't we see her?"

"Not bad," says Noonie.

"I think she's neat." Sarah takes a breath. "She told me you think she's infectious."

"Is that what she was telling you in Chicago?" Noonie asks through pursed lips.

(Noonie doesn't think this because she hasn't had this experience before, but seeing Sarah and her sister laughing on the seesaw is the kind of experience Rosie had over and over with Noonie and someone Noonie picked to be her friend, her companion: on the seesaw at school, at the movies, in their room with the door locked and the sounds of giggling behind it.)

Sarah doesn't answer, tosses her napkin away. "Can Brett spend the night?"

"Aren't you going to Daddy's?"

"He told you," Sarah says accusingly, defending him, as always. "He told you he was going to Kansas. He's helping Gramma Anna move."

"Oh." He did tell Noonie and this made her feel sad, another broken tie. She hadn't paid that much attention to her mother-in-law over the years, but Elsa's death has made her aware of the value of mothers.

"I'm supposed to have dinner at Lola's," she says.

"Oh, you have a date," Sarah says, mockingly.

"No, I'm just going to Lola's, Sarah. I'm sure I can pick you up at the party."

"Won't one of those creeps want to drive you home and come in for coffee?"

"That happened once."

"At least he was the right age."

"What does that mean?"

"Oh, you know what I mean," Sarah says, rolling her eyes. "I want to go home now."

Noonie has never discussed Tommy with Sarah; she sees him during the day. Once he came to dinner with them, but he was doing some repairs for her and it was time for dinner. Noonie thought Sarah had had a good time; Tommy gave her some of the Mexican beer he had brought and taught her to say "I am a grandmother" in Spanish.

"Oh, it's all right," Sarah says sarcastically. "Brett's mom can give us a ride. But can she spend the night?"

"You know I don't want anyone there when I'm not going to be home."

"Come on."

"No, Sarah."

"Get real, Mom," she says angrily, stamping her foot. "I'm late anyway."

"I'll be right down," Noonie says to Cliff, the man who drove her home from Lola's. "I want to make sure my daughter got back from her party."

She takes his coat and puts it over a bench in the hall. "Fix yourself a drink. The liquor's on a tray in the pantry."

Noonie runs upstairs; she hopes Sarah is asleep. She actually likes this man, she realizes—she feels happy. He is quiet, somewhat shy, and maybe she'd like to see him again. He has recently moved here with a ten-year-old son with learning problems and Noonie has just done a series on special schools. She opens the door to Sarah's room quietly. No one is there. She runs across the hall to her own, where she finds her daughter sprawled across her bed, snoring loudly. When Gus left, Sarah had started sleeping in Noonie's bed with her, which she knew wasn't a good idea, but she had been so lonely. But she hasn't done it for a long time. Noonie notices the bathroom light is on and that a lot of her clothes are lying around, but she doesn't want to take any more time. She closes her door.

"Did you find what you needed?" she asks Cliff.

"The gin seems to be empty. Do you have another bottle?"

"Yes, of course. I thought there was half a bottle. There's some wine in the refrigerator," she says, going into the kitchen, but she finds that is gone, too. "That's funny, I must have forgotten. Here's the tonic," she says.

"Thank you."

Noonie makes herself a drink, slices lime. They carry the drinks back into the living room.

"So, do you think I should change his school?" Cliff asks seriously. "We just moved here, he just started a new school."

"Mommy?" Sarah is leaning over the banister.

"Sarah. We're in here. This is Mr. Martin, this is my daughter . . ."

"Hello," Sarah hiccups. "Mommy, I feel so . . ." she begins, and runs away. Noonie hears the door to the bathroom slam.

"I'm sorry," Noonie says, "I'll be right back."

She runs up the stairs again. She finds Sarah holding onto the sink with one hand. Her face is very pale, under a lot of makeup, and her voice is low and wobbly. "Oh, Mommy, I feel so sick," she says.

"Do you feel like throwing up?"

"I did. Before."

"You never throw up," says Noonie. "What did you eat at the party?"

"Pizza. Pizza and potato chips and Chee-tos and Cokes. Lots and lots of Cokes."

"Do you want an Alka-Seltzer?"

"Will it make me feel better?"

"I think so," says Noonie.

"Okay."

Noonie runs back downstairs. "Look," she says to Cliff, "can I get you another drink or something?"

"Maybe I should go . . ."

"No, no, just a little upset stomach, I'll be right back. Please."

Noonie, going into the kitchen for the Alka-Seltzer and a tall glass, suddenly spots the empty gin bottle balanced on the side of the tray, runs quickly up the stairs.

"Sarah, what else did you drink at the party?"

"I told you," she slurs, "lots and lots of Cokes." She takes the Alka-Seltzer and drinks it down, making a terrible face. "Yick."

"Sarah," Noonie says, "I want you to tell me the truth." She grabs her by the shoulders. "What else did you drink?"

"Nothing," Sarah says, handing Noonie the glass. "I want to go to bed. I'm sleepy."

"You can't," Noonie says, blocking the doorway. "I want you to tell me the truth. Were you drinking at that party?"

"Oh, yes," says Sarah, crying suddenly. "Oh, Mommy, I feel so awful."

"Did you bring the gin?"

"Mmm. Wine, too."

Noonie sits down on the edge of the bathtub. "What did you drink?"

"Well, first," says Sarah seriously, relieved, chatty, now that the truth is out, "we tried some wine. But we didn't like the taste, so we poured a few gin-and-Cokes."

"Gin and Coke?"

"Uh-huh, it tastes just like Coke," Sarah confides. "You can't even taste the gin."

"How many of these gin-and-Cokes did you drink?"

"Oh, two or three . . ."

"Oh, Sarah," says Noonie.

"Oh, Mommy, I was so sick," she says. "I tried to clean up. I didn't want to bother you and . . . that man."

Noonie takes Sarah's hand, leads her back to the big bed, tucks her down comforter around her, brushes back her damp bangs, turns off the light.

"Oh, Mommy," says Sarah in a tiny voice Noonie has not heard for a long time, since sarcasm took up permanent residence, her eyelids gliding upward for one minute. "Oh, Mommy, will you ever forgive me?"

"I forgive you right now," says Noonie, her voice cracking. She is not certain it is the right response, but it is the only one she can give. "Go to sleep, Sarah."

"Natalie," says Cliff, who is standing in the hall with his coat over one arm. "I think I should go."

"I'm sorry," says Noonie, leaning over the balcony. "Thanks for the ride."

"Thanks for the drink. I can find my way out," he says, and does.

Well, that's the last of him, she thinks; Noonie feels incredibly alone. She wonders if she should try to find Gus in Kansas or call Sarah's pediatrician, or call Dr. Schnabel, dismissed several months ago, but theoretically available. (Of course, the person she would like to call is Elsa, who is definitely unavailable.) She knows by the time she starts telling this story—to Gus, to Lola, to her boss at the newspaper, probably puts it in a column—it will become funny, an amusing tale of adolescent experimentation that any of them can counter, and Noonie wants to take it seriously for at least a while. Something is wrong, her child is unhappy. And so is she.

Noonie goes into her bedroom, sits at the edge of her bed, pushes Sarah's arm. "Sarah. Sarah, are you all right?" She puts her hand in front of Sarah's nose to feel her breath, the way she used to when she was a baby, when she was so afraid she would stop breathing. She pushes her arm again, takes her little hand and waves it gently. How soft and firm her skin still is, her little nails . . . oh God! Sarah, in a drunken moment, has polished her fingernails bright red. Noonie laughs out loud, rests her head on Sarah's thigh. "Sarah?"

"Let me sleep, Mommy," Sarah murmurs.

"Sarah, are you okay?"

"I'm okay," she sighs, and rolls over.

Very gently, Noonie pushes her toward the far end of the bed and gets in next to her.

Gus is in Kansas. His mother has announced (suddenly, it seems to him) that she is selling the house and moving to a retirement home run by the Lutheran Church on the outskirts of town, near the shopping mall—Happy Groves.

Of course it is not sudden. Anna has been contemplating it for several years; a number of her friends have moved there. She is in her early seventies and you must pass an examination, mental and physical, to be admitted. They don't want anyone too sick or crazy, she tells Gus.

She passed with flying colors, she announces, and tells him with a great deal of amusement about the psychological testing: Rorschach inkblots and colored pictures and unfinished sentences. She tells him with delight about the psychiatrist, a young man with a goat's beard who picked at a sore on his wrist. He was a collector of antique colored glass—vases, lamps, hanging things—and asked many questions about the valuables she might be selling.

Gus is vaguely horrified by this, thinks of notifying the authorities, but his mother seems pleased with the story; she assumed these headshrinkers (a term he can't imagine her knowing) were like this and she is pleased when things run true to form.

On the other hand, she seems confused about his situation with Noonie; she wonders why he hasn't brought Sarah. Her favorite grandchild, she says without blushing. Oh, but don't tell your brother, she laughs naughtily.

Brothers, Gus thinks, closing the door on the room he shared with Thomas, sharers of a womb, sharers of a deep secret, so to speak, two boys who grew up cheek to cheek, without much to say to each other. (In reality, there are six years between them.) What was the point?

How spare everything is, and worn, with years of touch and care, plain and stark. He slides his hands over pieces of furniture, door mantels, window frames. He loves houses, he thinks, the courage of houses. Noonie is always tossing off names: Le Corbu, Biedermeier, Thonet. Pigeon loves coordinated colors: pink and green towels and rugs in her little bathroom. Fine. Gus cares about the way the planks are joined in his old floorboards—he can't believe

Noonie bleached them!—he admires the heft of the doors, the thickness of the walls, the way canvas was stretched under the ceilings before they were plastered. He will always think of that house as his. He misses it as he would a child; he aches with that loss. I learned about the value of that here, he thinks.

At the home, Gus is astounded by so many old familiar people, teachers, shopkeepers, the men from the Grange. Some of them call him Thomas.

"This is my second boy, Angus," Anna says, "the younger son, a teacher of English. Yes, Sarah's father."

Some of the old ladies reach out to touch Gus's sleeve as he passes in and out of the lobby with cartons, as if his tweed coat were a magic coat. A few stroke his face, not just the partially seeing. (Forty is kid stuff here.)

"Elsa's dead," Anna says in the car.

"Yes," Gus says gently. "She died a month ago."

"Too bad. I didn't like that woman particularly—flamboyant for my taste—but I don't like to see her dead, either."

Anna ties on her head scarf (strangely, it's an Hermès, a duty-free gift picked up at the last minute by Thomas, who does all of his shopping in airports). She sits very straight next to Gus in the front seat. He remembers when their roles were reversed and he sat tall, as she called it, beside her in their old Ford, his father's beloved Betsy, the only car they ever owned while Gus lived in that house. He is driving the maroon Honda that Thomas bought for her. (Thomas drives a Mercedes but buys his loved ones Japanese cars.)

They park at McDonald's, her choice; she likes it, she says shyly, recognizes the irony, even the absurdity that she might have done better. There are a few good "continental" restaurants around here, she admits, but Anna has become like a child who insists on the same peanut-butter-and-jelly sandwich for years and years.

Just yesterday morning, on his way into town, the windows of this McDonald's were strewn with grinning jack-o'-lanterns, the countergirls wore conical witches' hats; today, pilgrims and Indians decorate the aisles and there are plastic turkeys pinned to the shiny poly uniforms of the help.

Everyone in this country, Gus thinks, carrying the tray to the table his mother picked, is in such a hurry to obliterate the past, yesterdays, check off the days, jog from event to event, holiday to holiday. Gus imagines a huge national repository, a Pentagon, of Christmas trees, Easter bunnies, American flags, a jumble sale of symbols, all plastic, paper, disposable, and instantly replaceable.

Gus watches his mother bite into her apple turnover with her new porcelain teeth, remembers her pies: apple, berry, peach, rhubarb; remembers the broad brim of her straw hat, the soft dented buckets as they crept through the bushes. He remembers the bright stains of ripe fruit on his open palms, the dough being rolled and cut out on the wooden table, the fancy raised crimping along the edges, a dough cutout of the fruit inside wedded to the top crust by the glaze of a beaten egg.

Mother, he wants to cry, can't you tell the difference anymore? How can you eat this imitation of something you produced as if it were made of your flesh? His mother's hands rolling the dough, her wedding band so thin that one day it split and stuck in the crust. (Like an English pudding in a Christmas book of Dickens, she told him, laughing.) In a life as plain as the rough, unpainted hands of the woman across from him in the hard plastic booth, these pies shone like jewels, sparkled like precious objects in his dreary childhood.

"I'd like more coffee, son," she says.

"I'm sorry," says Gus, jumping up. "Milk and sugar?"

"No, I take a little Sweet 'n Low now," she says, carefully folding the little red box the tart came in.

Gus wouldn't be surprised if she put it in her pocketbook to take home, some crafts project for the fourth grade: Christmas decorations; he can imagine them with green painted stripes hanging from the tree in the school hallway or (horrors!) filled with fresh pencils in his Christmas stocking.

"Mother," he says, returning, hoping she doesn't pocket the stirrer, but she does. "I wanted to explain about Noonie, about what happened . . ."

"No need," she says stiffly. "Both you and your brother take after your father, men of the flesh, men of strong physical needs."

"Mother . . ."

"I've known about your brother for a long time, but you, well, I thought you were my son. So when that woman who ran the restaurant in town, Sugar Hansen, when she took you, too . . ."

(Sugar: can that really have been her name and is his mother talking about his brother or his father? Was there something planned, something ritualized in his seduction?)

"Your father, oh, he was the happy wanderer, a hand, an eye, always groping, creeping, a foot under the table, across the pews at church." She tilts back her head, laughs. "Little nosegays of flowers he left on their front porches, a scented hankie in the wash, a poem copied out in his hand, ah! His transgressions were so transparent, his sins so small for a man who needed the comfort of women. I needed comfort, too!" she says suddenly, straightening on her spine, her voice wobbly. Then: "About Noonie's mother," she says, her eyes watery, "I hope there wasn't too much suffering, at the end, that's bad. I'm truly sorry."

Gus offers to take down the screens and put up the storms for Noonie. It is late to be doing this, but he lucks out: it has been a mild fall and the first November Saturday is still amenable. He thought it would be a good father-daughter activity, but Sarah has better things to do and so it is Noonie milling about below, under the ladder, holding it, handing him things. Beneath his feet, he can see her in jeans and an old jacket of some man's, stamping her feet, impatient, scattered. The ladder shakes.

"I'm sorry," she calls.

Huge sunglasses obscure her face and there is something vaguely glamorous about her. "What made you cut your hair?" he asks, realizing what it is.

"It's the style," she says, shrugging. "It looks better with the new clothes, it's time for a change."

"I always liked your hair."

"Thank you."

"Did I tell you that when . . ."

"Oh, yes, you were always pretty complimentary about my hair," Noonie admits. "Can I leave this for a while? I have some phone calls to make."

"Oh, sure," says Gus, carrying down a stack of screens.

Doesn't everybody want a new life, he thinks, a second chance? It isn't only an escape but a moving toward something, recapturing something (youth) but also redefining it (life). Do you have to be Gauguin and show up with a cache of great paintings to get off the hook?

You aren't supposed to want it, of course, he thinks, climbing back up, a second-story man. The thing is, by this time, you are supposed to be living the life you want to be living. Or, as Elsa would have put it, you are supposed to lie in the bed you made. But the other beds . . . all those other beds. Men with strong physical needs, his mother had said, men who need the comfort of women.

The ladder sways slightly under his shifting weight and he thinks of his father falling to his death at forty-one; he had usurped all this, his new life was death. Gus can imagine some weary shrink, sucking on his pipe, nodding quietly: of course, if the father dies, mm-hmm, it makes it difficult to contemplate one's own transition, one's own mid-life passage. No role modeling. Gus thinks of Thomas, of stories he would confide late at night, when he was living with him that summer he met Noonie, brothers in front of late-night TV: sports, whiskey breath, beers, stories about women on airplanes, in airports. Gus can almost see Thomas, fat, glossy, overfed Thomas, the tassels on his highly polished Loafers bouncing as he turned to the woman next to him, his wide grin, his thick helmet of graying hair: a flight attendant in the first-class lounge, the Hertz girl in the back of a rented Ford, some busty secretary leaning over in a red lace teddy and garters as they pushed together the twin beds at a Holiday Inn.

But Thomas is still at the head of his table.

"Come to me," Pigeon had whispered, as in a dream, stretching her long arms out to him in a sleeping bag in the woods behind the school. (Gus has been reading *The Odyssey* with his tenth-grade class: Circe, the Sirens, Calypso. What a temptation, to see your own suburban longings as the travels of a classical hero!)

"I'm back!" Noonie calls. "Do you remember when

we were in Europe that year and we were in St. Tropez and we had lunch at one of those restaurants in the harbor and had bouillabaisse and there was that pink wine I liked . . . ?"

"The rosé?"

"In the scaly bottle, and I said I wanted to buy those pink-and-gold sandals but we didn't have the money and then we wandered into that little square and the men were playing *boules* on the gravel and there was a shooting range and a Ferris wheel and it looked like every little town in the world, you know, how every small town looks like every other small town . . ."

Gus laughs. "You don't come from a small town."

"Oh, but it's true," Noonie says. What has made her think of summers, of beginnings? She looks at the back of Gus's feet, heels, exposed in boating mocs, uncallused, smooth, soft as a baby's, whereas Noonie's are like cloven hooves.

(When they first moved here, they went to a welcome-wagon party on the next block. After everyone got there, all the husbands were instructed to sit on folding chairs in a circle and were asked to remove one shoe and sock. Then the wives were blindfolded, one by one, and each one had to crawl on the floor and pick out her own husband's foot. All the women chose the same foot: it was the biggest and smoothest. This foot belonged to Gus.)

Noonie wants to grab Gus, wind her arms around his calves and say, Let's start over, let's be friends, let's be lovers, let's have a wonderful life together, I want to be happy, I love you. "I made bean soup yesterday," she says. "Would you like some lunch?"

"Great," he says, "there are some things I want to talk to you about Sarah."

"Is something wrong?" Noonie wraps her arms around herself.

"No, I've been thinking we should be thinking about boarding schools."

"What are you talking about, sending her away?"

"Well, she has this opportunity, my old school, the scholarship, and I want her to have the best. She seems to like the idea."

"You talked to her about it?" She doesn't quite let the door slam on his face. (She wonders if it has something to do with Sarah's drunk; that he thinks Noonie can't take care of her.)

"Well, yes, several of her friends are applying."

"I thought you hated it so much," says Noonie. "Anyway, she never said anything to me." She feels angry—talking behind her back—throws the breadbasket on the table with such force that several pieces fall out.

"She's afraid of talking to you about it, Noonie, she's afraid you won't like it."

"I would be alone." Noonie sits down and looks at her soup plate. This was something she hadn't thought about. She guessed she didn't really think Sarah would stay home forever (Noonie hadn't wasted any time leaving her mother!) but she couldn't imagine life without her.

"Noonie," Gus says gently, "she can't stay here. She'll be going off to college in a few years."

"A few more years," Noonie says softly, "even a few years, so I can get used to the idea." She laughs. "Do you remember the first day of kindergarten, how we walked her to school, each holding a hand? But no one told me school was over at one that day, instead of two-forty, so while I was sitting here eating my lunch, the school called and asked if I was planning on picking up my child that afternoon. And there she was in this little blue knit dress and sandals and that little bowl cut she used to have, holding the teacher's hand and crying her heart out," Noonie says, wiping some tears from her eyes. "How can it be so long ago when I can remember it so well?" She is really crying now.

Gus is across the table before Noonie finishes her question, wraps his arms around her, lets her weep into his shirt, lets her weep until it is she who pushes him away, touches the soaked spot on his shirt, laughs suddenly.

"I did that to Rosie, too. I left her at school once, too." She is standing close to Gus, her hand flat on the breast pocket of his work shirt. "I must do that to people I love."

He smiles, takes her hand. "What time is Sarah coming home?" he asks as they walk up the stairs.

Noonie shakes her head. "Tomorrow morning, I think. She's staying at Brett's." He'll be gone long before that, she thinks.

Gus unbuttons his shirt, hangs it over the back of a chair, slips off his shoes, undoes his belt. Noonie hesitates, wonders if they should be doing this. Does this count as an affair or part of the marriage? She certainly understands the temptation, it is both forbidden and familiar, almost incest. She pulls off her own sweater and jeans, slides into bed with him.

Gus and Noonie sit up in their marriage bed, their backs against the pillows, the covers pulled up to and under their armpits like the couple in an antiquated stage play. (No need for such make-believe anymore. Sarah has witnessed more orgasms on celluloid than Noonie experienced in the first year of her marriage. Well, at least Sarah will know how to react; for such a verbal person, Noonie is strangely quiet during sex. She supposes it is because she learned about it from a nonaudiovisual medium: books.)

Gus is overwhelmed by Noonie, the luster of her coloring,

her skin, her scent—he had forgotten. Noonie would never guess, he thinks correctly, what is really unique, beautiful about her. Like many women, she takes her body apart like chicken pieces wrapped in Styrofoam and cellophane in the supermarket: breasts, thighs, legs, and rates them accordingly, and assumes men do the same.

"Do you ever think about what happened?" Gus asks, moving his hand across the sheet, taking Noonie's.

"What?"

"What happened to us, what went wrong?"

"Oh, come on," says Noonie. "All the time."

His other hand touches her neck, shoulders, pulls at the straps of her rather serviceable cotton bra. He pulls the barrette out of her hair. Noonie has forgotten how big he is, how much she loves the size of him.

"Hang on," he says. He turns on the small lamp next to her bed table. He reaches across and swiftly pulls a strand of hair from the front of her head.

"What are you doing?"

"Look," he says, "a gray hair."

"Don't be ridiculous, I don't have any gray hair. It must be very pale blond."

Gus laughs, "Noonie, look."

She squints at the hair. It is gray, whitish-gray, and the texture is different, coarser than her other hair. It is her first gray hair, and she feels as if she is another woman.

Gus puts his arms around her again. "You're shivering," he says, holding her.

Noonie loves too much. This is her curse, her cross, this huge need that can never be returned: no one can ever love her enough, fill her up—she is an empty vessel. (All this because of a missing father, a dead mother, an estranged sister, a wandering husband, a little girl who must grow up?)

"Is something wrong?" he asks, cupping her chin with his hand. "Do you think we shouldn't be doing this?"

Noonie shakes her head, but it is too late, Gus reaches down her back, slides her farther down the bed with the flat of his hand, raises himself over her.

This is what everyone is looking for, Noonie feels certain, this body so close, so familiar you can't tell which is your own elbow, your own knee; this connection so you won't have to be alone. This is all Noonie has learned in almost forty years on this planet: that she does not wish to be alone and that she must be. And that everything in her life is a reconciliation to this fact.

Gus remembers certain things. Some are new. Noonie feels strangely detached at first. She is more experienced than the last time, she has been opened in a way that doesn't have to do with anyone except Noonie. Gus pushes down on her shoulders; she thinks she hears the door downstairs.

"Wait," she whispers.

"I can't," he moans.

"Mom! Are you upstairs?" Sarah calls. "Is Daddy still here?"

Noonie hears footsteps, Gus pulls off.

"Mom!" Sarah pushes open the door to their bedroom.

"Sa . . ." Noonie begins, but the door is open and Sarah is framed in the mantel of the open door, one hand still resting on the doorknob.

"Shit!" Sarah screams, and runs down the stairs.

Noonie is dressing, ashen, shaking her head.

"We'd better go find her," Gus says. "We'd better talk to her."

"I hope you can think of something to say," Noonie says shakily.

Sarah is sitting in Gus's car; all the windows are rolled up and she has locked the doors. She is sitting in the driver's seat, her hands over her ears, sobbing, rocking back and forth. She looks out the curved tinted windshield, sees her parents: her mother is white-faced and trying to smile; she has been crying, for a change. Her father looks smoother, but worried. They are calling her name, opening and closing their mouths, and calling her name.

"Open up!" Gus is saying. "We want to talk to you."

They look like fish in a glass bowl, the fish she and Brett kept in their locker, Ichthyosis and Meshuggeneh; their mouths are opening and closing, their chests heaving with each breath; her mother looks cold. It is late in the afternoon and the temperature has dropped and their breaths are coming out foggy, clouding up the windshield.

"Go away!" Sarah shouts. "Go away, goddammit, just go away."

13

GREAT ESCAPES

"Gus?" Noonie is tentative, frightened; she is supposed to know where Sarah is.

"Yeah? Wait a minute, I have to go to the other phone."

Noonie hears the phone click against the night table, a soft mumbled explanation. Of course. He is in bed with Pigeon; that had not quite registered until this moment. Even in her terror, Noonie can imagine Pigeon's long tanned arm reaching across the covers, extended from a lacy pink gown. (Sarah has filled her in on jocky Pigeon's penchant for frills; Noonie is the kind of masochist who demands details. And it hurts more now, now that she has been with him again.)

"Okay," Gus says softly, and Pigeon hangs up.

"Gus. I'm sorry to wake you up . . . did I wake you up?" Noonie bites her lip, she is crying already. "Is Sarah at . . . is she there?"

He pauses for a moment and Noonie's heart leaps; in her mind she is rehearsing the answer, yes. It is obvious; maybe she really is an optimist.

"No," he says, "isn't she home?" (Home, he said it again, that place is home.)

Now Noonie's voice is really wobbly, very low, a guttural whisper. Gus has trouble hearing her. "She said she was spending the night at Brett's, but she forgot her Retin-A . . ."

"Her what?"

"Her acne cream, I found it when I went into the bathroom. She's been unhappy about her face lately, so I thought . . . I called Brett to say I'd bring it over to her, and Brett said she wasn't there. Brett didn't know where she was . . ." (She must know; Noonie thinks she's lying—she confided everything to Cheryl Ann—but Sarah is not like Noonie, she is more guarded, less needy.)

"Now, wait, take it easy, Noonie. Let's go back. What time did she come home from school?"

"Gus, can't you come here, please, come home? I'm really, really frightened, please, please come . . ."

Is Gus worried? He isn't sure, but as he pulls a pair of khakis over his pajama bottoms, he notices his hands are shaking badly. What could happen in this town? There is an occasional rape near the campus but mainly lots of robberies, shoplifting, burglaries; crimes of property.

Had he seen Sarah after he drove her to school this morning? He thinks he passed her in the dining hall at lunch, but she hadn't seemed to see him. Since last weekend, when she found Noonie and him in bed, she has been quieter but perfectly civil. He worries about that; he knows she inherited it from him, his passivity, this burying of pain. He leans over to tell Pigeon where he is going, but she acknowledges it only with a small wave of a hand, barely lifting it, and with a soft groan, she rolls back to sleep. That's how much she cares, he thinks, but that's not fair. She just probably thinks Noonie cooked this up to get him back in her bed. (Of course he told her about what happened putting up the storms. She sat on a kitchen chair, her mouth scrunched tightly, but she informed him in her flat way that it wasn't so unusual, from what she's heard. As a matter of fact, she had just read an article in *Cosmopolitan* about it, or someplace. It was the first real indication he had that she cared for him.)

Noonie is sitting on the floor in Sarah's room when Gus gets there. Her face is softening, he thinks, there is a short accordion of skin on the side of her face, and she was wrong, there is more gray hair. He can see it from the back.

"Noonie?"

"Oh, God," she cries and runs into his arms. "We did this, we did this."

"Now stop. Wait a minute. You're acting as if something has happened. You don't know that."

"I know, I know!" she shouts. "Look, she's gone. I called everyone." She throws the school directory at him. "Her backpack's gone, her savings book, her notebooks . . ."

"Did you call the police?"

"The police!" Noonie is truly alarmed.

"I think you should call the police."

"You," she says.

The police arrive in ten minutes.

"Five-five," answers Gus, flatly, "her eyes are blue."

"Not always, sometimes they're almost green, Gus, or gray, you know, she has eyes like that, that pick up the color of what she's wearing, the weather . . ."

(How does a mother give a description of her child,

the triangular beauty mark on her left shoulder, her height, weight, the color of her eyes, without imagining her lying dead on the highway or in a city alley?)

"Yes, ma'am," says the police officer, making notes. "Can you give me a description of what she was wearing?"

"Jeans," says Gus.

"Army pants," says Noonie, "a faded blue-jean jacket, a T-shirt from a James Taylor concert (Pigeon had taken Sarah and Brett this fall), bluchers . . ."

"I'm sorry . . ."

"They're the kind of shoes the kids wear, tie-shoes, the backs are broken down, they wear them like that . . . Oh, and red socks with Christmas trees on them." (A stocking stuffer.)

Gus is stunned that Noonie knows with such certainty, as if Sarah is a part of her. How does she know all this?

(Noonie knows because, to be frank, she snoops, something she feels uncomfortable about at times, but thinks it may be permissible on the grounds that she is being responsible. She has read enough about parents of drug addicts who haven't been in the teenage pigsty bedrooms for years and are amazed to see the needles and blackened spoons all around. No, Noonie knows just where Sarah keeps her pack of Camels—in the right top drawer of her desk—and the fancy bottle of rum from the Dominican Republic—the closet shelf—and the red-and-black dream notebook next to her bed, although she will not allow herself to read it. Thank God, Noonie assures herself, she hasn't gone that far, although now she wishes she had.)

And Sarah has stuffed it all into her blue backpack with a broken zipper. (Noonie had promised her she'd have it fixed months ago! Sarah holds it together with big safety pins. Is this the sin, a broken zipper, is this the punishment for being a negligent mother?)

Noonie thinks wildly of the thousands of lost children, like something out of *Peter Pan,* all those little children on the milk cartons, grocery sacks. Oh God, forgive me! she thinks, I shouldn't have ignored them; those hundreds of flyers in the mail she has tossed out with barely a glance at tiny Ronald Rodriquez or adorable Mary Beth Campbell, who, when last seen, had freckles and was missing two teeth—nine years ago!

How will I survive this? she wonders. I won't survive this, she thinks, knows, I've already lost one. What do they want from me? My baby, my baby, she thinks, tears falling down her cheeks, asleep in her carriage one minute, as Noonie runs into the pharmacy, and when she comes back, she is dead, cold, dead. My baby! Noonie had always thought this tragedy would protect her, that she had paid her dues. You can't have two things like this happen, it isn't fair! She still reads everything she can find about crib death; lately they have made some advances in understanding: Noonie has read of mothers who sleep with oxygen tanks nearby, intercoms on, so they can monitor the breathing of these tiny vulnerable babies.

"Is there something that recently happened, you know, at home, school," the officer is talking, "that might have caused her to run away?"

Gus looks at Noonie: do they have to know?

"She found us in bed," Noonie says flatly. "We've been separated, and she came home unexpectedly and we were making love."

Noonie is always courageous about the outrageous, Gus thinks. He used to think it was because of some childish desire to shock, but now he thinks it's because everything else floats between fantasy and reality for her, and only bold things really speak to her.

"Oh," says the officer, and flips his little notebook closed.

"Well, what we do at this point is notify the local police departments and the Port Authority in New York . . ."

The Port Authority—Noonie's heart really flutters with that—a launching pad for prostitutes and drug addicts; not a week goes by without a book, a movie, a television newscaster in the main waiting room to bring us more bad news about our society.

"Look," the officer says shyly, and barely touches Noonie's arm, "this is tough, but most kids are back in a day. We'll keep in touch." He tips the peak of his cap.

Now that he has left, Noonie's thoughts have moved from brain to mouth; she is really babbling now. They are in the kitchen, where Gus is making coffee. It is one in the morning, but it will be a while before they go to sleep, he knows.

"Do you remember when she took that bottle of baby aspirin at Lola's and Lola was hysterical and I called the doctor and he said it was okay, that's why they made the bottle so small, you know, twenty-six aspirins, because it was the last okay number. But he said I should make her vomit. 'How?' I said. 'Stick your finger down her throat,' he said. So I did. We were walking home and she was crying and I just stopped her, she was very small, six or seven, and I opened her mouth and stuck my fingers down her throat and she threw up in the Branons' bushes. Can you imagine a more intimate act?"

Gus is watching her sadly. "Noonie, did you get any dinner tonight?"

She shakes her head numbly. She is remembering when Sarah had a hundred-and-four-degree fever last summer and she had to bathe her in cold water. Noonie hadn't seen her naked in a long time. Sarah had been hiding. That's how Noonie knew she was so sick, because she let her handle her like that. Noonie had run the washrag over her child's new breasts and saw her pubic hair for the first time. It was a different color from Noonie's, that's what struck her, and she thought, This is my child, this is my child's woman's body. Sarah's eyes were closed with fever and Noonie wrapped her in a big towel and put her in a clean nightie and lifted her to her bed.

"Then she got better and she never let me see her again like that." Noonie looks through Gus, across the table from her. "How can I say goodbye to someone like that? How will I find that intimacy with anyone else? How can I lose her?"

"Noonie . . ."

"You hate me, don't you?" she says suddenly, in a completely different tone of voice. "You hate that I fucked up your life, not letting you go to work at GE or IBM and have a Mercedes and a tennis court, like your brother's life, don't you?"

"No . . ." Gus is stunned as always by Noonie's energy, her fury.

"I didn't understand. I thought you should be the writer because that's what men did. I thought ambition was something men had, like penises." She laughs, sits squatted in the middle of the kitchen floor, like a peasant woman in the marketplace, her hair wild in her face. "I miss my hair," she says, pushing the short strands out of the way, sighs. "Everything I wanted to do I thought some man would do for me. Discover me. All those years and years when all I wanted to do was open the door and find him there. 'Daddy! You're home! Daddy, I love you!' "

Gus reaches down, grabs her hands, pulls her up. He resists holding her close. "Don't think about it now. Here, Noonie, I made you some soup."

Noonie looks at him with a crooked smile. She is touched; he has never cooked for her before.

"Noonie," Gus says in the morning. "I have to go to school."

She has been asleep on the living-room sofa, the phone balanced on the edge, near her hand. (Gus has slept in a chair.) School. Oh, God, Sarah should be going to school.

"I'll talk to everyone," he says. "Maybe someone knows, maybe she'll turn up there, just show up at school. Noonie, that's a likely possibility."

"Call me," she says.

He is grateful he has someplace to go, something to do. He doesn't really think something has happened to Sarah, he doesn't think that way, anyway. Some piece of him thinks she'll be in school this morning, standing in front of her locker, talking to Brett before homeroom. "Will you be all right?"

"No," Noonie laughs, "no, I will not be okay." She shivers, wraps the afghan (her mother's work) around her more tightly.

"Do you want me to call the doctor and get you something, tranquilizers?"

"I have some."

"Oh." He didn't know that.

Noonie remembers when Otto died, and they sat *shivah,* seven days of mourning. They were not religious, but you did certain things then, followed custom, it was expected of you, even in modified form. She was small and the apartment was crowded with talk and smoke and there was a lot of food and every night she fell asleep under a pile of fur coats on her bed. When Elsa died, they didn't do much of anything; everyone had a flight to catch. In twenty-four hours they were gone.

So, I will sit in mourning for the missing, she thinks, for my mother and Sarah, for my tiny baby (she cannot say her name even now), for my father, missing in action, for my missing husband, for my lost sister, Rosemarie, for my life before this point.

Noonie in the bathroom mirror this morning is different, unknown, gray around the edges. The haircut was a terrible mistake; she tries to pull the ends back off her face. She splashes water over her eyes. She thinks she somehow looks masculine, her features sharper, her skin coarser. There is a tough white whisker on her chin; she plucks it angrily with a tweezer. She has noticed how androgynous people become with age—old men with fleshy breasts, old women with gray mustaches. She remembers Lola, several years older, bitterly warning Noonie that one morning someday she would not recognize herself in her own mirror.

Noonie wanders into Sarah's bedroom again, sits on her empty bed, looks through the books next to it. She took the damn Houdini. Fuck Rosie. Noonie remembers the trick Rosie liked best because she tried to duplicate it in their basement. There were several old trunks downstairs (this is where Noonie had seen the rolled-up backdrops Otto had used), big leather-and-brass bound trunks that had made the journey from Hungary to America, trunks like the one Houdini had used. But his had a trapdoor, of course, some secret passage; it must have been rigged. How could Rosie have thought she could do it, pull it off? All that positive thinking from her swimming coaches, probably.

It was the last time they had dressed up and played together in that way, Rosie as Houdini in an approximation of a dinner coat, Noonie as Bess in a strapless gown of Elsa's with a sequined rose on the bodice. After a week of being tied up repeatedly and put in a bag in the smelly old trunk, she refused to play ever again.

Last night Noonie dreamed she was in an old hotel and a fire broke out. Sarah was a tiny baby and Noonie grabbed her from her crib and wrapped her in a blanket and went down through the smoky corridors and stairwells to the lobby, where she deposited her safely. Then she had to go back for her mother. Elsa was heavy and sick, fragile. Noonie had to dress her and find her wig, and lean her against her own hip as she lifted her and carried her down the stairs. When she got downstairs, she remembered Gus, so she went back up. He was asleep with Pigeon, but she dutifully awakened them both and helped them through the corridors. Finally, choking with smoke, she fell into a chair in the lobby when Elsa, wrapped in a beautiful fur coat and looking young and healthy again, turned to her and asked, "Where's Rosie?"

Rosie, Noonie thinks. Of course.

Sarah feels free, freer than she has ever felt in her life, not scared, definitely not scared. She waits for the bus to New York. Maybe she would see someone, some friend of her parents' or a classmate's parent. But what does it matter? So she is going to New York, and she isn't being sneaky. She just wants to go, get out of here, and if her mother knew, she'd weep and scream and forbid it; that's why she isn't telling her. Not to be sneaky.

It is like a huge burden being removed, like when you have to carry your books around for hours and hours and then you get to put them down, or a long hike with a pack filled with ridiculous stuff: trail mix and matches in plastic bags and a bedroll. Gus insisted Sarah do a certain amount of summer camping, thought it encouraged a love of nature, developed character. Walking with a heavy pack is stupid, Sarah thinks, but the way you feel when you put it down isn't. It's a release, as if your body is made of feathers, can fly, lift off. That is fine. Maybe that's what Gus had in mind, comfort after discomfort—it only hurts when you stop, or is that the opposite? Anyway, this is what Sarah feels as she pays the driver and takes a seat toward the rear of the bus: it's as if suddenly you look around and notice all the trees are green and spring is here.

Her pack doesn't feel heavy today; there isn't much in it: a toothbrush, a hairbrush, a copy of a biography of Houdini her Aunt Rosie sent her for her last birthday, a box of granola bars (the unhealthy kind, with chocolate chips), her bathing suit and goggles (she assumes she will be spending a lot of time in the water from now on), a very dog-eared copy of *The Velveteen Rabbit,* surely one of the saddest of all childhood stories, but her little-girl favorite, and her dream notebook.

(*The Velveteen Rabbit* was an Easter gift from Gramma Anna the year Sarah was eight, recovering from scarlet fever. A totally tactless and scary book, Noonie thought; she was enraged at Gus's mother, went on and on about it. But she was wrong: that might have been true for Noonie, but Sarah was tougher, braver, an altogether more realistic little girl, and it served as a totem of survival.)

Sarah looks out the window; it will be familiar for about ten miles or so: their supermarket, a produce stand Noonie likes, the mall where she buys Italian coffee cups and fat candles for entertaining out-of-doors, the place they used to get the old Saab repaired, the miniature golf course Brett and she like a lot. Sarah watches the places of her life roll by: there is the orchard where they go, in the fall, to pick their own apples.

She remembers when she was a tiny little girl and Gus would carry her on his shoulders and lift her so she could pick the apples on the low branches. It always made Noonie nervous. She would be standing precariously on a ladder. (Noonie does not like heights. For all her dreaminess, she likes both feet planted on dry flat ground. For all her dreams of Paris, she is a Midwesterner.) Gus would say Sarah was the apple-cheeked apple princess and Noonie was the apple queen.

"Are you the king?" Sarah would ask, giggling so hard she could barely speak.

No, he would say, he was their humble servant.

Or sometimes, when she was even smaller, they would play a hide-and-seek game that frankly terrified her. Gus would be a bear or a lion and he was coming to eat her up. (Why do grown-ups say that to children: I'm going to eat you up, you look good enough to eat? That awful story of *Hansel and Gretel,* an early source of nightmares—the irresponsible father, the cruel stepmother, Hansel in a cage, Gretel part of the conspiracy, not by choice! Even Noonie, so supposedly sensitive to these things, would cackle and, pinching Sarah's little arm between her fingers, say, "Ha ha, we must fatten this one up!") Her father would chase her around the house (they lived in a smaller place then, an apartment, in another city—Ithaca, Sarah likes that name—while Gus got a master's degree) until he caught her, and fear and excitement were in her throat, and she was pale with that excitement. Then he would suddenly say her touch (one little hand held out in warning, warding him off) had turned him into a handsome prince.

Is he Pigeon's prince? she wonders. She doesn't seem

like the type. "Hero was a woman," Rosie told her the last time she saw her, at Grandma's funeral, "don't forget that."

Sarah likes mythology, but she didn't know that myth; she looked it up when she got home. Every night, Hero's lover, Leander, would swim the Hellespont to be with her and every morning he would swim back. (Did he have to go to work or did he have a wife at home?) One night he drowned, and when Hero heard she jumped into the sea, never to return.

Sarah knows why Rosie likes it—because of the swimming angles and maybe because of the lover part. Sarah can't imagine jumping into the water and dying for anyone—or swimming back and forth like that—although it reminds her of a story her father once told, how he was a camp counselor one summer and every night he and a bunch of his friends would row across the lake to visit the counselors of the girls' camp on the other side.

"Well, you couldn't have gotten into too much trouble, if you had to row back and forth," Noonie laughed when Gus told this story.

None of this mattered to Sarah, except she noticed her father quickly changed the subject.

Anyway, they acted like a family then, did family things, took picnics, trips, went to museums (she hadn't liked it so much then, but she wishes they could do it now); even going to the orchard would be a treat. She remembers she was supposed to help Gus do the storms that day, remembers seeing the ladder leaning against the house as she came in, before she saw them. Maybe, if she had been there, maybe it wouldn't have happened. She finds her Walkman and puts her headset on. The scenery is different now, they are on the turnpike.

Sarah walks into the ladies' room at the bus station. WOMEN, it says actually, and there are women, about ten of them lying in the corridor and entrance, using plastic sacks for pillows and newspaper for covers.

"Got some change, honey? Got anything?"

"Can you help out, sweet baby?" asks another.

Sarah doesn't know what to do. She thinks of her grandmother Elsa circling the toilet seat with squares of paper once when she went to the ladies' with her in a very fancy department store; Sarah hated sharing a booth with her. She can't imagine Grandma here: she wouldn't be able to touch the door handle. She wishes she hadn't died.

"What pretty hair," a woman next to Sarah at the long mirror says to her.

(Sarah thinks it's a woman, but no, maybe it's a girl, her eyes inside the huge silver and blue circles she is drawing are young. Normally Sarah would take this opportunity to put on her own eye makeup, but she suddenly wishes to fade away.)

"You should leave it down, honey," the girl says as Sarah combs out her braid.

"It's too long." Sarah giggles, uncomfortable. She doesn't really like strangers.

"Take off your glasses," the girl commands.

Sarah obeys, squints into the mirror.

"You have to wear your glasses all the time?"

Sarah nods dumbly.

"You should get some of those contact lenses. You real pretty, you know that. You had your nose done?"

Sarah laughs out loud now. "Look, there's a little bump on the top."

The girl nods, concedes the point. "You real cute, though, you could do something with yourself if you tried. Hey, watch out for the police!" she shouts as Sarah leaves. "They on the lookout for runaways."

Runaways! But that's what she is, isn't it? It seems so silly all of a sudden. Sarah feels she is sinking. It would be so easy now to call Noonie: Mommy, come pick me up, come and get me, I feel tired and afraid. There was a girl in the ladies' room who talked to me; she was so weird, she had so much makeup on, you wouldn't have believed it!

But she finds her way to the ticket counter and checks the schedule. Somehow she remembers Rosie checking buses in Chicago. She buys a bagel—cinnamon-and-raisin (her favorite, which Noonie says isn't really a kind of bagel at all)—with an inch of cream cheese and a can of Tab and finds the right terminal and gets on the bus that is waiting there.

Sarah picks a seat near the front, near the driver. She is a cautious child, after all; Noonie should not really worry about her. All the information that is pumped at children these days—only the most obtuse ignore it, only the most perverse pursue it. Sarah's heart is beating as the bus fills up, but no one bothers her—and why should they? It is Noonie who thinks one is a moving target in this world, a shining star, a piece of ripe fruit. And Noonie sends those signals; Sarah is a too-tall freckled thirteen-year-old girl with thick glasses and a blue backpack with a broken zipper.

(Noonie has told her that she would walk down the street as a child singing, in case a talent scout—a phrase wholly unfamiliar to Sarah—was lurking in the alleys and courtyards of Chicago. People did look at her mother, Sarah had to admit that, but usually because she was wearing something crazy—cowboy boots or riding britches; once she wore a man's tuxedo to a fancy ball. She didn't look like the other mothers, she didn't dress like them or act like them. Noonie imagined that she had escaped the curse of Elsa, but, in a fundamental way, she was more like her mother than she was like anyone else. Sarah is grateful to be pale and practically colorless, she doesn't believe that the girl in the restroom for a minute about having possibilities, she just wishes she weren't so tall.)

There are stops, rest stops, people get on and get off, and finally somewhere, probably when they leave Virginia, when they are south, it begins to look different: the sky, the landscape, and Sarah becomes excited. Suddenly she feels the passion of travel, that sense of adventure that even the most timid travelers of the armchair variety have. It takes over, and you think this is how it must be forever: you alone, traveling to strange and exotic places. (Even to begin to discuss travel as metaphor, the journey as the gentle unfolding of our lives, is pretentious, inappropriate except for only the youngest, most ignorant among us. But for Sarah, Sarah who is taking this first journey alone, it may still fit.)

For hours and hours Sarah sits and watches. Each of us is an explorer, a Byrd or a Scott. The first time we see it is the first time, and it becomes ours. Like all great adventurers, she is wary and open to the natives, their big toothy grins and drawls, the handsome lads with flat-top haircuts and thick arms in rolled up T-shirts, to the local delicacies, Dr. Pepper and Stuckey's peanut rolls.

In Miami she must change buses, in a terminal where Spanish fills the soft sleepy air and the coffee is thick and sweet and the men—there are so many men—follow you with their dark eyes and the women have crying babies in their arms. Then they are in Key West.

It is there, for a moment, one moment, in the Key West bus station (only a handful of streets away from her destination, although she doesn't know that yet), looking for Rosie's name in the phone book, that she almost panics, gulps, her tummy feels sick, but she remembers about Cook, Madge, and someone answers the phone.

"Yes," she says, "this is Sarah Bentley. Is my Aunt Rosie there?"

The phone rings. Noonie's heart beats wildly, as it has each time the phone has rung in the last two days. (Many times.)

"Yes?" she says, barely above a whisper.

"She just got here," Rosie says.

For two days, since Noonie has decided Sarah was going to find Rosie, in those two days, she has talked to her sister many times. Rosie, in turn, has been worried, responsible. But there was nothing either of them could do, and they remained serious, considerate of each other's positions. Now Noonie almost collapses. "Is she okay?" she asks shakily.

"Of course, she's fine."

Noonie recovers swiftly, snaps, without acknowledging her sister's identity. "Put her on!"

"Noonie, I didn't do this."

"Put her on!"

"Noonie, calm down, she's a little upset . . ." Rosie puts her hand to the receiver, whispers to Sarah, "I knew it, kid. You have to talk to her."

"Is she screaming?" Sarah mouths to Rosie.

"You bet, but she used to yell all the time at me. All bark, Sarah, no bite."

Somehow this makes Sarah feel better. She sniffles and dries her eyes, takes the phone. "Mommy?"

"Sarah! Are you all right?"

"I'm fine. I got on a bus in New York, it was neat . . ."

"Sarah!" Noonie grits her teeth. Now that she is relieved she is furious. "I was terrified! The last thirty-six hours have been hell for me and Daddy . . . !"

"If I told you, you wouldn't have let me go."

"Why did you do this to me?"

"You know why," Sarah says sensibly.

"Well," Noonie says, remembering to sound like a mother, "you could have taken a trip to Florida if you wanted. Why didn't you ask me?"

"You never would have let me go. You don't talk to her."

Noonie sighs deeply, she is confusing the issues already. "You just stay there, okay, and let me talk to Rosie. I love you, Sarah," she says in a different voice.

"Oh, Mommy, I know," says Sarah. "She wants to talk to you," she tells Rosie.

"I'm coming down," Noonie barks, "I'll get a flight tonight."

"Hang on, Noonie. Sarah and I had a little talk and I promised her I'd try to persuade you to let her stay here for a while by herself . . ."

"What are you talking about?" Noonie feels wild.

"You know, maybe a month, just to get some space between the two of you."

"You want my child . . . you can't have one . . . it's like those fairy tales, those old faggy women with some young beauty locked away in a tower. Or demanding the firstborn for spinning some fucking gold from straw . . . Rapunzel or Rumpelstiltskin . . . you've stolen my child!" She screams. "I hate you!"

Almost immediately she feels regret. "I'm sorry, Rosie, Rosie please, I'm sorry."

Rosie feels socked, sick, she feels the way she does when she is pulled out of the water in defeat. For a while she cannot speak.

"Rosie, please, talk to me."

"Yeah?"

"She has to go to school."

"There are schools here."

"Not like her school."

Rosie recovers with that. It is so much like Noonie, she has to laugh. "Oh, Noonie, stop it. Where did you go to school?"

"That's what I mean. I want different things for her."

"It's almost Thanksgiving. She doesn't even have to go to school."

(Thanksgiving is three weeks away.)

Noonie lets out a deep breath. "I have to talk to Gus, Rosie," she says quietly. "I'll call you back. Tell Sarah I love her again."

Being Rosie and Madge's little girl, this is different. Sarah sleeps in the narrow bed in the sewing room with new pink sheets and flowered curtains Madge made the first day Sarah was there. Madge had gone out right away and bought a muffin tin with animal shapes: a rhinoceros and a hippo, a lion, a tiger. Sarah doesn't have the heart to tell her it is for little kids; she just eats her corn lion and then a bear.

Rosie buys her funny presents: stuffed animals, T-shirts, heart-shaped sunglasses, a key chain with a tiny plastic clog on it. (Sarah wonders if it would fit her dolls—where are her dolls, anyway? She hadn't liked them that much, but she wonders where they are.) Rosie and Madge take delight in tiny vegetables, too: carrots the size of baby fingers, little eggplants, yellow cherry tomatoes, and Madge makes a good salad of weird peppers: orange and green and red and yellow, all tossed together in a big wooden bowl—it looks like a salad from outer space. (When she tells them that, they love it, dub it the Outer Space Pepper Salad, call all their friends.)

Madge makes Sarah French braids every morning before she goes off to school, threads silk ribbons through them. Madge buys her T-shirts, too (these are a little small), to match the ribbons, but Sarah understands that they need her to be a little, little girl, so she can grow up in a more natural way; it would be too strange to have a teenager plunked down in their midst. These are women who did not appreciate their adolescence for a minute.

There is nothing natural about adolescents; Sarah knows that no one of any free will or choice will go out and adopt someone thirteen years old (she reads stories in the newspaper all the time about the difficulty of placing these unlucky orphaned children). Evidently, the only way parents can maintain a love for you during those years, twelve to seventeen, is if they keep conjuring up the memory of you as a smaller, tidier, more compliant and adorable human being.

Noonie calls every other day; sometimes she forgets (she says) and calls the next day, too. Gus calls less often and once he and Noonie are together when they call. Rosie lets her call Brett a couple of times and Brett says no one was mad at her but everyone is pretty jealous and Brett thinks she should bring back some presents—maybe some grapefruit or T-shirts—when she comes back to school. Sarah knows her mother is coming for Thanksgiving and then she will have to go home with her.

In the meantime, she is just having fun. She hadn't realized how much she needed a vacation until now. The weather is very hot and sunny, it is like summer and she and Rosie hang out all day at the beach and eat breakfast out a lot (Rosie is a lot more like Gus than like Noonie, she thinks) and they eat ice cream religiously, once a day. When Madge comes home from school, they all go out, too; they go to the grocery store or over to a friend's who has a pool and swim laps. (Trillions of laps.)

Madge and Rosie are a couple, Sarah can tell that. There is a kindness, a gentleness between them that she has never noticed between her parents. Between Noonie and Gus, there are sparks, heavy fire. Gus frequently touches Noonie, but not with the teasing ease that these women have with each other—Madge tugs Rosie's short curls, Rosie pinches Madge's floppy waist. Gus touches Noonie with a purpose—it leads to something but it is not pleasure for its own sake. It is as if Rosie and Madge are playing house, while Noonie and Gus are playing war.

14

HOMECOMING

Noonie is alone for the first time in her life. Like many women her age, she merely went from her childhood bed to her marriage bed without skipping a beat. There is so much time, now; she has to learn about time. At first she was euphoric that Sarah was all right, then angry that she wasn't home, then weepy, sad, lonesome.

In the time that Sarah is gone, Noonie learns something about families. She finds herself looking very carefully at the families she sees: babies—so many of them again, all of a sudden!—in backpacks, toddlers in strollers, mommies and daddies. They are always shopping together and holding hands and crossing the street and laughing and licking ice cream. There are balloons tied to the strollers or the children's wrists, balloons from the shoe store where Sarah's shoes came from, too. Noonie, shopping alone, stares at them like a starving tramp contemplating an elaborate feast. (Newborns simply make her weep.)

Noonie used to think there had to be some special activity

to be a family, something planned (a vacation, a party, a museum trip). She hadn't understood that being together was enough; she hadn't known that being together wasn't forever.

Had she imagined that life could stand still on some one day of her choosing? Had she thought time was like the sets of slides in the carousel reels in the boxes in the attic: Noonie and Gus on their honeymoon (Europe!), Sarah as a baby (Ithaca, New York), Sarah at camp (Cape Cod)? Of course, the camera is like that, photography lies, it gives a false sense of security, a false impression of the stasis of life. And the preponderance of gaiety: who brings an Instamatic to a funeral?

Noonie realizes now what an act of courage it was for Elsa to make an attempt at a normal home: the good sit-down meals and day camp and Girl Scouts, when the truth was far from that. When Gus left, Noonie had wanted to bury herself in the farthest region of her bed. She had never thought how alone her mother was for most of her life, and how grateful for Rosie and Noonie she must have been, what they meant in her life. Elsa had run a business, she had her network of gentleman callers, she had made a real life for herself in a time when women didn't do that very often. Noonie had mocked her mother's pretending that they were like other families, but she sees now, they were a family: they had loved one another and cared for one another. It was the only way they could have survived.

Noonie begins to contemplate a life alone: without her child, without Gus. She knows she will have to take her work more seriously and wonders why she never has. Elsa worked all her life; Noonie's and Rosie's lives were punctuated with their mother's schedules and deadlines, the calendar marked with weddings in June and First Communions in the spring and those family portraits at Christmas (always a rush!). The newspaper Noonie writes her column for has just purchased a cable-television franchise and wonders if Noonie would like to expand her university interviews into a weekly program. There are day trips she could write about for the *Times*.

When she thinks of Tommy she still gets warm, flushed; she feels a sensation in her lower parts, but this is high school stuff. She has noticed now that she isn't sharing Tommy with Sarah, she is sharing him with Gail.

Tommy is around a lot; he and a friend of his are working on the garage. He has convinced Noonie to turn the big empty room upstairs—a room with hooks and low cupboards for tack, harnesses, and saddles, and a low small stove where the stableboy made his tea (Noonie loves these English-novel details)—into a space for a boarder. He'd like to live there, he suggests.

"With Gail?" Noonie asks coolly, a lot smarter than she was last year at this time.

Gus stops by on his way home from school. To chat, he says, but Noonie knows what's bothering him.

"What are you doing to the garage?" he asks, after a few seconds.

"I'm turning it into a rental property," she says, officially.

"Did I say you could do that?"

"Do you live here?" she says, angrily.

"Noonie, I still own this house. I mean, we both do. I don't think you can do this without my permission."

Noonie guesses this is true, but they have avoided doing anything official about the separation, ending the marriage (she wasn't going to be the one to bring up the subject!).

"Hey, Noonie, we're going to break now," Tommy calls,

walking over to where Noonie and Gus are standing in the driveway.

Gus puts out his hand. Slowly Tommy reaches for it and shakes it.

Noonie hasn't realized how much alike they are; standing in the cold November sunshine, Tommy is a younger, less complicated version of Gus.

"My brother's name is Thomas," Gus says to Tommy, although these introductions are perfunctory. Each knows what the other is. Contrary to what Noonie suspects, Sarah has never told Gus about Tommy, but, of course, Gus knows immediately his wife is sleeping with him—he knows by the way her body arches toward him, like a plant toward the sun. Gus can feel the heat she is giving off standing there between them. (Noonie has never been subtle, sexually.)

"We'd better talk about the garage," Gus says sharply. "I'm calling Sarah tonight, so you don't have to," he says, also, and walks away.

Gus is sitting in his car. He has parked near a playground where he used to take Sarah on the Sunday mornings they let Noonie sleep late. He feels angry, angry with himself, and sad: sadder than he has ever felt in his life. He feels like crying.

He did something like this once, dumped a date off on a roommate because some campus beauty had indicated a desire to go to a dance with him. Of course, once she got to the dance, he discovered she had only wanted to be seen with him to make someone jealous. She had left after fifteen minutes.

But this isn't some girl, this is Noonie, his wife, Noonie, whom he picked up off a path in a city park so many years ago. He had felt as if he was carrying something so damned breakable, he could feel her breathing against his chest. (He hadn't ever carried a person before.)

He can still see Noonie in that crowded funny apartment, with her strange cagey mother and her silly little sister; Noonie coming shyly to the door. He could have smacked her, standing there with that boy. He should have put a fist through the garage or into Tommy's face. He knows Tommy would have defended Noonie with everything he has: his voice, his fists, his youth. He knows this because Gus would have done that and Gus can recognize himself or what he used to be.

Noonie wishes she could take the bus to Key West, trace Sarah's steps, experience things as she did, as if that were available to any of us: the old dream of Metamorphosis. But she is really too impatient, too old.

On her flight, she is seated next to an old woman on her way to her grandson's wedding. She is nervous—this is her first flight, she confesses to Noonie even before she sits down. She reaches across the armrest and touches Noonie's hand, her fingers stiff and crooked from some form of arthritis, small diamonds sprinkled on several of the crooked fingers. Apparently, she wants Noonie to hold her hand during takeoff.

In the air, she talks nonstop (except when she is served her lunch, which she finds charming, a doll's meal; she unwraps her tiny utensils with glee), presents a litany of women's troubles: broken promises and engagements, abuse, stillborns, betrayals, mastectomies, hysterectomies. All this matches Noonie's experience, too, but faced with such realism, she needs to refute it. She asks in a small voice about happiness, about pleasure, about the impending wedding of the grandson-in-uniform (she has seen a few dozen snapshots by now). The report is equally fulsome, detailed, but it is always of a moment, something short, something temporary, as fleeting as a child's kiss blown across the room.

Many women's lives must be like this, Noonie thinks, a string of memories, like beads, and as you become older, they become clearer, more memorized efforts to remember a little girl's profile as she bends to collect seashells on a sunny beach, or the weight of the beloved's arms as you lie under the shade of a spreading tree, as if the only real danger in life is forgetting.

Wearily, Noonie gets off the plane and sees her sister standing behind the double doors of the gate at the airport in Key West.

"Where's Sarah?" Noonie demands immediately.

"She's fine. She's home."

Noonie bristles at the use of the word, embraces Rosie loosely, follows her to her car, where she snaps her seatbelt on loudly—she doesn't think much of Rosie's driving.

"I wanted to talk to you alone," Rosie says. "Sarah's very hurt, but she chose her words carefully, you should know that. She isn't disloyal, your daughter, she's a big fan. She says you've been screwing around."

Noonie nearly chokes. "That's choosing her words carefully? She said that?"

"That's my word," Rosie says. "And then she found you and Gus in bed. She says you're not a family anymore, so she felt free to try something else, too."

Noonie is so angry she can barely hear what Rosie is saying. She wants this sermon to stop so she can see her child.

"Of course, Sarah can't stay here," Rosie is saying.

"Oh, thank God, I thought you might . . ."

"I didn't steal your child, Noonie. I'm not some evil character in a story. She wants to go home. She misses you and she misses her friends. This isn't the right place for her. But she's not going back until you and Gus start behaving."

"Great. You tell Gus." (Why does this family think she is to blame, why are men allowed all kinds of dispensation? It's so normal for them to be missing! She knows Elsa carried this theory about Gus and Noonie's marriage to her grave.)

"And what's this boarding-school crap?" Rosie asks, starting up her car.

"It's not my idea. She and Gus cooked it up."

"I think she wants to be told that you can't live without her, that she can't go."

Noonie is listening to Rosie now; they have pulled into the carport and she can see Sarah, tanned, even taller, her hair bleached very blond from the sun and in tight French braids, waiting under the porch light.

As soon as she is secure in her place with Sarah again, Noonie begins making demands. She insists they sightsee a bit: the sunset at Mallory Square, Mel Fisher's Treasure Exhibit, Fort Zachary Taylor, the Half Shell Raw Bar, where Sarah poses in a cut-out billboard of a half-dressed waitress with the slogan EAT IT RAW above her head.

Noonie insists they see Hemingway's house, a perfect opportunity for her to lecture on Life and Letters. The house is a mess. It obviously hasn't been cleaned since his second wife, Pauline, left in a huff (maybe the staff is too busy reading all the books in the gift shop). There are hundreds of cats in the garden and dozens of containers of dried cat food in skillets and aluminum take-out pans; litter boxes are strewn around. Noonie corrects the tour guide *sotto voce* on dates and titles as Sarah tries to ignore her, moving slightly ahead, so people might think she belongs to the nice young family with two toddlers ahead of them in line. The tour ends at the pool, the enormously expensive pool (a town scandal, all that water, all those young workmen!) Pauline had built for Papa while he was off carousing with Martha Gellhorn one year. Oh, well, thinks Noonie, she can understand a gesture like that; there was a chance he might have preferred a swimming pool.

"Do you want an ice cream?" Noonie asks.

Sarah sighs. It is ten-thirty in the morning. "Do you?"

"Yes, I think there's a place around here . . ."

"Just across the street," says Sarah. (It is her town, not Noonie's.) "When are we going home?"

"I thought at the end of the week," Noonie says delicately. "Saturday morning?"

"Am I in trouble at school?"

"No. You may have to make up some work, but . . ."

"Why don't we ever see them?"

"Rosie and Madge?"

"Yeah, I like them. And now that I know them, I want to see them. I want them to come to our house, too."

"Why do you think," asks Noonie, "we don't see them?" Sarah's ice-cream cone is dripping, and instinctively Noonie reaches over and licks the cone.

"Rosie says you don't approve of her lifestyle."

"Did she describe it as a lifestyle?"

"Not exactly," Sarah says.

"She isn't talking about her swimming, Sarah."

"I know," Sarah snaps, "she means about her and

Madge, that they're gay." She says it seriously. A month ago she would have had to swallow a giggle. "But why don't you like them?"

"I do like them, it's just . . ." Noonie sighs. What is it, this disappointment, this betrayal? Why does she feel Rosie has escaped something, escaped having to grow up?

"She told me she loved you so much that the night you and Daddy were married she got very drunk, just so she wouldn't think you were gone. She was so jealous of him that you would be his."

Noonie is stunned. But what a thing to say to a child. After the wedding. Of course she had never thought about after the wedding, what happened to anyone else, the absolute vanity of brides. It seems so archaic these days: going to your wedding night a virgin, the fear, the trembling, the twin desires to hurry and to flee. She remembers a song Cheryl Ann and she used to sing in high school, thinking they were all-knowing and supercool: "Oh, how we danced on the night we were wed, we danced and we danced, 'cause the room had no bed."

(Well, now Noonie knows you don't need a bed, although maybe she and Gus do. Do Gus and Pigeon do it on the floor, the kitchen table, the shower stall, up against the closet door, hanging over a chair?)

But what the others did after the wedding—Elsa and Rosie, Uncle Tootie and Aunt Tatie—she had never even thought about it before.

(This is what they did: they had the rooms at the hotel until the next morning, so Elsa and Rosie went back to the room, Rosie ordering up room service and watching *The Maltese Falcon* on TV, finishing the hors d'oeuvres and drinking the rest of the half-empty bottles of warm champagne. About ten—just as Noonie and Gus were finishing dinner in a hotel not far from this one, but fancier, in the bridal suite, a gift from Gus's brother—Rosie was very sick. Elsa dumped her into the shower and got her into bed and went out for a late supper at Fritzel's with Tatiana and Tootie.)

"I didn't know that," Noonie says to Sarah, "you can't fault me for that." She says it in a joking way, but she can see Sarah's face is dark and her eyes are filling with tears.

"Then you just forgot about her," Sarah says, "the way you forgot about Daddy. You were too lazy to even give me a sister."

"What?"

"Why am I an only child?"

"But I tried." Noonie is flabbergasted. "You know that, don't you? I've told you that, haven't I?" Noonie sits down on a bench on the corner near the ice-cream store. She is completely bewildered, she has told dozens of people in her life. Hadn't she told Sarah?

"You never told me."

"I had a baby, a little girl, three years before you were born and she died, she was only six months old, crib death, they call it, only she wasn't in her crib. She was in her carriage . . ."

Sarah is looking at her feet, kicking some stones with the toes of her tennis shoes.

"I never told you this? Then I had a miscarriage after Emily died—that was her name, Sarah—it was another girl, she was big enough for them to tell. And then I had you and I was just so grateful. I didn't want to seem greedy and maybe I was a coward, I'm not brave like that, so I just stopped." She grabs Sarah's knee so she will stop kicking. "I never told you any of this?"

"No! Just junk! You just told me what you wore on Halloween and what you ate at your wedding and what I said when I was a baby, but nothing important. You never told me about this baby or why you don't talk to Aunt Rosie or what's going on with Daddy and you!" Sarah's shoulders are shaking and she is sobbing. Noonie is afraid she will fall, she is waving her arms around so wildly. "So much crap! Just crap!" she screams at Noonie.

"Stop it!" Noonie shouts. "You sound like Rosie. Stop sounding like Rosie!" Noonie commands, and she remembers a dream in which she is shaking Rosie, shaking her and shaking her so that her speech becomes slurred and her head is banging against the sidewalk and just as her skull is about to break open like an egg cracking, a black curtain opens and reveals a blue cloudless sky. Noonie grabs Sarah sharply, wrapping her arms around her daughter's forearms tightly, locking them to her sides, as if her own arms were tight bandages.

Sarah is crying, "I'm sorry I ran away." She is sitting on Noonie's lap on the bench, but she is so tall her legs dangle over one side, and she looks like a large rag doll on the lap of a tired tiny child. Noonie has no Kleenex for a change, so she is wiping Sarah's eyes and her nose on the edge of her shirt.

"Get Daddy back for me," Sarah says.

Noonie sighs. "I'm sorry I didn't tell you true things," she says.

"You love me too much," says Sarah accusingly, pulling away from Noonie's embrace. "You love me instead of loving everyone else."

Noonie thinks how wise that is—the love she denied Rosie she put into Sarah, surely, and the sleeping baby girl, maybe even Gus, but it isn't just love. Sarah is the only one, she thinks, holding her almost grown daughter on her lap, the only single person who has never let her down, never disappointed her, because Noonie has no expectations, only that Sarah be who she is.

Every day Noonie sits waiting for Sarah to come home from school, her heart in her throat until she hears the door. She assumes she will stop at some point—maybe a hundred years from now.

(When you have been truly scared, your foundations shaken to the core, you do not forget, and when you have a strong inclination for guilt, longing, exaggeration anyway; you will clasp this memory like a friendly demon to your bosom and not part with it easily.)

Sarah seems resigned to this guardian behavior. She is quieter; she learned some things in Florida—she learned about her own privileged existence and her mother's weakness for her. So she just sighs when she sees Noonie busily cleaning the kitchen counters. She knows her mother has been sitting in the shadow of the kitchen clock for half an hour, waiting, and has just leapt up to look busy.

"Hi," Sarah says.

"Oh, hi," says Noonie, "did you have a good day?"

"Okay." Sarah stuffs a cookie in her mouth.

Noonie has been baking up a storm, making up for years of not baking cookies, all of Elsa's recipes, filling tins with cookies. (Noonie has put on about six pounds, although it is Sarah whom she wants to feed to make it harder for her to flee.) "How was your math test?"

"Gross," says Sarah, balancing two cookies on her pile of books. "Oh, Mom, I got my period."

"Are you all right?" Noonie feels faint.

"Sure. It's not a disease or anything, is it?"

"Don't be silly. Do you need pads or something?"

"No, I've got everything. They hand out those starter kits at school. I went to the nurse."

Noonie follows her out of the room. "Do you want to talk about it? How do you feel about it? Do you feel happy?"

"Mother," says Sarah, about to ascend the staircase, "I really don't think I have any choice."

Noonie sits on the bottom step. She hears Sarah's door snap shut. What choice does she have about it, anyway? (What choice did Noonie have?)

Noonie remembers very well when Elsa told her about menstruation. She had come into the steamy bathroom to pee while Elsa was taking a bath (oh, the indignities of those one-bathroom days!) and as she was finishing (embarrassed, eyes closed), Elsa had said firmly, "Sit down, there's something I've been meaning to tell you."

Noonie was nine or ten at the time and she doesn't remember anything Elsa really said, although she imagines it was a fairly factual description of the process—Elsa tended not to romanticize bodily functions. No, what she remembers is her mother's large slippery body, her long full breasts and dark nipples and the fierce triangle of black hair. Elsa must have been droning on for twenty minutes when Noonie finally caught on and started to cry.

"I don't want to bleed!"

"Don't be silly," Elsa said briskly. "Don't you want to have babies?" she asked coyly.

"No!" Noonie sobbed. "I don't even want to grow up!"

As if she had a choice.

Noonie has no one but herself to blame for this tendency not to believe in reality, for her inability to understand history as an ongoing, ever-changing phenomenon. (There is no way to go in reverse except in your imagination.)

"Sarah!" she calls from the foot of the stairs. "Do you want to have dinner out?"

Sarah appears, her expression suspicious, cagey. "To celebrate?"

Noonie shrugs. "I didn't make it to the store today."

"Okay." She narrows her eyes. "Is Tommy coming?"

"Tommy finished everything he had to do here," Noonie says.

"Oh . . . Hey, are you going to tell Daddy? About me?"

"Do you want me to tell him?"

"Maybe."

"Sarah got her period," Gus tells Pigeon, hanging up the phone.

"Well, she's thirteen. I don't think that's so unusual. What kind of cheese do you want in your tacos?"

"Do we have any of the stuff with the jalapeño peppers?" Gus folds the paper napkins thoughtfully.

"Um-hum. I thought she'd be taller than this."

"What?"

"Girls usually stop growing when they begin to menstruate, hormonal stuff. I didn't get mine until I was fifteen. I thought I was a freak of nature or something."

Gus smiles; he knows enough to give Pigeon a compliment. "Pretty good-lookin' freak," he says, but he is thinking about Sarah not growing. "Do you think I should buy her a present or something?"

Pigeon groans. "Don't you dare! When I finally got mine, Daddy came to my room, very serious, and gave me a little talk about growing up and the responsibilities of being a woman. As if he would know." Pigeon makes some choking noises as if she is about to vomit, and puts a plate of tacos in front of Gus. "I'd ignore it if I were you."

"You would ignore it, wouldn't you?"

"Huh?" At first, Pigeon thinks she hasn't heard him—Gus doesn't ask questions, he usually nods yes or no, mainly yes.

"I'm tired of ignoring things," he says. "I've been ignoring things for months and months." He throws down his napkin, watches it float to the floor. "I don't want to eat this! Why can't we have real food, a leg of lamb or a pot roast," he shouts, "real grown-up food!"

When Noonie goes out to get the paper Sunday morning, there is Gus parked at the curb in his car. The top is down and he is squinting into the cold sun, his head bowed slightly.

Noonie holds the paper to her chest; she is wearing one of Sarah's nightgowns and an old sweater of Gus's over it, and she instinctively holds the paper tighter, as much for warmth as protection on this chilly day.

"Noonie," Gus says, getting out of the car.

"Yes?"

"I want to come home."

"Home?" she says softly, as if she doesn't understand.

"Home. Where you are, I want to be where you are."

"Oh."

"Can we at least talk about it?"

"I guess so. Do you want some coffee?"

"That would be nice," he says. All his things are in the car: his typewriter, boxes of books, his briefcase, his tennis rackets, duffel bags—everything he had taken from this house fifteen months ago is in his car. He hopes Noonie hasn't seen.

(Of course she has: Noonie has the powers of a clairvoyant, a radar system developed on Mars.)

"Have you had your breakfast?" she asks without turning from the sink, an odd thing for her to say—it is an expression of Gus's mother's.

"No, ma'am, as a matter of fact, I have not," Gus says in a deliberate drawl. It is a game they played early in their marriage, the southern sheriff and the schoolmarm, the courtship of Gus's parents. (*High Noon* is still his favorite movie.)

Oh, Christ, Noonie thinks, we're going to end up in bed at this rate, and Sarah is asleep upstairs. So she says, "Eggs? Fried?"

"Yeh, thanks."

"I don't have any bacon or sausage. We haven't been eating a lot of meat, but I have some English muffins and juice . . ."

"Anything you have will be all right with me," he drawls.

Noonie thinks about all those fairy tales she loved: "And they lived happily ever after." No details, however, no bulletins from the palace after the wedding, nothing about the boredom and the anger and the daily betrayals. Even if Gus is back, there will always be a piece missing, fifteen months of Gus, fifteen months of Noonie—that will not belong to the other, the way their lives before they met did not, the way Sarah's life could not belong to Noonie forever. We can never completely belong to another.

15

THE ROSE TREES OF THE WIDOW

Noonie has put off going through Elsa's things for a long time after her death. She spent a lot of time in her mother's apartment when she was sick, and now that it has officially become the past, she is worried it will look like a stage setting or a museum exhibition and she is afraid of what she might discover. Elsa had a healthy fantasy life and Noonie is terrified Truth will come popping out of drawers and cartons and vault boxes.

Her mother's attorney, another old admirer, keeps calling, pressing her, anxious for her to give it a "little look-see." There is all that photographic equipment and he thinks Noonie should take advantage of "the photography boom." Besides, he reminds her, she must sell the building: "the neighborhood is changing."

Except for a few Oriental rugs and some of Grandma's Meissen knickknacks, there is little of value. Noonie is mainly interested in a pair of earrings, large rose-cut diamonds that had belonged to her grandmother. When

Grandma died, many years ago, Elsa would not let Noonie have them because her ears were not pierced.

Noonie and Rosie were supposed to have their ears pierced and share the earrings. What Elsa meant was that Noonie would have them for a month and then Rosie, although how this transaction was supposed to take place long-distance was never fully outlined. Noonie suspects it was in the tradition of the grandmother's traveling eiderdown. Rosie liked to believe that each of them was supposed to receive one earring and have one ear pierced.

When they were children, Elsa would tell them a Hungarian folk story about royal twins, separated at birth, one raised as a gypsy, the other the inevitable princess. They were reunited only because a clever nursemaid had placed identical rings on their tiny fingers at birth. Noonie was certain she would recognize Rosie anywhere, but Rosie wasn't so sure.

"Had your ear pierced?" was Rosie's greeting years ago in airports or over long distance.

Noonie wanted to mention the earrings to her mother in the hospital, but she was afraid Elsa would rise from the pillows and sigh in a vibrant contralto, "But what has changed? Have you pierced your ears?"

Finally, Noonie makes plans to meet Rosie in Chicago. She takes the airport bus, wondering if she will ever come back to this city again; no one is left.

The driver, a man in his fifties, his gray hair neat under a blue cap, lifts her suitcase, cups her elbow as she climbs the steep steps. Sometimes she imagines going home with a man like this, a man with a good tenor voice, a lean spare body, strong hands with square clean nails. She imagines lying down with him on a stripped mattress, an open window showing a full moon and a fire escape, an Edward Hopper painting. It is a scene from the thirties or forties: working people, a hospitable city, a round and healthy woman in a full slip of shiny fabric with thin ribbon straps, a pale scarf tied around a full head of curly hair.

It is Elsa's life she is imagining. Elsa is the woman in Noonie's fantasy, a woman who had always trusted men, although she didn't need them, a basic woman who selected real things for her environment, who had no shame of a body that stretched and expanded and sagged and eventually turned against her. (To the end Elsa kept her nails painted.)

Noonie doesn't really trust men, but she needs them badly, and her taste is so effete she has eliminated color from her life. Elsa would bring pillows and wall hangings to enliven the large empty white interiors of Noonie's house, filled with white sofas and black canvas chairs.

"Black and white," Elsa always snickered. As a photographer, she recommended color to all her prospective customers.

Noonie finds the earrings in a musty box in the vault and goes directly to Wolfson's Jewelers.

"Hi, Natalie," says Mr. Wolfson as if it were yesterday, not looking up. (Noonie and Rosie used to stop in frequently to try on engagement rings, although they did their buying at Kresge's; but Noonie's real ring, Noonie's and Gus's wedding rings, came from here—at cost.) Noonie blinks back tears. Without a word, she puts Grandma's earrings on the blue velvet plaque, noting the darned spots.

"Noonie," he says unhappily, "are you in some kind of trouble?"

"What?"

"You shouldn't sell your grandma's earrings, no matter what," he counsels. He fits his loupe to his eye automatically. Rosie used to say he had a wooden eye with threads in the socket that he screwed it into, which always made Noonie look away, as she does now. "European . . . rose-cut diamonds, half a karat each, give or take, set in eighteen-karat yellow gold. Look at the old-fashioned backs, you don't see those much anymore." He begins polishing the stones, shakes his head. "I remember your grandmother in those earrings. What little ears she had, like little seashells, you too, Noonie." He sighs. "Ah, women in those days were so pretty, little hands and feet and soft in-between. Nowadays," he says, shrugging, "the boys come in for earrings. So?"

"I don't want to sell the earrings. I want to wear them. But see, no holes."

"Mother," he shouts into the back of the store, "I think I have a customer for you."

Mrs. Wolfson comes running, wiping her hands on an apron. "Oh, Noonie," she says, embracing her, "I didn't know it was you."

"Noonie wants to wear her grandma's earrings, Ida."

"Oh." She smiles, shaking her head approvingly. "Come with me," she says, taking Noonie's hand.

Mrs. Wolfson, Ida, has taken a course in ear-piercing in her spare time and she is happy to practice on Noonie. She hands her the certificate.

"Very nice," says Noonie, but she feels rather cold.

"It only takes a minute," she says, pushing Noonie onto a stool near the Mr. Coffee machine. She picks up what appears to be a large metal drill. "Now," she says, remembering, taking something out of her pocket and leaning toward Noonie's cheek.

"Wait!" Noonie screams, grabbing her wrists.

"This is just a pen, Noonie. You wouldn't want one earring up here and the other way down there?" She points to the ceiling with one outstretched hand and toward the floor with the other. She draws X's on Noonie's ears, and before Noonie can protest again, swiftly punches a pair of tiny gold balls into her red lobes.

"There," Mrs. Wolfson says with pleasure, washing her hands professionally. "Want some coffee?"

Noonie nods her head yes; she actually feels a little faint. She remembers lying on a cot at a Red Cross station for hours one year when she felt particularly guilty and gave blood. "Thank you. Luckily, I don't have to drive home," she jokes.

"Sit a few minutes and relax," Ida says to Noonie, bustling out.

When Noonie emerges, she hears her saying to her husband, "Now, dear, just put your head between your knees and breathe deeply. That's a good boy." She smiles at Noonie. "He does it every time."

"You're bleeding," Elsa's attorney notes unhappily over scrambled eggs and lox at Katz's deli the next day.

Noonie touches her ear. Despite Ida's instructions, she has hastily switched the gold balls (too prepubescent) for the diamonds, which are heavy and will leave keyholes in her earlobes. "I had my ears pierced so I could wear my grandmother's earrings. Elsa never let me have them."

He purses his ruddy lips. "Did you come to some conclusions?"

"About the stuff?" (He can't know about Gus moving back.)

"Yes, yes, the stuff, the building," he replies, impatiently, wiping his mouth. "What should I do with it, Natalie? Prices are falling, it may be red-lined—you don't want to hang on to that building forever. What are you going to do, move here yourself?" He lets out a big laugh; a belch escapes. "Come on," he says chummily, "you can't go home again."

"Excuse me," Noonie says, slides out of the booth.

In the ladies', gritting her teeth, she pulls the earrings from her sore ears, wipes at the blood with a paper towel. (Weeks later, sending this coat to the cleaners, she will find them in the coarse bloody paper in the pocket.) She wipes her nose, too—it is running, a Chicago cold—applies some lip gloss, a comb.

"Did I order this?" There are toasted bagels at her place.

"No, I did. You haven't eaten anything. I can tell. Here," he says, handing her a box. "I found this in my office."

Noonie takes it gingerly. It is an orange Agfa paper box. She opens it, remembers thinking her father's ashes might be in the valentine candy box under Elsa's bed. Few surprises here: a second set of house and studio keys, a rounded plain gold band that might have been Grandma's or Elsa's—did she slip this on for illicit liaisons in highway motels with Mr. Kleinert or Mr. Horowitz or Chick O'Connors or was it really her wedding band? Noonie slips it absentmindedly on her own hand. Here, in little leathery jewelry boxes are Noonie's baby curls and Rosie's; she winds them around her finger: soft. In another box, snippets of Sarah's fine blond hair: no curls. There is a stack of Noonie's report cards and Rosie's medals and clippings and a folded copy of a photograph from a women's magazine of Rosie and Noonie and Elsa, startled—there are so few photographs of her.

Noonie remembers it was taken one strange day in

Florida many years ago, after the Channel victory, by a very successful photographer, a young foreign woman with piles of dark hair, who posed them in a triangle on the dock. Rosie is standing, dripping wet in a racing suit and goggles around her neck, slashes of black grease under her eyes, as Noonie and Elsa, in summer dresses, sit politely in wicker chairs. Elsa, so used to being behind the camera, was suddenly shy, quiet, uncooperative. There was a reporter, too, another amazingly self-possessed young woman in fabulous French clothes with a tiny tape recorder, but Elsa answered curtly: Yes, Rosie had always liked to swim. No, no one thought it was a talent. No, no one in their family had been a swimmer. (How ridiculous!)

The magazine folded shortly after this piece ran, so it just survives in a box of memories, the only existing photograph of Elsa and her daughters, after Otto died, and she started taking pictures. Here, also, is a soft and yellow newspaper copy of Noonie's prize-winning World War II essay and a silhouette of Aunt Tatiana's elegant profile in a veiled hat made at a country fair in Wisconsin, and Noonie's Brownie beanie and pin.

There was a part of the Brownie initiation ceremony, Noonie remembers decades later with chagrin and embarrassment, in which each girl was turned around and around and the troop leader pointed her toward a mirror on the floor that was disguised with crepe paper and leaves and twigs to resemble a pool of water in the woods.

> "I look in the mirror and see an elf,
> Turn me around and I see . . ."

Noonie, usually so clever with words and rhyme, could not come up with the missing word. "I see . . . I see . . ." She knew exactly what she saw: the little brown cotton dress with an orange tie, orange elves bouncing on the scallops of her cotton socks (she had been allowed to wear her party shoes), the pointy felt Brownie cap.

"Myself!" Elsa shouted from a folding chair in the front row, Rosie dangling dangerously upside down on Elsa's shiny leg. "I see myself, Natalie!" Elsa hissed.

In her mother's things, Noonie sees herself. The bond—stretched, damaged, ignored, battled, lost—is strong. Noonie is suddenly the keeper of her own past.

Rosie is sitting in the front room when Noonie gets back. Noonie hugs her quickly. Rosie is sitting surrounded by the dozens of bottles of liqueurs.

"What is this junk? Cactus?"

"She and Aunt Tatie used to buy them as gifts and forget to give them away."

"You look like you got into a fight."

"I had my ears pierced so I could wear the earrings, but they were too big." Noonie pinches the lobes gingerly, caked blood flakes off.

"Aha, the earrings," Rosie says.

"Look, we can go back downstairs. They're yours, too."

"No thanks," says Rosie, shivering, "I don't go for all this bloodletting. Besides, she'd want you to have them."

"You don't know that, Rosie."

"Can you see me swimming with them? I'd be dragged to the bottom of the sea."

"What are you going to do about your swimming? Want coffee?"

"Tea, if there's any." Rosie follows her into the kitchen. "I don't know. Madge is trying to get me to go to college, get a degree in phys ed or something."

"That's a good idea." Noonie holds the blue-and-white coffeepot in her hands. She guesses she wants this, too.

"There's going to be some money, if the building's sold."

"Maybe I'll go back and do the Channel—you know, the oldest girl to swim the Channel." She looks through the cupboards for honey. "I lost my nerve, you can't do that."

"I was always jealous of your swimming," Noonie says.

"You were?"

"Sure. I wanted to be special and here you were. Special." She finds the photograph of the three of them, but Rosie doesn't look at it.

"I'm not sure I can do this," Rosie says.

"I got some big boxes," says Noonie, "and we can just throw the stuff in them without looking. Is there anything you want?" She feels very protective of Rosie all of a sudden.

Rosie looks confused. "Yes," she says finally, "I want my mother's blessing. I should have gotten it in time; I didn't think it would matter, I didn't think I'd care."

"Oh, Rosie," says Noonie, and puts her arms around her.

Noonie and Rosie walk down the stairs to Elsa's studio. Noonie opens the door with the key and turns on the light to the darkroom for the first time in her life.

They spent their childhoods in this darkness: one red light bulb, like the holy lamp over the ark in the unfrequented synagogue, dangling over their heads. Their playthings were the props in the corner trunk: paper wedding bouquets (two choices: roses and spider orchids), a molding mortarboard, a white furry rug and alphabet blocks, the black-velvet shoulder drapes that hid the brassiere straps of girl graduates and made them look all creamy shoulders and swan necks, the fabric melting into the corners of the picture like warm chocolate.

"Ho ho!" Elsa would laugh. "Ach!" she would exclaim. "Look at that!" She would point to something particularly disfiguring or hideous. "Twenty-one, my foot!" she would spit.

She would lean over the steel sink in her flowing blue-serge slacks; her haunches were like the spheres of the globe flattened into a map in Noonie's school atlas: tapering nicely at the top and the bottom but encompassing the entire earth. Noonie would watch in amazement as Elsa washed away the imperfections: receding hairlines, deepening wrinkles, warts, moles, would all disappear in the warm wash of the sink.

Here is Elsa's blessing: Rosie was never dead for her. Clipped to the line above the sink, Rosie is alive and well: Rosie as a pageboy in a school play, Rosie on Cloverleaf (a horse) at overnight camp, classic Rosie, dividing the waters with one bent elbow, pursed lips, mouthing her siren's song. In Elsa's studio, Noonie is still a bride, Sarah is a baby, Gus poses in a handsome camel's-hair coat the winter they returned from England. Aunt Tatiana, in a polka-dot sundress and platform shoes, waves as she steams into the harbor of Havana.

Noonie has been left in a world without her mother's magic. Elsa has thrown her into unknown waters, scantily clad in a discarded life vest, a prewar relic, when Noonie will need to stay afloat into the twenty-first century. Rosie watches in horror as Noonie pulls the photographs from their clips, grabs the big brown bottles from their shelves, empties chemicals into the sink, and watches them disappear down the drain.

"You remember the next part. One night a bear comes into the house and they're frightened," Noonie tells Rosie, "but the mother says, Nonsense, anyone can see he's a friendly bear, so feed him and dry him off and let him lie by the fire."

"I'm not sure what you're getting at," says Rosie. They are wandering around O'Hare. The airport is fogged in and everything is backed up several hours.

"There's more, of course, a pet lamb and a dove and a cruel demented dwarf and bags of pearls and gold and stones . . ."

"You're nuts," says Rosie. "Hey, let's get a drink."

"Where?"

"Here, in the bar. Come on, they're kind of fun, airport bars."

Noonie squints; it's very dark and there are businessmen mostly, looking very rumpled and tired and slightly disoriented. Large color cutouts of frosted drinks hang from the ceiling and decorate the tiny tables along with half-empty bowls of something salty and a candle in a red glass cup.

"Come on," says Rosie. "I know it's a tad déclassé for the likes of you, Natalie."

Noonie sticks out her tongue, sits. Rosie orders a Tom Collins.

"What do you want, Noonie?"

"I don't know, a glass of white wine."

"You don't drink wine here. She'll have a whiskey sour," Rosie tells the waitress.

"You don't remember the adventures of Snow-white and Rose-red?"

"I remember your conversing with that moth-eaten bearskin rug," says Rosie agreeably. "I was quite knocked out by that."

"Anyway, the bear's really a prince, a prince in a bear

suit, and when the dwarf dies . . ." Noonie suddenly laughs, recites in a low voice: " 'Snow-white and Rose-red, don't beat your lover dead!' See. The prince is in the bear suit. And he has a brother for Rose-red."

"Aha, that's what you're getting at. That's what you bought, Noonie, hook, line, and sinker, and that's the part I hated. Of course," Rosie says with a big grin, "if things had been a little different, I might have liked Gus; I can imagine loving a man like Gus."

"Do you think I should have let Gus back?" Even as she says this Noonie is astonished: she has never asked Rosie's opinion of anything—ever—not even whether to wear a red ribbon or the blue, the black shoes or navy!

"You love Gus, don't you?" Rosie is chewing on the cherry she took from Noonie's drink. "So, he hurt your feelings. Big deal. You don't stop loving someone because of that. You aren't used to having your feelings hurt—if you were, you'd know that loving is worth anything in the end."

"Do you think about that, loving a man?"

"Oh, Noonie," Rosie says, shaking her head. "I think for you, love is something completely different. It's tied up with fairy tales and men in bear suits and being rescued. For me . . . for me, the happiest moments of my life were in our kitchen at home on Devon Avenue with Mama baking something and tapping her shoe to some music on the radio she danced to as a young girl. Remember how she taught us to dance?"

Rosie tosses back her head, her lovely curls, and Noonie reaches out to touch them, as she used to when Rosie was small and soft. Rosie rises from her chair and lifts her arms to dance around the little table; "Star Dust" is playing on the stereo system in the bar. Noonie hesitates, looks around, but it is so dark in here, anyway, what could it matter? (Why are you so sure they're looking at you? Elsa used to say.) So after a few minutes, she joins Rosie, and they dance around the table, the way they used to at family parties: Noonie leading, Rosie on tiptoes, following.

"I don't know how you believed all those fairy tales," Rosie says when they sit down. (They get some scattered applause.)

"Oh, come on, you locked me in a trunk every afternoon for a week." Noonie leans over, asks seriously, "How did you think you were going to do it, Rosie?"

"I didn't think I could, I thought you could, Noonie; I thought you were magic, I thought you could make it happen. Boy, you were powerful. You came on like Minerva, Diana, like a ton of bricks, you were so positive, so confident. I don't know why I'm the way I am, whether it's physically based or just psychological or what. But I know what I wanted: I wanted to feel comfortable, and you wanted to feel stirred." Rosie sips her second drink. "You were obsessed with finding our father, with the stranger out there. I never knew him and I didn't care. You and Elsa were enough for me. You always wanted out, you always wanted more."

On their way to the gates, Rosie buys Madge a Bears T-shirt, Noonie buys one for Sarah and a baseball cap for Gus. He can wear it on the beach next summer.

Noonie walks Rosie to her gate; the plane for Florida leaves first.

"And Sarah can come for her spring break?" Rosie asks.

Noonie nods. "Do you have your boarding pass?"

"There's plenty of time, Noonie."

"No, I think you should get on now," says Noonie, the older sister.

Rosie laughs, shakes her head. She puts her arms around Noonie and hugs her hard. "You'll never change."

"You're right," says Noonie, hugging back. "But there's plenty of time."

3 3311 00253493